**Praise for *New York Times* bestselling
author MAGGIE SHAYNE**

"Maggie Shayne is better than chocolate.
She satisfies every wicked craving."
—*New York Times* bestselling author
Suzanne Forster

"Shayne's talent knows no bounds."
—*Rendezvous*

"Suspense thrums throughout due to Shayne's...
seemingly effortless skill at teasing readers with
surprising but believable plot turns."
—*Publishers Weekly* on *Thicker Than Water*

"Maggie Shayne demonstrates an absolutely
superb touch, blending fantasy and romance into
an outstanding reading experience."
—*Romantic Times BOOKreviews*
on *Embrace the Twilight*

"One of the best of the decade as the magnificent
Ms. Shayne demonstrates why she is ranked
among the top writers of any genre!"
—*Affaire de Coeur*

"Shayne's gift has made her one of the
preeminent voices in paranormal romance today."
—*Romantic Times BOOKreviews*

Dear Reader,

Take a break from all the holiday shopping and indulge yourself with December's four heart-stopping romances from Silhouette Intimate Moments.

New York Times bestselling author Maggie Shayne kicks off the month with *Dangerous Lover* (#1443), the latest in THE OKLAHOMA ALL-GIRL BRANDS miniseries. An amnesiac seeks the help of his rescuer, but the bewitching woman might just be a suspect in his attempted murder. Next is Lyn Stone's *From Mission to Marriage* (#1444), the new installment in her SPECIAL OPS miniseries. A killer vows revenge, and as the chase heats up, so does Special Ops agent Clay Senate's desire for his sexy new hire.

In Nancy Gideon's *Warrior's Second Chance* (#1445), a determined heroine must save her family by turning to the man she left behind years ago. But will her secret douse the flames of their newly rekindled romance? And be sure to pick up *Rules of Re-engagement* (#1446), the final book in Loreth Anne White's SHADOW SOLDIERS trilogy. Here, a wanted man returns to save his country…but to do so he must reunite with the only woman he's ever loved— his enemy's daughter.

Starting in February 2007, Silhouette Intimate Moments will have a new name—Silhouette Romantic Suspense, but we will continue to deliver four breathtaking romantic-suspense novels each and every month. Don't miss a single one! Have a wonderful holiday season and happy reading!

Sincerely,

Patience Smith
Associate Senior Editor

Please address questions and book requests to:
Silhouette Reader Service
U.S.: 3010 Walden Ave., P.O. Box 1325, Buffalo, NY 14269
Canadian: P.O. Box 609, Fort Erie, Ont. L2A 5X3

MAGGIE SHAYNE

Dangerous Lover

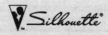

INTIMATE MOMENTS™

Published by Silhouette Books

America's Publisher of Contemporary Romance

 SILHOUETTE BOOKS

ISBN-13: 978-0-373-27513-7
ISBN-10:   0-373-27513-7

DANGEROUS LOVER

Books by Maggie Shayne

Silhouette Intimate Moments

Reckless Angel #522
Miranda's Viking #568
Forgotten Vows...? #598
Out-of-This-World Marriage #633
Forever, Dad #694
*The Littlest Cowboy #716
*The Baddest Virgin in Texas #788
*Badlands Bad Boy #809
*The Husband She Couldn't Remember #854
Brides of the Night #883
   †"*Twilight Vows*"
*The Baddest Bride in Texas #907
*The Outlaw Bride #967
*Angel Meets the Badman #1000
Who Do You Love? #1027
   "*Two Hearts*"
**The Brands Who Came for Christmas #1039
**Brand-New Heartache #1117
**Secrets and Lies #1189
**Feels Like Home #1395

*The Texas Brand
†Wings in the Night
**The Oklahoma All-Girl Brands

MAGGIE SHAYNE,

a *USA TODAY* bestselling author whom *Romantic Times BOOKreviews* calls "brilliantly inventive," has written more than twenty-five novels for Silhouette Books.

Maggie has won numerous awards, including two *Romantic Times BOOKreviews* Career Achievement awards. A five-time finalist for the Romance Writers of America's prestigious RITA® Award, Maggie also writes mainstream contemporary fantasy and romantic suspense for MIRA Books, and has contributed story lines to network daytime soap operas.

She lives in rural Otselic, New York, with her husband, Rick, with whom she shares five beautiful daughters, two English bulldogs and two grandchildren.

Chapter 1

"There's something incredibly freeing about being naked outside," Selene said.

She adjusted the sarong skirt where it was knotted at her side. It was the only piece of clothing she wore. "Well, *nearly* naked."

"Naked enough to get the idea," Marcy said, giggling as she spun with her arms open wide and her head tipped back beneath the stars. "This is awesome. It's…primal."

"I'm not sure I like it so much." Helena had finally stopped crossing her arms over her chest, but it had taken the better part of the ritual before she'd let the energy take away her inhibitions. "I mean, among you guys, sure, but I don't know that I'd do it with anyone else.

"Well, we couldn't have known what it would be like unless we tried it," Erica said, and she whipped off the skirt and stood in the moonlight, completely naked, while the others gasped and laughed. "And I *love* it. It's like—a rebellion. It's like shouting in the moonlight, 'Take your stupid phony standards, society, and cram them where the sun don't shine!' Who the hell ever decided clothes were necessary, anyway?"

"Probably the first caveman to get caught naked in a snowstorm," Selene said. Everyone laughed, and the ring of that laughter, feminine and secretive, filled the clearing. Beyond it the thunder of the nearby waterfall pounded. It was constant and powerful, and the main reason the women—Witches all, and every one of them completely hidden within the depths of the proverbial broom closet—had chosen this spot for their secret gatherings.

They came here once in the month, when the moon was full. And no one else knew. No one ever would. They had too much to lose. Here they came, to cast a circle of invisible power. Here they called on the elements of nature to meld with their own energies, so that they could be closer to the Whole. Here they worshiped the Moon Goddess. They called her Diana, visualized her as a powerful huntress. They saw her not as a separate being, or a deity dwelling somewhere in the cosmos. To these women, Diana was the deepest, most powerful part of themselves. And she was also the collective soul of womankind. The secret rituals they held here were sacred and beautiful.

Trying the nudity was an attempt to learn to see and love the beauty of their own bodies—a direct challenge to the way society taught women to think of themselves. And it was also to satisfy the curiosity they'd all felt when reading that some Witches practiced their rites *only* in the nude.

"Magical requests, before we close?" Selene asked. She felt incredibly free and slightly wicked standing bare-breasted in the moonlight. Not that she hadn't done ritual in the nude before. She had. But only when she was all alone and certain no one would ever find out. This was entirely different.

Marcy raised her hand, knowing full well that wasn't necessary. "I know I ask every month, but could we just *try* to turn my ex into a toad?"

Selene shook her head slowly. It was an old joke, but still funny. They didn't do harm. They just didn't.

"Fine. Then let's work to ensure my custody battle gets settled in the best possible way for the boys."

"Works for me," Selene said, and she stepped aside. Marcy moved to the altar at the center of the circle taking with her a photo of her sons, Jack and Joey, both blond, blue-eyed angels, six and eight respectively. She removed the drawstring pouch from the sash at her waist, and laid that beside the photo. Everyone knew it contained a lock of each boy's hair. Then she stood, hands extended to feel the energy, and she led the chant.

"Be it me or be it him, give my boys the best for them."

"Be it her or be it him," the women repeated, "give her boys the best for them."

The others began to move in a clockwise circle around the altar, chanting with Marcy in a slow and steady rhythm. Selene picked up a rattle. Erica kept time on a small drum. Their movements grew faster as the rhythm picked up. Faster. Louder. The rattle became more urgent, the drum more frantic. And the energy rose. Marcy's hands rose with it, and when she sensed the power peaking, she shouted "Release!"

At the moment of that shout the others went still and silent, expelling their breath and relaxing their bodies with such a rush of release that two of them even sank to the ground. And in the same instant, Marcy drew her hands downward quickly, aiming them at the photo on the altar, pushing all the energy they had raised into the photo and hair, which stood in as representatives for the boys themselves.

She sighed, and let her head fall forward, spent. "That was intense," she muttered.

"I sure felt it," Helena said. She was one of those on the ground, but she got up now, smoothing her sarong and brushing twigs and leaves from it. "You're selfless, Marcy, you know that? Most people would be working magic to win custody. Not to do whatever's best for the boys."

"They're what matter," Marcy said. "They're all that matter."

The others nodded. If the doe-eyed brunette, Helena, felt the energy, it had been real, Selene was sure of that. Helena was the most sensitive, and her impressions were usually accurate. As for Marcy, she came off as the most fiery, the most hot-tempered and impulsive, and her coloring matched her personality. Flame-red hair, bright-green eyes. But there was nothing she wouldn't do for her kids. Nothing. And inside a circle, she could generate magical energy like nobody's business.

"Anybody else have magic they need done tonight?" Selene asked, looking around the circle. "You, Erica? How are things with your father?"

"He's still the local minister," she replied, as she gathered up her sarong and tied it around her waist again. "And I'm still keeping the truth from him."

Selene had to wonder how. Erica with her dyed black hair, straight down her back to her waist, and her overly dramatic application of eyeliner, her Stevie Nicks wardrobe and her collection of goddess-symbol jewelry, seemed to be doing everything except painting the word *Witch* across her forehead. But her father didn't see it, or didn't want to. And she didn't come out and tell him. Mostly, they didn't communicate at all.

She was the youngest of them all, still in college, living in her own apartment with some other juniors, and having as little as possible to do with her father, though she still went home on weekends.

"You, Tessa?"

The butterscotch-blonde sighed. "I just want to keep this part of myself private. Chet would never understand."

They'd been married less than a year, and Tessa lived in fear of losing him. Selene thought he would understand, and was probably much more deeply in love with Tess than Tess could comprehend, but she was going to have to come to that conclusion on her own.

"I just want to work to keep this part of my life secret. Just a little bit longer."

"And anything else?" Selene asked.

No one had anything, until Marcy said, "What about you, Selene? Isn't there something you want to work for?"

"Yeah, or maybe some*one*?" Helena added.

The others laughed softly. Selene rolled her eyes. There were no secrets in this circle, that was for sure. "I want to find the love of my life. The perfect mate for me. The man I'm destined to be with. But I don't want to work magic for that. I know he's out there, the Universe has been telling me so my whole entire life. I want him to come to me exactly when and where and how he's supposed to. And until then, I can wait."

"How can you be sure he hasn't already, though?" Tessa asked. "I mean, how can any of us be sure the one we pick is the right one? You should at least ask for a sign."

"I agree," Marcy said. "A clear, unmistakable sign to let you know when he arrives."

Selene smiled. "That wouldn't be a bad idea. What kind of a sign though?"

"Have him fall at your feet the first time he sets eyes on you," Helena said with a breathy sigh.

"Have a fork-tailed comet shoot through the sky when you meet."

"And make sure he absolutely can't live without you," Erica tossed in. "We like our men a bit needy, right?"

"You guys are a riot. What do you say we just do the secrecy charm and close the circle?"

"Fine," Marcy said. "Have it your way. But remember we're between the worlds. Whether we cast a spell or not, we've created a thought form. You're going to get a sign."

Helena nodded her agreement, went to the altar, knelt beside it and took the wine from the ice bucket nearby. She poured it into five wine glasses, and each woman came forward to take one.

They returned to their positions around the circle, then. Selene in the west, probably because her silver-blond hair, pale-blue eyes and even her name corresponded with a moon goddess, and because the moon was most closely associated with the west, and with water. Helena stood in the east, home of the element of air. Marcy was in the south with fire, and Tessa in the north, the home of earth. Erica took center, and the position of spirit, though her own spirit seemed awfully unsettled tonight. Probably she was excited about the four-day camping weekend she'd be spending at a Pagan festival, down at Merry Meet Campground in Texas. She was leaving right from here. And only her fellow Witches knew where she would be.

They lifted their glasses as one, and Selene said:

"Elements and Deities gathered this night
We bid you farewell and give thanks for your light,
Our secrets we ask that you help us to keep,
Until the time comes when fate deems we must speak.
Hail and farewell."

The others repeated, "Hail and farewell," and then they gathered closer to the center, clinked their glasses together with their favorite toast, "May you never thirst," and drank deeply.

But Selene stopped with her glass halfway to her lips, and lifted her head, her eyes probing the darkness beyond the altar and the ring of candles that marked the boundary of their circle on the ground. "Someone's coming," she whispered.

Marcy shot her a look, then quickly grabbed the double-edged dagger from the altar, and thrust it into Selene's hand. "Better open the circle, hon, so we can get this site cleaned up and get out of here."

She nodded, and moved to the edge of the circle, lifting the blade, and trying to keep her focus on the task at hand, rather than out there, in the night, where something was happening; something that made her stomach clench tight, and her nerves tingle. She pointed the blade outward, and moved slowly, counterclockwise—or what the Witches called *widdershins*—around the circle, drawing its energy into the blade. When she returned to the north, she pointed the blade down and whispered that she would send the excess power back into the earth mother as she prepared to drive the athame's tip into the ground at her feet.

But before she could bring it down, someone came. Crashing, stumbling, careening, he came and he fell. Right there: right at her feet at the edge of the circle's boundary. He rolled onto his back, knocking lit candles over in the process, and she stood blinking down at him even as he opened his eyes. He gazed up at her, his unfocused eyes on her body, her unclothed breasts and then her face, and finally, as they found the blade in her hands, his eyes went wide.

Something flashed overhead, so bright she jerked her head up, and she saw the comet, its forked tail glittering behind it as it jetted across the sky. "Ohmygoddess," she muttered, and, as she lowered her head again, Selene realized that the man was bleeding. And not just a little bit. His shirt was soaked in blood.

He'd fallen at her feet. A fork-tailed comet had shot across the sky. And he would almost certainly die without her.

"Damn," Selene muttered. "As much as I tell myself I believe, it still gives me goosebumps the way this shit works." She drove the blade into the earth beside him and whispered, "The circle is open. So mote it be."

He'd found himself stumbling through the woods, a burning pain in his gut, his shirt and his hands soaked in blood. And he'd known—though he wasn't sure how—that someone was chasing him. He had to run. He needed help. He was injured. Those were his thoughts then. And those were the thoughts that had driven him down from the steep, wooded hillside into the clearing.

He'd heard them, clearly. Voices, like tinkling bells:

women, laughing and talking, chanting and singing. Beyond the voices there had been a roar, like rushing water, but it was the voices that drew him.

They held in their female lilt the promise of aid, so he'd fought his way clear of the undergrowth, pushing aside branches to try to catch a glimpse of his salvation, better to pick his way closer.

The women danced in a circle of candles, bathed in moonlight, naked, except for sarong skirts, and one hadn't even been wearing that much when he'd first glimpsed them. For a moment he thought he must be hallucinating from the blood loss, imagining he'd stumbled upon an enchanted grove full of fairies. Their backdrop was a thundering waterfall, the source of the rushing, roaring sound. But the women were far more interesting. Their bodies swayed and moved in time with the haunting and primitive sounds of rattle and drum, and their voices rose in some mystical cadence, though he couldn't make out the words. The sight of them, the feeling of something primal and forbidden, something *powerful*, sent chills racing up his spine.

But he needed help, he couldn't be choosy. If they were real and not just a delusion, they would help him. God, please, he thought, let them help him.

A branch snapped behind him, and that, if nothing else, propelled him into motion once again. He headed down the hillside, in far too much of a hurry to pick his way with care, so he slid and stumbled often.

Finally, he was there, on level ground, in the clearing. The women—and he was fairly certain now that they were women, not fairies—at least he didn't *see* any gossamer wings sprouting from their backs—didn't see him. They were too involved with whatever it was they were doing. He fell to his knees, and darkness closed in around the edges of his vision. He'd lost too much blood. He wasn't going to last much longer. No time for caution. Dragging himself to his feet, he lurched forward, making it almost to them before he fell again, landing hard this time.

Silence. Dead silence.

Forcing himself to make his body move, he pushed, rolled over onto his back and blinked up at the woman who stood over him. He saw wide, surprised eyes, their color nothing more than a reflection of the candlelight around her, so they seemed to blaze with an inner flame. Her hair was long, perfectly straight and very pale. The spun silk of angel hair, he thought. Her breasts were small and unclothed, round and perfect, her waist, just the right size to hold in his hands, and her arms were slender but strong.

He saw the rest, went still and sucked in a breath, a *painful* breath. She had a blade raised up above him, its tip aimed squarely at his chest. And the way she clasped its handle in both fists suggested she was about to bring it down *hard.*

"He's hurt! He's bleeding!" Selene drove the blade of her athame into the earth beside the fallen man, even as his eyes fell closed again, grounding the energy it held and freeing her hands at the same time. She dropped to her knees, tore his shirt open. "Get a light over here. And someone grab my cell phone."

Marcy came running with a candle, and held it up high as the others gathered closer. At some point she'd tied her sarong back around her waist. The man had a hole in his belly and spurts of blood pumped out of it in time with his pulse. Someone handed Selene something, a baby T-shirt, she thought, and she wadded it up and pressed it hard against the wound, then focused there, to keep him from bleeding to death. "What's the chant? What's the damn Pow-Wow bleeding chant?"

"Um—uh, wait, lemme think," Marcy said.

Helena leaned closer. "Blessed Mary, Mother of God, who stoppeth the pain and stoppeth the blood," she whispered. "What's the rest?"

"Women's mysteries fine and strong, stop this blood by female song," Selene said as the rest of the charm, long used by the Pennsylvania Dutch Pow-Wow Healers came back to her. She nodded hard, and repeated the words, pressing against the wound and falling into a steady cadence. "Blessed Mary, Mother of God.... "

"Here," Helena said, drawing Selene's gaze upward. She was holding out a cell phone. Selene kept chanting as she took it. She chanted and chanted and the blood slowed more and more.

"Put the phone away," Marcy snapped.

Selene shot her a look, breaking her chant. "I have to get him some help."

"You make that call and we're all outed as Witches, Selene. There's no way we'll have time to clean up the site and get out of here."

"We're talking about a man's life," Selene said softly.

"We're talking about me losing custody of my kids." Marcy looked at the man, her expression torn. Then she glanced at the others. "And about Helena losing her job. How many schools are going to employ a kindergarten teacher who's known to frolic naked in the moonlight? And what about Erica? Her father's the town minister for goddess' sake."

Selene looked from one of them to the next, then nodded slowly. She had no small stake in keeping this secret herself. Her mother was going to have a freaking breakdown over this. But she didn't see that she had a choice. "Look, this is my problem, not yours. I'll cover you."

"What makes it your problem?" Marcy snapped.

"Marcy, hell, didn't you see the comet?" Helena whispered.

Erica nodded. "He's the one. Fell at her feet. Going to die without her. We asked for the signs, and we got 'em in spades," she said. "Poor guy probably doesn't even know he just fell into his destiny."

"Just go," Selene said. "All of you. Gather up as much of your stuff as you can and get the hell out of here. But hurry.

I'm making that call right now. You should have a good ten
minutes before they get here."

The women scattered, gathering clothes, handbags, ritual
tools even as Selene punched buttons on the cell phone. She
gave the information calmly and slowly and then disconnected. Helena came to her as she folded the phone and set
it down. The others were already running along the path back
to the road where their cars were parked.

"You should go, too. They'll be here soon."

Selene looked up at her friend, then down at the man, at
his face, for the first time. "I can't leave him. I can't."

"Well at least gather up the rest of the ritual gear, hon.
Good luck."

"Merry part, Helena."

"Yeah, and merry meet again—I hope," Helena said. She
handed Selene her blouse. "Better put this on before they get
here." And then she hurried away.

Selene told herself to follow her friend's wise advice, and
she got as far as pulling her blouse on before she got distracted. But then the candle flickered in the breeze, and
painted the fallen man's face in amber glow. He wore a day's
growth of beard. Some men thought that look was sexy.

She thought it was sexy. Even lying there, unconscious,
he was sexy. Hair cut short, kind of brushed back on the
top. Dark, dark hair. And a luscious, thick brow line. Everything in her was drawn to him, physically drawn, as if
he were magnet pulling her body closer. And even as she
wondered whether that was only because she knew he was
fated for her, she gave in to it. She leaned closer. She closed
her eyes and inhaled him, and something in her knew that
scent. She ran a hand over the smooth, strong chest, and
something in her knew that silken steel against her palms.
Something in her knew the pounding of the heart that beat
beneath his skin.

He opened his eyes, dark like his hair in the light of the

candle glow, and he stared into hers, but he was unfocused, blinking, clearly confused and in pain.

"Don't be afraid," she told him. "Help is on the way. I'm not going to let anything happen to you."

"You…you…." He gave up his effort at speech, his eyes falling away from hers, sliding over the athame that was thrust into the ground near his head.

"What's your name?" she asked.

He jerked his eyes back to hers. "I…I don't know," he whispered. And then he looked panicky again. "I don't know—"

"That's okay," she told him, keeping her voice calm, soothing. "I know who you are."

That thick brow bent in the middle. "Who…am I?"

"You're the one," she said softly. "You're the one I've been waiting for."

His confusion didn't ease. In fact, it seemed to increase as he stared up at her. And then she heard vehicles arriving, sirens wailing, doors slamming. Feet came running in time with the bounding flashlights. Paramedics were pushing her out of the way, and kneeling around the man. She stood a few feet away, watching them, willing him to be all right. And then a hand fell onto her shoulder.

She turned, startled.

"Ma'am, do you mind telling me what's—" The police chief stopped there, pushed his wide-brimmed hat back on his head, and blinked at her. "Miz Brand? Selene Brand?"

She nodded. "Hello, Chief Wheatly."

"Well now, what in the name of all that's—"

"Chief, he has something to say," one of the medics called.

Chief Wheatly sighed. "You stay right here, Selene," he said, patting her shoulder. And he went to where the medics worked on the man. They spoke in low tones. She heard her beloved's voice, strained and whispering. When they all kept looking back at her, and then around at the circle, with its candles, and its altar full of Witch tools, she felt a ripple of warning move along her spine, and she went closer to try to hear what was being said.

The chief pulled her athame from the ground, eyed it, and dropped it into an evidence bag.

Uh-oh.

The chief got up, turning toward her, holding up the bag. "This your knife, little lady?"

"Yes, Chief, it is, but it's not—"

"So we'll find your fingerprints on it, then."

"Of course you will, but not because I—"

"You do realize that young feller over yonder has been stabbed, don't you, Selene?"

She blinked. "Not by me," she said.

"Well, now, that's good to know. Good to know." Chief Wheatly took her arm, and drew her with him as he moved closer to the altar, and nodded at the tools there. There was a goblet full of moon-water; a silver censer, still emitting a thin spiral of fragrant smoke, a magic wand, unmistakably phallic in shape and size, a candle snuffer that looked like a Witch's hat dangling from the end of a broomstick handle; a dinner-plate-sized circle of crystal, etched with the five-pointed star, or pentacle, a hollow half sphere of quartz-lined stone called a geode, with a few pinches of sea salt inside; a statue of a beautiful naked woman, with hounds at her sides and a bow in her hands; a statue of a beautiful, naked man with a full beard, horns on his bushy head, and hooves instead of feet. They were Diana, the Huntress, and Pan, her lover. They were images representing the Goddess and God.

Selene doubted the chief would see them that way, though.

After looking the items over carefully, Chief Wheatly turned to face her. "You care to tell me what's been goin' on out here tonight, Selene?"

She pursed her lips and tried to swallow against the dryness in her throat. "I'll be happy to tell you, Chief. I was here

minding my own business when this man came stumbling out
of the woods bleeding, and fell at my feet." She shrugged. "I
called you. End of story."

"That's not the way he tells it."

She lifted her brows, her eyes shooting back to the man.
They were lifting him now, onto a gurney, and then hauling
him toward a waiting ambulance. "How *does* he tell it?"

"Someone stabbed him. He thinks it was you."

She thought she could have fallen over dead from shock.
"Why would he say something like that?"

"Well, now, that's a mighty good question, Selene. You
were here alone, you say?" Even as he said it, he was looking
around at the ritual site. Without even trying, Selene could
find evidence of others there. Two pairs of shoes, a couple of
blouses. She prayed her friends had taken everything that
might possibly identify them by name.

"Do you see anyone else?" she asked, not exactly lying.

"No, ma'am, I don't." Chief Wheatly clearly saw everything she did, though. "But uh, this ground is gonna give up
plenty of tracks, you know. And if there were cars parked
nearby, we'll know. Looks to me like there were at least a few
others out here with you."

She glanced at the chief, met his eyes, and lowered her
own. She couldn't understand why the wounded man would
think—then again, he was hurt, confused, and he'd looked up
at her to find her standing over him with a blade poised over
his chest. "He's confused, Chief. I would never hurt anyone.
And as to what the ground is going to give up, there has to
be a trail of blood leading from the woods to this clearing."

"That there is. I've got men on it already."

"Doesn't that prove my story?"

"Only proves he was stabbed elsewhere. Doesn't prove
you weren't the one who did it, though frankly, Selene, I'd
be pretty shocked." He shrugged. "You didn't see him until
he came out of the woods, you say?"

She nodded.

"Fella says you told him you know who he is. That true?"

She pursed her lips. "I think maybe I'd better shut up now, Chief. I'm awful sorry and I hate to be rude. But you know, my brother-in-law, Caleb, would be pretty mad at me for talking to you without him here, given what you think might have happened out here tonight, him being a lawyer and all."

"Uh-huh."

"You wanna do me a favor and call him for me?"

The chief eyeballed her. "You could call him yourself from the station, Selene. I'm gonna have to call your mamma anyway." He pursed his lips, shook his head. "And I don't mind tellin' you, that's one call I don't look forward to makin'."

No, she wasn't looking forward to that, either. Her mother was going to have an absolute hissy over this. She would never understand.

"I suppose you're going to confiscate all my things," she said, nodding toward the altar.

"Afraid so, Selene. This is a crime scene."

"It's not, really. I told you, he was stabbed somewhere else. He just stumbled in here."

"Still—"

"Yeah, I know." She stared at the statues on the altar. "These things are…they're sacred objects, Chief. This spot is as holy to me as a church is to other folks. I don't expect you to understand that, but—"

"So then, this *was* some kind of…occult ceremony."

She licked her lips. "I'm just asking you to take care with my things, is all. Maybe…maybe you could have Jimmy take charge of collecting the evidence? As a favor to my family?"

"That would put him in an awful position, Selene, him being your brother-in-law. Suppose he finds something incriminating?"

"You know Jimmy Corona, Chief. He's a good cop. He wouldn't tamper with evidence—not even for me."

"No, I don't suppose he would. All right, out of respect for your family, Selene, I'll have Jimmy oversee things here. He's off duty so I'll call him in. And....," the chief thinned his lips, sighed, "while I'm at it, I'll have him tell Caleb to meet us at the station."

"Thanks, Chief Wheatly."

He harrumphed, taking her gently by one arm, and leading her toward his black-and-white SUV. "I've known your mamma a long time," he said. "It's not her fault if you've fallen into some kind of satanic cult, girl."

"I have not fallen into any—"

"She's done the best she could by you girls. It can't have been easy raising five kids all alone. I just hope we can find a way to get you back on the straight and narrow. Vidalia Brand is a good woman. She doesn't deserve this." He opened the door, eased her into the passenger seat, closed the door and then got behind the wheel. He took his radio mike from the dashboard, and put in a call. "Sally, I need you to put in a call to Jimmy Corona. Tell him to meet me at the station and to bring Caleb Montgomery with him. Tell them Selene Brand is being brought in for questioning in relation to an attempted murder with...ties to the occult. And uh, maybe you'd best put in a call to Reverend Jackson, as well."

Selene shot him a look. "You ever hear of separation of church and state, Chief?"

"Aw, c'mon, Selene. Your mamma would want him there."

She pursed her lips, folded her arms across her chest, and leaned back in the seat. This was going to be a hell of a long night.

Chapter 2

Selene sat in the small room alone, waiting for the ax to fall. She knew her mother was in the next room. She didn't know about anyone else in the family, but she could feel her mother's presence. Goddess, what must Vidalia be thinking right now? To get a phone call from the police in the middle of the night, to be told her youngest daughter had been brought in for questioning regarding a stabbing with Chief Wheatly's so-called "occult ties." Poor Mamma.

She could deal with her mother, though, and she would. At least that was something she *could* deal with. That poor man in the hospital, that was something almost entirely out of her hands.

Almost.

She could still send magic. She whispered charms and sent healing energy to him on the web of the night. But she wished she could do more. All night she'd been thinking about him. She wondered if he was all right, if he was in pain, if he had remembered what had really happened. She wondered if he really thought she had been the one who'd hurt him.

That bothered her, knowing he thought that. It was no way to start out a lifetime together, that was for sure.

She tensed when the door opened, then relaxed when she saw it was only Caleb, her brother-in-law. One thing about it, she had a family made for getting a girl out of trouble. Of her four brothers-in-law, one was a cop, one was a PI and one was a lawyer. The fourth was a mechanic, but in most circumstances, his kind of help was all she needed. Tonight was certainly different.

Caleb smiled, but it didn't meet his worried eyes. "Hi, Selene. You okay?"

She closed her eyes, nodded slowly. "Thanks for coming, Cal."

"Not a problem. Uh, Vidalia's here, too. Chomping at the bit to get in here."

"Thanks for making her wait."

"It wasn't easy." Caleb pulled out a chair and sat down. "It's just you and me here. No one's listening in. So uh, you wanna tell me what happened out by the falls tonight, Selene?"

She watched his eyes, looking for any sign that he no longer trusted her. She half expected the entire family to turn on her once they knew the truth. But she saw nothing to tell her that was the case with him. "What's the chief saying?"

He lifted his brows. "Some pretty farfetched stuff. Says it looks as if there was some kind of satanic ritual going on out there, with you right smack in the middle of it."

She said nothing. He stared at her, waiting.

Finally she sighed. "There was a ritual. But there was nothing satanic about it, Caleb. Just because something is different doesn't mean it's evil. Just because someone has a different way of worshipping, that doesn't make them satanic."

He held up a hand. "Hey, you don't have to convince me. I believe you."

"You do?"

"Come on, Selene. You've been messing with herbs and spells for as long as I've been in this family. I'm not ignorant."

She was stunned. "You…you knew?"

He nodded. "I figured if you weren't ready to talk about it out loud, then that was your business. So I never brought it up. But look, that's me. The chief and the rest of the good folks of Big Falls aren't necessarily as familiar with alternative belief systems. And—well, a stranger was stabbed tonight. People are muttering about a botched human sacrifice."

She shot to her feet. "That's insane!"

"Well, sure it is, hon. I know that. Everyone else will, too, as soon as you fill us in. What happened, Selene?"

"Bring my mother in." He just looked at her, unsure. "Bring her in, Cal. I don't want to have to go through this more times than I absolutely have to."

He nodded, got up and left the room. A second later, he returned with her mother and Chief Wheatly. She paced away from them, trying to form words in her mind to explain herself. But she could have spent all night planning her words and still not got them quite right. So she just started talking.

"You all know me, right? You know I'm always brewing herbal teas and making charms and reading cards, right?"

"Yes," Caleb said. "We love those things about you, don't we Vidalia?"

"It's always made me nervous. You know that, child."

"Those things are…well, they're…they're folk magic. They're what a lot of people call…witchcraft." She turned and looked her mother dead in the eye. "I'm a Witch."

She'd thought Vidalia would faint dead away. Instead she folded her hands around her tiny silver cross pendant and closed her eyes.

Caleb nodded slowly. "What, exactly, does that mean? To you, I mean?" he asked. And she knew he was asking only to give her the chance to explain things to her mom and to the chief.

"Well, I'll tell you what it *doesn't* mean. It doesn't mean I worship the devil and it doesn't mean I would ever hurt anyone or anything. The only commandment in the Craft is 'Harm none.'"

Caleb sat calmly in the chair, his eyes following her agitated pacing. The chief stood, his gaze shifting from Cal and Vi to Selene and back again. Vidalia just sat there, head bowed, eyes closed, muttering what might have been a prayer under her breath.

"Wicca is about empowering the divine within ourselves and respecting it in others. It's about attuning to the cycles and seasons of nature. It's about finding the magic in everything around us. It's about—" She stopped there, turned to stare at her mother. "We were just observing the full moon, Mom, just relishing the fact that we're alive and in such a beautiful place, enjoying God's creation. We were just laughing and talking and casting a few positive spells—which is just like praying, only a little more proactive and a little less dependent. We were doing nothing wrong."

Caleb nodded as if he fully understood. The chief said, "We, huh?"

She bit her lip and turned away from him.

"Look, Selene, the chief knows there were others out there with you tonight. If you'd just tell him who else was with you, and one of them could vouch for your story—"

"It's not a story, Caleb, it's the truth. And I'm sorry, but I won't tell anyone who was out there with me."

"You most certainly will, young lady!" Vidalia's outburst shocked them all. She'd jumped to her feet as she spoke, and Caleb got up, too, and put a calming hand on her shoulder.

"Vidalia," the chief said. "Now I told you, if you want to be here for this, you're going to need stay calm, all right?"

She pursed her lips, lowered her head and slowly sank back into her seat.

"Now, Selene," Chief Wheatly said, "those others who were out there with you, they were witnesses to a crime."

"There was no crime. No one witnessed any crime. We witnessed a man stumble bleeding from the woods and collapse on the ground. I tried to stop his bleeding and called for help. I didn't see anyone or anything else. No one did."

The chief nodded and glanced at Vidalia. "There is a blood trail leading from the woods to the spot where the fellow ended up, Vi. I tend to believe your daughter is telling the truth, if that helps you any." Then he focused on Selene again. "Selene, will you at least tell me why it is you won't give me their names so they can tell me this for themselves?"

She met his eyes, held them steadily. "Because they don't want it known. They don't want their friends and relatives and employers thinking the same things about them that this entire police department, not to mention my own mother, are thinking about me right now." She lowered her head, closed her eyes. "Hell, given the efficiency of the Big Falls grapevine, half the town is probably thinking those things about me by now."

When she looked up again, it was to find the chief staring at her almost as if he felt a bit sorry for her. Meanwhile, her mother was staring, too—looking at her as if she'd never seen her before. That look hurt. It hurt deeply.

There was a knock at the door, and then it opened, and Jimmy Corona came in. He wore his uniform, but didn't hesitate to cross straight to Selene and give her a bear hug that squeezed the breath out of her. She held on and he picked her right up off the floor for a moment, then set her down again with a peck on the cheek. "All your stuff is safe, Selene. Don't give it another thought."

"Thanks, Jimmy."

"How's the victim, Corona?" the chief asked.

Selene searched Jimmy's eyes, hoping he'd say the man was fine. All he needed to do was get over the shock and recover a little, and he would be able to tell the police what had happened, that she hadn't been the one to try to hurt him tonight.

"He's gonna recover from the knife wound. It's his head that has them worried, Chief."

"He has a head injury?"

"He was apparently drugged. Had a bad reaction to it, and right now, he can't remember a damn thing."

"What do you mean?"

Jimmy shook his head. "Amnesia, Chief. The doc actually used that word. *Amnesia.* This guy doesn't know his own name, much less what happened out there tonight."

Selene looked from one face to the next, and felt as if her hopes were dying a slow, painful death. "Amnesia," she whispered..

Jimmy cleared his throat. "He only remembers being chased through the woods, bleeding. Beyond that, all he's been able to tell us so far is that he wound up on the ground with you standing over him holding a dagger, looking for all the world like you were about to use it to gut him."

She closed her eyes slowly. "I imagine that's about what it did look like, to him. But it wasn't the case. Not that I expect any of you to take my word for that."

"Your word's good enough for me, Selene," Caleb said.

"And me," Jimmy added.

Vidalia was still silent. Selene felt as if a dagger were being driven into her own belly. "Aside from the lack of memory—is he all right?"

"He will be," Jimmy promised.

"Look, Chief." Caleb walked to her side and stood there, shoulder to shoulder, facing the chief. "You took her dagger, right? Surely you've given it the once-over with some Luminol by now. Was there any trace of blood on the blade?"

"No," the chief said. "And from the photos of the wound, it looks like a single-edged blade made it. Probably a hunting knife. Selene's knife was double-edged. Now, that doesn't mean there wasn't another weapon. A prosecutor would say she ditched it somewhere."

"Maybe so," Caleb said. "But aside from her being on the scene, there's no evidence against Selene. She tried to give aid. She called for help and then stayed with the victim until it arrived, when she could have taken off to keep her secrets intact. Are those the actions of someone who'd just knifed a man?"

"Caleb, we're just trying to get to the bottom of this."

"The bottom of this is that a stranger was attacked in the woods by the falls by an unknown assailant, and that he probably would have died without Selene's help."

"And the real criminal is probably getting away while you waste time grilling my daughter," Vidalia said softly. She got to her feet, her eyes raking Selene, then hardening before she turned back to the chief. "I don't know what all is going on here, Chief, but I do know Selene. If she finds a spider in her room she carries it outside and turns it loose. She doesn't eat meat, and argues against cutting down live Christmas trees every year. She won't even swat a fly. There's no way she harmed that man."

"Well, now if she'd just give me the names of the other witnesses, they could vouch for that and I could let her go," he said. Then he looked at Selene.

"One woman could lose her kids in court if this comes out," Selene said softly. "Another could lose her job. Giving their names could make trouble for them, a lot of trouble. I can't betray them that way."

The chief sighed. "Selene, darlin', will you tell me if I have the others leave the room?"

She met his eyes, shook her head. "I'll only tell you this. There was nothing dark, nothing satanic. It was a group of women honoring nature and communing with the divine, a group of women who've made two very solemn vows—never to betray each other's secrets, and never to harm any living thing. That's all."

He nodded slowly. "So, for the record, it was a group of women practicing what you might call…Witchcraft?"

She lifted her head, held his gaze. "Yes."

Vidalia's eyes filled and she closed them tightly.

Caleb seemed ready climb the walls, but he kept his cool. "Chief, this family has a lot to work through tonight. You know Selene. You've known her all her life. You know she's not going anywhere. You've got no evidence to hold her. So why not let her go home and get some rest, huh?"

Caleb was good. He was eloquent and he was on her side. Thank the Goddess someone was.

The chief nodded. "You have anything you want to add, Selene?"

"Just that I didn't hurt that man. And that…I'm a good person." The last was said with a look in her mother's direction, but Vidalia refused to meet her eyes.

"All right, Selene. You go on home with your family. But now, listen, this is important. You can't be leaving town. We're gonna need to talk to you some more as this investigation moves along. All right?"

"I promise."

"Good."

Selene rose from the chair and walked with her mother and Caleb to the door. In the waiting area of the police department, her sisters Kara and Edie waited, and they came to hug her hard as soon as she came within their sight.

"Are you okay?" Kara asked. "I told Jimmy not to let you out of his sight while you were in this place."

"I'm fine, and Jimmy was with me every second since he got here." Selene glanced behind her to see him coming out of the interrogation room, looking tired.

Vidalia was heading for the exit, not even pausing to talk to the girls. She was embarrassed by her youngest daughter tonight. That was a first. She paused only long enough to send the girls her patented get-moving-already look.

Selene frowned. "I'll be home soon, Mom. I have something I need to do first."

Vi stared at her for a long moment, then just lowered her head and shook it slowly, as she turned and left the room.

"Damn, she's upset," Edie said. "I've never seen her this bad."

"She'll be all right once she gives me a chance to explain," Selene said. "But you two better go with her. See to it she gets home all right. I'll be along later."

Caleb put a hand on her shoulder. "Your car's been impounded, hon."

She took that in stride, she thought, barely flinching. "Then someone will have to loan me one."

Kara handed her a set of keys. "I'll ride home with Mom and Edie. Keep it as long as you need it, hon," she said.

"Thanks, Kara."

"You want to tell me where you're going?" Caleb asked.

She met his eyes, shook her head side to side, and left the police station.

He lay in the hospital bed, staring at the ceiling. But the ceiling held no answers. His mind was gaping black hole. He had no idea who he was, but there was a deeper and more frightening lack. He didn't know *how* he was, either. Was he a serious man or a playful one? Was he hard-working or lazy? Was he a friendly, easy-going type or a grouchy SOB? He had no clue.

"How are you feeling?"

He drew his focus up out of the abyss that was his inner psyche and shifted his gaze from the ceiling to the nurse standing beside his bed. She must be close to retiring age, he thought. She was silver-haired, bone thin and slightly stooped, but smiling.

"How would I know?"

"Well, are you in pain?"

"No." He glanced down toward his belly, though it was

currently covered by a layer of bandages, a hospital gown and a white sheet. "But I have no doubt you're here to start poking at the hole in my belly to change that, just like you've done every time it's stopped throbbing for more than five minutes."

"I'm afraid so." She peeled back the covers.

He yanked them back over himself again. "I'm afraid not."

"It's necessary, son."

"I'm not your son. At least, I don't think I am."

She scowled at him, her patience clearly wearing thin. "Listen, I have other patients to take care of."

"Then go take care of them and leave me the hell alone."

From behind the door there was a commotion. He frowned in that direction, hearing the cop who'd been posted outside telling someone they couldn't come in. Then he glanced at the nurse. "See who that is, would you?"

"Oh, so now you *want* my help?"

He just held her gaze until she rolled her eyes and turned to go open the door. "Prince Charming in here wants to know who's trying to see him. I figure it's gotta be someone with a penchant for self-flagellation, because he's—oh. Aren't you—?"

She didn't finish the question. And because Nurse Ratchitt was blocking the partially open door with her body, he couldn't see who it was. Maybe someone who knew him. Maybe—

He tried to get out of the bed, but when he started to sit up, it felt as if his stomach muscles were ripping apart. Dammit.

"Let them the hell in, whoever they are." He made the demand in a voice that hid his pain as he fell back onto the bed, one hand on his belly, waiting for the pain to ebb.

The door opened the rest of the way, and the nurse stepped on the doorstop to keep it there, then stepped aside. The woman stood there staring in at him. She had eyes as pale blue as a springtime morning, and that silver-blond hair that made a man think of angels. She was wearing a blouse this time, with the sarong skirt she'd been wearing earlier, but he remembered clearly what she'd looked like without one. Wild and free and enticing.

He also remembered opening his eyes to find her standing over him with a knife in her hands.

"I'm going to have to search you, ma'am," the cop beyond her said.

She sighed and raised her arms outward toward her sides. "Just keep in mind that if you touch anything you shouldn't, my brother-in-law will kick your ass."

"Which one?" the cop asked with a crooked grin.

"All four of them," she said. "I can't guarantee in what order, though."

He shrugged, and proceeded to run his hands up and down her sides, and her front and her back. He didn't grope her, but he didn't skip any parts either. Seemed all business. Then he nodded and looked past her at him. "You sure you're okay with this?"

He didn't take his eyes off the woman. And hers were on him now, steady and probing as he nodded.

"Okay, then," the cop said. "I'll be right outside the door if you need me."

"Okay."

The cop withdrew, pulling the door closed behind him.

He lay in the bed, waiting. "So?" he asked after a long moment.

She shrugged and came closer. The way she looked at him suggested that she knew him. "So." When she was standing right beside the bed, still probing his eyes and drinking in his face as if she were trying to memorize it, she lifted a palm and lowered it onto his shoulder.

It was an odd thing to do. And even though there was a thin hospital gown between her skin and his, he felt the heat, and wondered what the hell it was about. He had to grab hold of himself, shake himself a little, before he could speak. "So what are you doing here?"

"I wanted to see if you were okay. It's not every day I have wounded men falling at my feet."

"Just healthy ones, huh?"

She smiled a little. "I guess it's a good sign you have a sense of humor."

He shrugged. "Do you know me?"

Her smile died. "No. I'm sorry, I wish I did."

"You said you did. You said you'd been waiting for me."

She lowered her eyes to hide them from him. "Well, waiting for a dark, handsome stranger to fall at my feet, anyway. Though I'd have preferred a less wounded one." Lifting her steady gaze to his again, she went on. "It must be awful, not being able to remember."

"It'll come back to me."

"Sure, I know that." She pursed her lips a little, lowered her head, repositioned her hands, so they were resting on his chest now. "I'm Selene, by the way."

"Yeah, I heard that somewhere along the line. What is it you're doing, exactly?"

He nodded downward at her hands on his chest as he asked it.

"It's a healing modality." Then she thinned her lips, and lifted her hands. "I'm sorry. I should have asked first."

"Healing modality?"

"Yeah. So do you mind?"

Did he mind? Her hands on his body were not exactly a hardship. "No, I don't mind."

"I knew you wouldn't. That's probably why I didn't ask." She laid her palms on his chest again. He wished he wasn't wearing a hospital gown. Her hands got warm, tingly against his skin before she moved them lower, kind of bracketing the bandaged section of his waist, knowing where that spot was without being able to see it.

"So…about what you told the police—"

"Right. So you're finally getting to the reason you're really here, then."

Her brows crinkled over her pale, spooky eyes. "I came because I was compelled to come to you. And I think you know it."

"I do?"

"You're kind of grouchy, you know that?"

"Yeah, well, getting stabbed in the belly will do that to a guy."

She held his gaze, her own steady, unflinching. "I didn't hurt you, you know. I only tried to help you."

"And if you had, you'd have come here to admit it?"

"I know how it must have looked, but it's not what it seems."

"Well, let me recap for you. Someone stabs me in the belly. I run away, aware only that I'm hurt and bleeding and being chased. I collapse, and when I look up it's to see you standing over me with a dagger raised up head high, ready to bring it down. I can see where that set of circumstances could confuse the hell out of me."

She lowered her head. "If you would just stop thinking so much, you'd know the truth. Look at me. Look me right in the eyes." He did, but he found himself getting lost in those eyes of hers. "Keep looking. And open up your senses. Feel me. Sense me. You know I didn't hurt you. Can't you sense that? I couldn't hurt you if I wanted to."

He felt himself nodding in agreement, then snapped his gaze from hers. What the hell was she doing? Trying to hyp-notize him or something? The cops had said there were occult connections to this woman, and the others who were with her out there tonight. It gave him chills.

"Look, I don't remember what happened. And staring into those blue eyes of yours isn't going to help."

"It might be the only thing that does," she whispered.

He shot her a look. "What's that supposed to mean?"

"Look, would it help if I told you the police didn't find any blood on my athame?"

"Athamay?"

"My…blade. My dagger." She held his eyes, finally lowering hers. "This isn't going to be easy if you insist on thinking I tried to kill you tonight."

"What isn't going to be easy?"

She frowned, sighed. "Never mind. I have to um … go home. Face the music, you know? But I'd like to come back and see you again."

"Why?"

She made the cutest face he'd ever seen, then. She pursed her lips and moved them all the way to one side, as if straining hard to think of an answer to his question. It disarmed him completely, shot down his suspicions and almost made him smile. He had to fight hard to keep a straight face. Finally, she said, "I don't think I can tell you that yet. But it's important. To me and to you. So don't…you know, disappear, okay?"

"I don't think there's any danger of me going anywhere tonight."

"I'll be back tomorrow, then."

He almost looked forward to it. "Okay."

She turned for the door, and he said, "Selene?"

Stopping, she faced him slowly, and he went on. "What were you and those other women doing out there by the Falls tonight?"

She smiled slowly. "We're Witches."

He felt his face go blank. She said it as if that was supposed to explain everything. It didn't.

"Yeah, I know. You don't know what that means. But I have to tell you, it feels good to say it like that. Just say it right out, and not worry about the reaction. That's the first time I've done that. I like it."

"I am completely confused."

"I know. Look, we can talk more about that the next time I see you, okay? I mean, you really do need to know."

"I do?"

She nodded. "Yeah. You do. You more than anyone. Good night, C. I'll come by in the morning."

He frowned hard. "Did you just call me C?"

"Yeah. I don't know the rest. But I'm sure your name starts with a *C*. A hard *C*, not a soft one."

"And how do you know that?"

"I told you, I'm a Witch."

"Right."

She sailed out of the room, but paused in the doorway to send him a long, searching look. He felt something in that look, and for just a second, believed she really was what she said she was; a Witch.

He sure as hell wasn't going to make this easy on her. She didn't think he was used to trusting his senses, and he was going to have to learn to depend on them, to make up for his lack of memory. Convincing him of that would be a challenge.

Selene drove her sister's car back toward home, and tried to focus on the man in the hospital room because it was a lot more pleasant than focusing on what awaited her at her house.

She was going to have to try to explain herself to her mother. And Vidalia Brand wasn't exactly known for being open-minded.

Selene rounded a curve and gasped at the number of cars in the driveway. My God, she thought, her mother must have called the entire family from the police station. Everyone was there. Then she noticed an unfamiliar brown SUV and wondered who owned it.

She squinted in the headlight's glow and read the customized plate. WWJD-3. "What *would* Jesus do," Selene wondered aloud. "If he were smart, he'd probably turn around and head for the hills." She sighed deeply, knowing by the plates that the SUV was Reverend Jackson's car. "God, this is an ambush."

She pulled into the driveway, but didn't shut off the engine. She could turn around and leave. But, no. No, that wasn't going to solve anything. She was going to have to face this sooner or later, and if this was the way her mother wanted to do it, then fine. This was the way they would do it.

She shut off the engine, stiffened her spine, got out of the car, and marched toward the front door. Pausing with her hand on the knob, Selene took a deep breath and tried to exhale her anger and her hurt when she let it out again. She took another and visualized pulling a shield of positive energy around her with the air. She lifted her chin, whispered an invocation to the Goddess, and opened the door.

The murmur of voices fell silent when she stepped through the door. Her home was filled with familiar faces. Her oldest sister Maya sent her an encouraging smile, Caleb stood behind her, with the twins at his feet. Seated at the kitchen table beside Maya, were Melusine and Alex. Kara and Jimmy sat on the opposite side of the table with little Tyler between them, and Edie and Wade stood near the freshly filled coffee pot. Vidalia rose from her spot at the head of the table. At her shoulder, Reverend Jackson seemed to be presiding over them all.

The men quickly got up. Jimmy hauled Tyler up into his arms, and headed for the door. He paused to kiss Selene on the cheek as he passed. "We're outta here. Give you females some time to talk. But if you need us, we'll be within shouting distance."

"Good idea," Caleb said. He scooped up a twin in each arm. "We can go up to my place. Come on, guys." With that he and Jimmy went outside and started toward the house Caleb and Maya had built just up the hill, behind Vidalia's.

Wade and Alex came to the door to follow suit. Wade chucked her on the chin and gave her a wink. Alex whispered, "They give you any trouble, baby, you just whistle."

She nodded as they passed, grateful. But then she turned to face her mother and sisters again, and her heart fell. Reverend Jackson stood there looking for all the world as if he were gearing up for a full-blown sermon. Before he could say a word, she got her own in. "Reverend, it's wonderful to see you, as always. But I'm afraid you've come at a bad time. I really need to have a private conversation with my mother, if you don't mind."

Vidalia gaped, and Maya put a hand on her shoulder as if to calm her.

"I'm well aware of that, Selene," the minister said. "That's why I'm here, in fact. To talk with you about this…this Wicca nonsense."

"Wicca is my religion, Reverend. And calling it nonsense is as offensive to me as calling Christianity, Judaism or Islam nonsense would be to a practitioner of any of those faiths. And every bit as wrong."

He nodded slowly. "I understand the point of view, Selene, but—"

"I'm not going to discuss this with you, sir. I don't mean to be blunt, but it's none of your business."

"Selene!" This time Vidalia jumped to her feet, mortified.

"Mom, I want to talk to you about this. I do, but not like this. Please, ask him to leave so we can just sit down and—"

"He's a *minister*, Selene!"

Selene closed her eyes, and felt the sympathetic gazes of her sisters on her. Lowering her head, she gave up. "I'm going to my room. Good night."

"Selene, you come back here! We're talking about this right now."

She glanced at her mother, shook her head slowly, and just kept on walking.

"Selene!"

"Mom, come on. Let her go," Edie said softly.

"I told you this was a mistake," Maya put in. "You should give her a chance. This wasn't fair."

"Girls, girls, your mother is only concerned about your sister's soul."

"Our mother has raised her daughters to think for themselves," Melusine snapped, her tone shorter than any of the others' had been. "It amazes me to realize that that value only holds as long as we agree with her point of view. I never would have believed it."

"Me neither," Kara whispered.

Selene closed the bedroom door, no longer able to hear their voices. She needed time. She needed distance.

She needed, she thought, to get the hell out of here.

Chapter 3

It was quiet in the hospital. He supposed he'd been a difficult patient, but it was difficult *being* a patient, given the situation.

According to the police chief, who'd finally come to fill him in on what was known about his case, the gorgeous blonde who'd saved his life was a self-proclaimed witch who'd been engaged in some sort of Pagan rite about the time he'd been stabbed. Chief Wheatly claimed Selene Brand was a good girl, but had always been "a little odd" and that he had to wonder if his stabbing had been some sort of occult blood rite, though he hastened to add that there had been a blood trail leading from the woods to the site where the women had been gathered, and that there was no evidence Selene had been the one who'd stabbed him. Her blade held no trace of blood, and didn't match the wound in his belly.

He hated to think she might have been his attacker. Granted, when he'd opened his eyes and seen her standing

over him with that knife in her hand, that was exactly what
he'd thought. But not instantly. His initial thoughts had been
far different ones. He'd been looking up at a half-naked babe,
with her breasts exposed to the night and to his eyes, after all.
And he was only human, as far as he knew. And she was hot.

But was she a beautiful, insane killer?

It made him angry that he would know for sure if only his
mind was anything other than a dark, black hole. He didn't
remember a damn thing about the stabbing. Nothing. Except
that the wound they'd patched up had already been inflicted
when he'd fallen at the woman's feet, and he'd confirmed with
the doctors here that there had only been one. The nude
madwoman could have inflicted another while he lay there.
God knew she'd had the time. But she hadn't. She'd helped
him, instead.

The question remained, though, had she inflicted the first
one? Had he run off into the woods, become disoriented and
stumbled right back to her, having forgotten what she had just
done? Had she been the one pursuing him through the night?

This was ridiculous. He didn't need to be in a hospital. He
needed to be out of here, figuring out what the hell had
happened to him. And who the hell he was.

He peeled back his covers, and sat up, moving carefully,
one hand over his bandaged abdomen. It hurt, but not too
badly, so he kept going, swung his legs over the side, and sat
up that way for a minute, just to take stock.

Yeah. He was all right. He needed to talk to someone about
getting out of here.

A young screech owl gave three cries from somewhere just
outside the window. Most people got chills when they heard
a screech owl, wondering what sort of creature made such a
sound. But he knew.

There was a big plastic bag lying on the stand beside his
bed, marked Patient's Belongings, and he reached for it,
tugged it open and began pulling the items out of it: a pair of

jeans, shorts, socks, shoes. The shirt was missing. He checked every pocket for clues, hoping for any personal item that might help him out. But there was nothing. Either he'd had nothing on him, or the police had taken everything except these clothes. He was surprised they hadn't taken all the clothes, but then he figured by the time he went from the woods to the women, to the ambulance to the ER, any evidence on the clothes would have been useless.

He put on the shorts and jeans, socks and shoes. He was just reaching for the call button when the door opened, and his lights went out.

He squinted, but couldn't see more than a silhouette in the doorway, backed by the light from the hall. And then the silhouette lifted a hand, and he saw the unmistakable shape of a gun. He hit the floor just as it went off—two shots without a single bang. Two thuds into the pillow of his bed. He yanked the first thing within reach—the bedside phone—and hurled it at the door, but by then the form was gone, and a half dozen nurses were rushing into the room as the lights came on again. His police guard came on their heels.

Hands were on him, helping him up, voices were asking what had happened. His belly was bleeding again. He got upright, and stared at the holes in his pillow. As the nurses and the cop followed his gaze he muttered, "Someone just tried to kill me. Again."

"Man! I only went to the restroom," the cop muttered.

"Yeah, maybe not such a great idea."

"Was it one of the women? One of the…the witches?" the cop asked.

He met the officer's eyes, and thought it was odd that although he'd seen all the women, four or five all told, when the chief had asked him to describe them, he'd drawn a complete blank. The only details he remembered were the ones pertaining to her. Selene. The silver-haired wood nymph.

"It was a man. But I could only see him in silhouette." He

looked at the nurses. "No one saw him? He shot twice and ran. You telling me no one saw him?"

They all shook their heads. He thought then that it was a damn good thing his pillow bore the bullet holes as proof, because he didn't think they would have believed him otherwise.

Selene retreated to her bedroom and locked the door. She was upset. She'd been meaning to talk to her mom and sisters about her beliefs for ages, and just had never managed to work up the courage. Now she was paying the price, and she wasn't naive enough to think it wasn't her own fault. She should have come clean long ago. Having them find out like this—she couldn't really think of a worse way for her secret to be revealed.

But damn, her mother's stubborn refusal even to hear her side of things had thrown her. She had never expected that. It felt like a betrayal, and it hurt. At least Vidalia had come through at the police station, stating firmly that she didn't believe Selene would ever hurt anyone. Thank Goddess for that.

Still, it didn't change the fact that her mother thought she was doing something wrong. Probably thought she was damned to hell for her most deeply held beliefs.

Right now, though, there were more important things to deal with than her own hurt feelings. She picked up the telephone in her bedroom and dialed Tessa's number.

Tessa picked up on the first ring.

"Hey, hon. It's me."

"Selene? Are you okay? What happened?"

"It's a mess," Selene said. She turned a full circle and sank onto the floor, pushing a hand through her hair. "The guy— you know the one who was hurt?"

"Your soul mate? Yeah, I remember him. Vaguely."

"He doesn't remember anything, Tess. And the police seem to think I tried to kill him as some kind of Pagan sacrifice."

Her statement was met with dead silence. Selene closed

her eyes, drew a breath. "They know I wasn't there alone, Tess. But I didn't give up your names, and I won't. I promise you that, no matter what."

"Oh, God, Selene—"

"My mother knows, and she's acting all crazy. Had Erica's father here waiting for me when I got home."

"Reverend Jackson? Oh, hell, Selene."

"She's not even giving me a chance to explain. Tess, I have to get out of here."

Tessa sighed. "Selene, if you tell them who else was there, wouldn't that help you out of this mess? I mean, we're all witnesses to the fact that you didn't do anything to hurt that man. Hell, you put yourself on the line to try to help him."

"You think they'd believe you?" Selene shook her head and sighed. "Because I don't. If it was a ritual sacrifice gone wrong, we were all involved, and we'd cover each other. I don't think the word of a Witch is going to go far in this town, Tess."

"Five of us, all telling the same story, and no evidence to the contrary? Come on, they're not cavemen. They'd listen."

"Maybe." Selene sighed. "Let's wait and see. I'm hoping it clears itself up and no one else needs to be outed. They know he was stabbed in the woods—there's a clear blood trail. And they know my athame wasn't the weapon. So that's a plus. Just let me be clear on this, Tessa, I'm not giving up your names, no matter what. If it gets really down-and-dirty, and you decide to do that, it's up to you. Not me. I won't do it."

"You need to keep me posted, so I know if it's necessary."

"Yeah, that's why I called. I want you to get in touch with the others, tell them what's going on, everything I've told you. I'd do it myself, but I just need to get out of here."

"I'll tell them. Except for Erica. She's headed down to that Pagan festival in Texas, remember? She'll be gone four days."

"Right. I forgot, with everything else."

"Where are you going to go, Selene? I mean, if you take off, won't that make you look even more guilty?"

"I don't even care. But the chief told me not to leave town, so if I go too far it might just give him an excuse to arrest me." She closed her eyes. "I just can't stay here. Not with Mom acting all crazy on me. I need some time, you know? And Kara loaned me her car, so…"

"You can go to the cabin," Tessa said.

Selene lifted her brows, surprised. "Your husband's hunting cabin?"

"Yeah. Chet isn't using it until next week. You remember where it is?"

"Yeah."

"Key's in one of those fake rock thingies to the right of the door. The place is fully stocked. And I won't tell a soul that's where you are."

"Thanks, Tessa."

"It's the least I can do. Stay in touch, okay?"

"Yeah. I will. Thank you, Tessa. You're…you're like a sister."

"Better. Good night, Selene."

"'Night, Tessa."

Selene hung up her phone, reaching the stand without getting up. She felt drained, emotionally more than physically. To meet the man fate has chosen for you, only to realize he thinks you tried to kill him. Well, hell, it didn't get much worse than that, did it?

She couldn't stop thinking about him. Couldn't get those dark eyes out of her mind. He was something. He was…everything.

She really needed to be doing something, getting ready, though she would have to wait until everyone was asleep before actually leaving the house. And she was going to have to borrow a car since hers was still impounded.

Chet Monro's cabin was a good option. The perfect hideaway, really. Not technically outside of town, and yet isolated enough to give her the time she needed to work through some things.

On the way, though, she had one stop to make.

She needed to see that stranger. She needed to go to the hospital. She'd promised him she would see him tomorrow—so she had to tell him tonight why that wasn't going to happen.

He was nervous as hell, and the damn cop stationed outside his door wasn't doing a thing to ease his mind. Someone was trying to kill him, and right now, that someone knew exactly where to find him.

He didn't intend to wait around for the bastard to try again. No way. He didn't know a hell of a lot about himself right then, but he felt very much like the kind of guy who wouldn't go down without a fight. And that fight would be on his terms. Term one being, it wasn't going to take place in a hospital room where he was defenseless.

No way in hell.

He had to wait, though. He'd been quizzing nurses about the schedule here, claiming he needed to be left alone to get some rest. The doctor had made his evening rounds at nine, and at two—just ten minutes from now—his nurse would be in to check his vitals and administer his meds. He'd have four hours from then until the next time he'd be bothered. And that was when he would make his move.

Until then, he lay in the bed feeling very much like a man with a glowing neon target painted on his forehead.

Finally, the nurse came in with his meds, and damned if he didn't tense up when the door opened. He damn near threw himself over the side onto the floor in case the newcomer turned out to be his would-be assassin back for a third try.

But it was just his nurse, her smile wary, since he'd basically been biting her head off every time she came in, up to now. He was glad to see her this time, though. Get this over with so he could move on with his plan.

"How are you feeling?"

"Fine." Monosyllabic answers might speed this along.

She came to his bedside and took his wrist in her hand, then gazed at her watch for a few seconds. "Pulse looks a little high. You been up running laps around the room?"

"No."

"Talkative tonight, aren't you?"

"Just wondering if you people are ever going to leave me alone long enough to get some sleep."

"Well, then you'll be pleased to know I'm your last visitor for a few hours. Arm please."

She had the blood pressure cuff in her hands now, and he obediently held up his arm so she could get her kicks by cutting off its circulation for a few seconds. She pumped and watched the dial, and pumped some more. Then she whipped the thing off him and hung it from its hook on the wall. "A little elevated."

"Hadn't you heard? Someone took a shot at me a few hours ago."

"I suppose that would account for it." She turned to check the IV.

"Leave me a Band-Aid, huh?"

She frowned at him. "You have a cut somewhere?"

"Might have, after I shave. There shaving gear in there?" he asked with a nod toward the bathroom attached to his room.

"No, but I'll get you some." She smiled. "And a Band-Aid. Be right back."

She left, and was back moments later with the requested items. "You need some help getting to the bathroom?"

"Not in this lifetime."

She rolled her eyes. "Men are the worst patients. Okay, then. I'll leave you to it."

"And will you try to keep everyone out of here for a few hours? I really need some rest."

"I will. Good night, Mr....um, good night."

"Yeah."

She left. Alone at last, he sat up and carefully slid the IV line from his arm. Then he quickly applied the Band-Aid to keep it from bleeding all over the place. He put his jeans back on—the damn nurses had insisted on restoring him to hospital garb after the "incident." Socks and shoes were next, even though it hurt like hell to bend over. He didn't have a shirt to wear, and he didn't much give a damn. He just needed to get out of there.

He went to the window and slid it open. Small-town hospital—one sprawling story. Lucky for him. After a quick look around, he climbed out, wincing as his wound felt the strain, then closed the window behind him, and headed across the parking lot.

It was a cool night. A little too cool to be running around with nothing on from the waist up except for some white bandages that were almost sure to get him spotted. If his attacker returned, he'd still make a pretty easy target. So the goal was to put distance between himself and the hospital and find a damned shirt and a place to hole up until he figured out what to do next.

He crossed the hospital parking lot, hit the sidewalk, and picked up the pace, one arm crossed over his middle. Ten steps later, give or take, he heard other footsteps on the sidewalk a short distance behind him. Stopping short, he turned to look back. No one in sight. He started walking again, and again, heard the footsteps behind him.

Dammit.

He walked faster, heading for the road to cross to the other side without even bothering to look for traffic first. Brakes shrieked, tires skidded, headlights blinded him. A car bucked to a stop just short of hitting him. Turning, he lifted a hand to shield his eyes from the glare of the headlights, but he was damned if he could see a thing. So he shifted his gaze to the sidewalk, and saw a shape, pausing there, watching him.

Probably debating whether to shoot him right there in front

of a witness, or wait for the car to move on. He decided to choose door number three, and went to the passenger side of the car, opened the door and said, "I could sure use a ride, pal."

"Well, then get in, buddy."

That voice.

He squinted in the interior lights and saw her, the blond babe from the nymph brigade, sitting behind the wheel. And there was no way in hell this was a coincidence. So the question was, was she working with the bad guys, or seriously into helping him out?

Footsteps came closer—the SOB on the sidewalk realizing he was about to lose his best shot. So he got into the car, slammed the door and said, "step on it, okay?"

She stepped on it.

Selene's passenger kept looking behind them as she drove away, and she glanced into the rearview mirror to see what had his interest. "You running away from someone?"

He looked at her sharply. "Had a visitor in my hospital room earlier. Took two shots at me in the bed."

She swung her head around and gaped at him. "Someone tried to shoot you?"

"Fortunately, he missed."

"He?"

He slid a sideways glance at her. "Eyes on the road, huh?"

She readjusted her focus, realized she'd been drifting into the wrong lane, and corrected the car's position. "So you, what, ducked the bullets and ran for it?"

"Ducked the bullets and waited it for an opportunity to get the hell out of there. I don't know for sure, but I think he spotted me, was following me. And then, *coincidentally,* you pulled up."

"Oh, there's no such thing as coincidence."

"So you admit you were here for a reason."

"Yeah. I thought the reason was to see you again, and tell

you why I wouldn't be coming tomorrow, as promised. But now I'm thinking the real reason was to save your life. Again."

"Again?"

"Yeah, I'm the one who kept you from bleeding to death the first time, as you already know."

"Yeah. I remember it hurt like hell. Direct pressure?"

"And Pow-Wow charms."

"Right. I seem to recall some chanting."

"Exactly."

"But you're also the one who was standing over me with a knife out there."

"An athame."

"Excuse me?"

"It wasn't a knife," she said, wondering why she bothered. "It was an athame. A double-edged blade used to control and direct energy during Wiccan rituals. It's never used to cut anything physical, much less harm anyone."

"Uh-huh."

"I was just grounding the energy."

"Right."

"Look, I'm not the one who stabbed you, okay?"

She felt his eyes on her, felt him staring as if he could see the truth if he just looked at her hard enough and long enough. It was frustrating as hell.

"And you would tell me if you were?" he asked.

Glancing sideways at him, just long enough to look him dead in the eyes when she spoke, she said, "I don't expect you to believe it. But yes, I would."

His reaction was one of surprise, and then speculation. "If you saved my life out there, then thank you."

"Gee, the gratitude laced with doubt thing is touching. But you're welcome."

He sighed. When he spoke again his voice was kinder. "It's Selene, isn't it?"

"Selene Brand," she said. And she offered her left hand,

reaching across her body while keeping the right one on the wheel.

He clasped it. His grip was warm and surprisingly strong, given what he'd been through today. His big hand enveloped her small one completely, and she barely suppressed the shiver of response that wriggled up her spine.

"Wish I could introduce myself in return," he said. And he hadn't released her hand yet.

"Still with the memory, huh?"

He nodded.

"What about the ring?"

"Ring?"

She turned his hand in hers, and nodded at the ring he wore. He stared down at it for a moment, then, frowning, slid it from his finger, and turned on the overhead light. "I hadn't even realized—"

"You've been wearing it for so long you don't notice it anymore. It looks like a class ring."

He frowned as he turned the ring in his hand. "There's an eagle on one side, and an elk on the other."

"Big speckled stone there," she said. "I've never seen a crystal like that and I thought I'd seen them all."

"It's not a crystal. It's a fragment of polished dinosaur bone," he said.

She shot him a look. "You remember that?"

"I don't know. Maybe I just know by looking at it." His brows drew closer. "Above the stone are the letters NOWO. And below...."

"What? What's below?"

"A name. Cory."

She smiled a little. "Cory. Does it ring any bells?"

"No. Do I look like a Cory?"

"Yeah. You do. Besides, it's a hard *C*, just like I told you it would be. Is there a last name anywhere? Anything engraved inside?"

He turned the ring over and peered at the inner part of the band. "Twenty-four karat, Endymion."

Her throat went utterly dry and she swerved a little. "Endymion?"

"Yeah. Must be the brand name or the jeweler or something."

"Yeah. Must be."

He tipped his head to one side, studying her face, which she was certain had gone pale. "Does that name mean something to you?"

"I just...well, yeah. I mean. Endymion is the name of a God. He's the lover and mate of the Moon Goddess, Selene." She slid her eyes his way very briefly. "Crazy coincidence, huh?"

"I thought you said there was no such thing as coincidence."

There wasn't, she thought. This man was fated to walk into her life, she knew it with everything in her.

"There isn't," she said.

Chapter 4

"So where are we going?" he asked.

He watched her face, wondering what the hell to make of her. It was tough to tell, because she was focused entirely on two things: the road and his torso. He wished he'd put on the bloody shirt. She didn't even try to hide her interest. Just stole glances that skimmed from his chest to his abs, and burned with their intensity.

So he returned the favor, checking her out just as openly. She was no longer dressed in the sarong skirt. Too bad. He could ogle her much better if she were shirtless, like before, those round breasts bouncing in the moonlight. Then again, he didn't imagine she made a habit of driving through town that way.

But you could tell a lot about a woman from her clothes. She was a beatnik, he thought. A new-ager. The term *dirty hippy* came to mind, and he wondered where he'd picked that up and whether he really felt that way about her kind.

She wore jeans, faded to near white, with holes worn right

through the fabric on the right thigh and the left knee. He wondered if the ass cheeks were worn through as well, and promised to take a gander when she got up. They were too long, their hems nothing but pale fringe. On top she wore a peasant blouse made from what looked like a pile of paisley-print handkerchiefs sewn together. Big sleeves that came to points, V-neck, and a V hemline front and back.

No bra.

He liked that. The free way her breasts moved underneath that loose fabric. Nothing holding them, binding them. It made him have to shift in his seat to think too long about them, moving around under there with every bump in the road.

So he changed his focus to her hair, which was loose and shiny, clean and silky, and totally unadorned. Then to her face, which was pretty much makeup-free, except for maybe a hint of mascara, because he didn't think her lashes would be naturally that thick or that dark. Not with her blond coloring. He studied her hands, with their long, slender fingers and neatly trimmed nails, on the steering wheel. She wore a necklace, a silver star enclosed within a circle, suspended from a chain around her neck. No rings on her fingers. Earrings, though, lots of them. She had four holes in the ear on his side, three in the lobe, and one up top. The top one had a crescent moon in it. The three holes on the bottom had one large wire hoop, one dangling strand of amethyst beads, and one diamond stud.

It occurred to him that she hadn't answered his question. "Selene?"

"Yeah?" She glanced at him again, eyes on his belly. God, the look in them was so blatantly horny he thought he would blow a gasket.

"I asked where we're going?"

"Oh. Yeah." She looked at the road again. "I'll take you wherever you want to go. After that, I'm going up to a secluded cabin for a few days. Now that my family know I'm a Witch, living at home is impossible."

"They didn't know?"

"No."

"And I take it the news wasn't well received."

She glanced his way, looked him in the eyes for once, smiled a little sadly. "My mother had the local minister waiting for me when I got home from the police station. She thinks I'm going straight to hell."

He frowned at her, ignoring the hell comment, though it struck him as sad. "You were at the police station. What, giving a statement or—"

"I was being questioned. The chief thinks I stabbed you. But you know that, right? I mean, you're the one who gave him that idea in the first place."

"Hey, I only told him the truth. That I woke up to find you standing over me with a knife."

She shrugged. "Whatever."

"What about your friends?" he asked. "The women who were out there with you, doing the nakey-dance thing."

"Nakey-dance thing?"

He ignored the sarcasm in her voice. "They must have been able to back up your story, right?" If it were true, at least, he thought.

"Their families don't know they're Witches either. I refused to give their names."

"Even though they could verify your story?"

"Even though."

He sighed. "So, then…I'm a little hazy on what happened and when. But…they left before help arrived, didn't they?"

She nodded, then glanced sideways at him. At, more accurately, at his chest. A long, burning look at his chest, before she jerked her eyes back to the road again. "I told them to go. One could lose her job, another, custody of her kids. There was no need for all of us to be exposed."

"But you stayed."

"I couldn't just let you lie there alone, bleeding. Someone had to stay with you."

He mulled that over in his mind. "Okay, someone had to. But why you?"

She shrugged. "You fell at my feet," she said as if that explained everything. "I'm the one who was supposed to stay."

"I suppose that's something only a Witch would understand."

"It was a sign. We'd just finished discussing signs, and then there you were, and every sign we'd mentioned came along with you. I was the one you came to. There's no question."

"If you say so."

"I say so. And you know what else?" she continued. "If I'd wanted to kill you, I had enough time to do it before the ambulance arrived. Hell, the way you were bleeding, I probably wouldn't have had to do anything. I could have stood there, done nothing, and let you go. But instead, I stopped the bleeding. Do you remember that?"

He thought back, recalled her hands on him, pressing something to his wound, remembered her chanting intensely, rocking back and forth. Something about Mary and Women and Blood. "I think I do," he admitted.

"So why would I do that if I was the one who'd stabbed you in the first place?"

She really wanted him to believe her. It was clear in the intensity in her voice, in her eyes. She was damn near willing him to believe her. He just wished he knew why that was so important.

"Look, I don't even know you," she went on. "What possible reason could I have to want to—"

"How do I know that?" he asked.

"Know what? That I don't know you?"

He nodded. "If I remember right, you said you did know me. You said you'd been waiting for me, or something."

"I did say that. But I was referring to the signs. I felt you coming before you got there. I saw the signs when you arrived. That's all I meant, not that I had ever seen you before."

He sighed, shaking his head and settling back in the seat. "You have no idea how frustrating this is—not to remember anything about myself. Not to know who I am, or what I was doing out in the woods or what happened to me out there. I know it's obnoxious as hell of me to mistrust you—particularly if you saved my life last night. So forgive me if I'm suspicious. But someone is trying to kill me. Right now I don't trust anyone, or anything."

She sent him another look, but this one was softer, and only lingered for a second—on the spot where his belly met his button fly this time—before shifting to his face. "You're right. I'm asking a lot of you, huh? You wake up with a stab wound and see me with a knife, and I'm expecting you to believe I didn't do it just because I say so." She returned her gaze to the road, drew a deep breath, and finally blew it out again. "I can't blame you for being suspicious. And that's sad, because I really think I could help you."

He was surprised, both at her immediate dropping of the defensiveness, and her sudden offer of help. "How?"

She shrugged. "You think this killer is still after you, right? You can't stay in the hospital—he'd know where to find you. Where are you going to go? You don't know anyone here."

"I don't know anyone anywhere."

She nodded and slowed the car as they approached a dirt road that turned right from the paved one they were on. "You could come with me to the cabin."

Having reached the turn, she brought the car to a stop. There was no other traffic in sight. She turned in her seat, and fixed her eyes on his.

"It would be a safe place to hide out. This guy, whoever he is, would have no idea where to find you."

Unless you're working with him. He found it tough to believe she might be, but hell, he didn't know if he could trust his own instincts right now. He wasn't even sure what his instincts were telling him, besides that he didn't approve of her sort, even while he wanted to jump her bones in the worst possible way.

"And maybe we could figure some things out while we're hiding out up there."

"I don't see how. You don't know any more about me than I do."

She shrugged. "Hey, you know your name now. That's more than you knew when you got into this car with me. I helped you figure *that* out, didn't I?"

He nodded.

"Come on, Cory. What other options do you have?"

He sighed. "I'm pretty sure the guy saw me get into your car."

"It's not my car. It's my sister's. Mine's been impounded by the cops. And even if he did see you get in, he wouldn't know the car, much less be able to follow us. He was on foot. And, besides, I've been watching the rear-view. I seriously doubt this would-be killer of yours is a local who knows his way around."

"What makes you so sure?"

She shrugged. "Well, *you're* not a local."

"How do you know that?"

"It's a small town, Cory. I've lived here all my life, was born here. If you were a local, I'd know you. And if it's that you still don't know whether to believe me or not, then ask yourself why no one else knows you, either. No one at the hospital, no one on the ambulance squad. No one at the police department. It's a tiny town, Cory. If you were local, someone would have recognized you. You're not. And if you're not, it stands to reason that whoever is chasing you around trying to kill you isn't either."

He nodded slowly. "That makes sense, I guess."

"So I've helped you figure out something else already. See that? I'm good at this stuff."

He stared at her, completely unsure which way to lean as far as she was concerned.

"You think I might be working with this guy, don't you? You think I'm going to take you up into the middle of nowhere and somehow signal him to come and finish you off."

He met her steady, light-blue gaze, studied her face in the glow of the panel lights. "It had crossed my mind."

She nodded, and glanced behind them. "If you're afraid I'm going to call him as soon as your back is turned, you needn't be. The cell phone reception is very hit and miss where we're going, and the cabin has no phone. But just so you're sure...." She nodded at the bag, a denim backpack, that rested on the back seat. "Take my phone out of my bag. It's in the side pocket."

He reached back and tugged the bag up onto his lap, then felt around for the phone, and pulled it out. When he did, a small drawstring pouch came out as well. It was brown, with a feather tied in its string, a feather with distinctive rust-colored stripes across its base

"Are you a Native American?" he asked her, looking up at her blond, blond hair and doubting it.

"No."

"Then this is illegal." He held up the pouch, let the feather spin slowly from its string. "It's from a redtail hawk. You can't legally possess one."

"Yeah, not until someone takes it to court and wins. Like a Native American, Cory, that feather is a part of my religion. An important part. The hawk is my animal spirit guide. That feather was a gift, from her to me, dropped during a meditation right where I could find it. I think I have a pretty good case."

He shrugged. "Maybe you do, but until then, it's illegal."

"So you going to arrest me?"

He looked her in the eye, then sighed and shook his head.

She thinned her lips. "You know about hawks. You recognized the feather. And you seem to be rather conservative, kind of a stiff-assed, by-the-book stick-in-the-mud. Probably a Republican."

"You say that like it's a bad thing."

She shrugged. "It's just a couple more things we know about you. You stick with me, we'll have all those blanks filled in before you know it." She took the pouch from his hand, and dropped it into her lap, then nodded at the cell phone he held. "Does that ease your mind any?"

"It assures me you can't call and tell anyone where we are. But I suppose he could already know where you're taking me."

"I couldn't have planned for you to run out in front of my car, Cory."

"No, I don't suppose you could."

She tapped the steering wheel, still sitting still in the middle of the road. "It's not my cabin. It belongs to the husband of a friend of mine, and she's the only one who knows I'll be using it for a few days. I don't have any way to prove that to you, though."

He looked at her and finally, he nodded. "All right."

"All right?"

"Yeah. I'll come to the cabin with you. I don't see anyone making me any better offers right now, do you?"

Her smile was quick and unplanned and it damn near floored him when she flashed it, because it reached her eyes, and made them sparkle. "I'm *really* glad."

Yeah, and he knew why. She wanted him. Was as turned on by him as he was by her. And who the hell was he kidding? He'd taken her up on the offer mostly because he was pretty sure he'd get laid before it was over. And he could hardly wait.

She turned the corner and took the dirt road, which wound uphill, through ever thicker woods. "I know I can help you figure this out."

"And what makes you so sure?"

She smiled even bigger that time. "I'm a Witch," she said, as if it made all the sense in the world.

It was really a crying shame she was a card-carrying lunatic, he thought. A *crying* shame.

Vidalia Brand couldn't sleep. She'd tossed and she'd turned and she'd worried for hours, and finally decided she couldn't wait any longer to have a long-overdue talk with her youngest daughter. She'd raised her girls well. Too well for this nonsense. Well, she would be damned herself before she'd stand by and watch her youngest headed straight for hellfire. Not without a fight.

She flung back her covers, got out of bed and stood for just a moment, looking at herself in the full-length mirror and feeling way older than she ever had. Her nightgown was flannel. Her bathrobe, terry. Her slippers were fuzzy blue ones, and her hair was pulled into a long, still-black ponytail on one side of her head.

When had she stopped wearing slinky satin nighties and slippers with heels and clingy red robes? It had been awhile. It had been awhile since she'd had any reason to wear them, anyone to wear them for. For a time, it had been enough to wear them for herself, to remind herself that she was a woman, not just a mother or the matriarch of the Oklahoma branch of the family. But a woman.

And then, slowly, it had kind of stopped mattering so much.

She sighed, and refocused on her daughter, the current problem of the day. She knew Selene was awake. She'd heard the sounds of her steps in the house for the past fifteen minutes or so, first in the kitchen and then in her bedroom. It was a good time to talk. And yes, maybe she'd made a mistake in having Reverend Jackson waiting for her when she got home. Maybe it would have been better to talk to her privately first. Witchcraft. What was that child thinking? If that wasn't enough to throw a God-fearing parent off track, Vi didn't know what was. So she'd messed up. But hell, she'd never claimed to be perfect.

Yanking the bathrobe's sash tighter, she opened her bedroom door, and strolled to the kitchen to make hot cocoa. Maybe if she showed up at her daughter's door with an offering, the way she used to when Selene was little and pouting over some dead 'possum she'd seen along the roadside on the school bus ride home or something—maybe then they could have a civil conversation.

Selene had always been different. Always.

Vidalia filled the kettle from the tap, and set it on the burner, then turned to the cupboard to get down mugs, and set them on the table.

And that's when she saw the sheet of paper, folded once and resting on top of a book on the kitchen table. Frowning, she glanced toward the stairs. She could still hear Selene moving around up there. What on earth?

Unfolding the note, she read the words in Selene's elegant handwriting.

> Mom, I love you, but I can't be around you right now. I just need some time to get my head together. And don't worry, I'm not leaving town and breaking my word to the chief. If you ever calm down enough to want to know exactly what it is I believe, take a look at this book. It'll answer a lot of your questions. I'll call. Don't worry. Love, Selene.

Vidalia's hand was shaking as she folded the note and glanced at the book on the table. *The Truth About Wicca.*

"Nonsense."

A thump from upstairs made her look up sharply, and then she frowned. If Selene had left, then who was in her room?

She glanced at the hook near the door, where Selene's jacket had been hanging. It was gone.

Her brows drew together as she noticed the marks on the door, and the fact that it wasn't closed tightly.

Swallowing hard, she turned, opened a drawer, and took out the metal mallet she used to tenderize beef. Then she moved toward the phone, picked it up and hit the pre-programmed number 1. Maya's number. She and Caleb were closest, after all.

Maya picked up and answered with a sleepy "Hello?"

"Someone is in the house."

"Huh?" Then, with alarm in her tone, "Mom? Caleb, wake up, it's mom."

"Send Caleb down. And call the police. Lock your doors and hold your babies, honey."

She hung up before Maya could reply, then she turned, and started for the stairway. She supposed a wiser woman would just slip outside, or hide in a closet until the intruder left. And she was wise, most of the time. Right now, though, righteous indignation was taking wisdom's place. Some intruder was in her house. Her *home*. No one messed with Vidalia Brand, and the son of a gun upstairs was going to find that out in no uncertain terms.

She started up the stairs and got halfway up them before a man appeared at the top, his face covered by a ski mask. She had only a moment to take him in. He wore gloves, but she glimpsed pale skin at one wrist, just below the cuff of his dark shirt sleeve. Dark clothes. Nothing remarkable. Large man, though it was tough to judge. She glanced at the wall behind him and made a mental note that his head was about level with the tiny tear in the wallpaper there.

And then her time for observing was done, because he came barreling down the stairs, hitting her full force before she could bring her mallet down on his head as he so richly deserved. He hit her hard with both hands, and she flew off the stairs—literally *flew*. She landed with a huge impact, heard furniture breaking beneath her, thought *God, not my coffee table*. Then she heard footsteps racing through the house, the door slamming, a car squealing away.

And what seemed like about a half a second later, Caleb was kneeling beside her. "For God's sakes, Vidalia— What happened?"

She lifted her head and speared her son-in-law with her eyes. "Don't you take the Lord's name in vain in my house, young man." And then she passed out.

"This is it."

Cory—he was beginning to feel comfortable thinking about himself by that name—eyed the log cabin in the headlights' glow. It was small, square, with dark-green shingles on its roof. The shutters that flanked the windows were green as well, each with a pine-tree-shaped cutout in its center. The driveway was barely one. More like a worn spot on the forest floor. A pair of massive antlers were mounted above the entry door.

The woman beside him made a disgusted sound, and he glanced her way quickly. "Not up to your standards or something?" he asked. The place was exactly what he would have expected of a hunting cabin.

She lifted her brows. "My standards? Wow, you have a lot to learn about me, you know that, Cory?"

"Yeah? Like what?"

"Like that I'm as content in a pup tent as I would be in a five-star hotel. More content, actually. The cabin is fine. It's the dead animal parts as a decorating theme I don't like." She nodded toward the antlers over the door.

It took him a minute to shift his gaze there, because when she nodded like that, her corn-silk hair fell over her face, and she had to push it back with one hand. And for some reason his gaze got stuck on her face, on the way she grimaced at the antlers.

Then he managed to look back to the rack again.

"Poor freaking deer," she muttered.

"Elk," he said.

"How do you know?" she asked.

He shrugged. "Good question."

She frowned at him for a moment, then sighed and got out of the car, hauling her backpack from the rear seat and slinging it over her shoulder. "I guess we might as well go in. It's too late to seek alternative options tonight. But I swear, if there are animals' heads mounted on the walls, I'm sleeping outside."

He nodded, and told himself it was pretty clear she'd never been up here before, or if she had, it had been awhile. He didn't think she was faking her reaction to the elk rack. And he saw further evidence of it when she picked up three or four rocks from the ground near the door, before locating the one that wasn't a rock at all, and took the key from within it. Then she unlocked the door and stepped into the utter darkness inside.

"Wait a sec. I don't know where anything is here, but—" He heard movement, the sound of a zipper. Then there was a click, and she was aiming a flashlight beam around the place.

He spotted a kerosene lamp. There was a book of matches beside it, so he went to it and lit it. As he did so, she was lighting another, and pretty soon they had four of the lamps burning and filling the place with soft, yellow light.

No animal heads graced the walls, he noted, and was grateful for reasons he couldn't have named. Just relieved on her behalf, he guessed. They'd walked into a large living room with a cobblestone fireplace as its focal point, and comfortable-looking furniture all around.

"Tessa said the place was well-stocked. Are you hungry?"

"Starved. Who is Tessa?"

She stiffened enough to tell him she hadn't meant to mention the name. "She's a friend of mine. This is her husband's cabin."

"I see. Is she one of the other nude-nymphets from the woods?"

She sent him a frown. "We were not nude."

"Nude enough."

Shaking her head she said, "I'm not telling anyone who else was out there with me, so there's no point in asking."

"I don't need to ask. You just told me."

She rolled her eyes. "I didn't tell you anything. And I'm not going to."

"Then you admit you have something to hide."

"I don't have a thing to hide, Cory. But some secrets just aren't mine to tell. I promised those women I would keep their names out of it, and I keep my promises. Now, why don't you start that fire and I'll go see what I can find us to eat."

She walked away, across the room and through a darkened doorway, carrying one of the kerosene lamps with her. The kernel of a thought came into his mind that she suddenly seemed to know her way around this place pretty well, but before it became a fully developed suspicion, she reappeared in the doorway, looking sheepish.

"Nothing to eat in the bedroom," she said.

"Oh." She shot his newborn theory down with a self-deprecating grin that did something to his insides. "Try that one," he suggested, pointing out another doorway, at the opposite side of the room.

"On it." She crossed the room in front of him. "Holler if you need me."

He watched her go, and for a second, the image of her, dancing half-naked in the forest, wearing nothing but a colorful cloth tied at her waist, that long silvery-blond hair falling around her shoulders, grabbed hold of his mind and wouldn't let go.

He took a mental grip on himself, reminded himself he could be fantasizing about his would-be killer. Or his would-be killer's accomplice. At the very least, he was fantasizing about a woman with a slight mental break from reality.

She thought she was a Witch, for heaven's sake.

Chapter 5

By the time Selene had fixed him canned beef stew and located some crackers, her guest had a huge fire burning in the fireplace, and the living room was toasty warm and much brighter than it had been before. He was sitting on the sofa, staring pensively into the flames.

For just a moment, she paused in the doorway and looked at him. He had a strong jawline, gorgeous cheekbones and soft eyes that were muddled brown and green—eyes that could melt a woman with the right look, she thought. Though he hadn't sent that look her way—yet. He was still shirtless, and his chest drew her gaze almost irresistibly. It was a strong chest. Not bulging with muscle, but lean and tight. Nice shoulders, too, especially undressed. Smooth skin. Tapered waist. Taut abs that made her fingers itch to run over them. Looking at his belly was as erotic to her as watching a porno film would have been, though she couldn't be sure, having never watched one.

But she could imagine. That belly—well, the parts not covered in bandages, at least— So hard and smooth, and flat, and the hairs under his belly button making a dark path downward until they vanished behind his button and zipper. And damn, she wanted to touch him there.

"Do I pass inspection, then?"

She jerked her gaze upward, and felt her face heat. "Caught me, huh? Well, hell, Cory, if you don't like me looking, you should put on a shirt. 'Cause, um, I'm not having much luck keeping my focus elsewhere."

"So who said I didn't like you looking?"

She allowed her smile to erupt, and then she crossed the room to set the bowl of stew on the coffee table in front of him. "It's hot."

"You can say that again."

"I meant the stew." She looked at him, his face, not his abs. "Why don't you go check out the bedroom, find a shirt. I'll get some of the astral gunk out of this place while your stew cools off."

"Astral gunk?"

"I can tell just by sitting here that it hasn't been cleansed in awhile. I don't think Tessa gets up here much. It's mostly Chet and his guy friends."

"I have no idea what language you're speaking. But, uh, yeah. I'll go find a shirt."

He got up and went into the bedroom. She got up, too, dug into her backpack and located a plastic bag full of white sage she'd grown and dried herself. She plucked out a bundle of it, leaned close to the fireplace and held it to the flames until it blazed up. Then she drew it close to her face and blew out the flames.

Thick swirls of fragrant smoke wafted from the bundle. She smiled, satisfied, and walked around the room, wafting the smoke high and low and blowing it into the corners.

She felt his eyes on her within a minute or so. He'd come

out of the bedroom, a shirt on, but unbuttoned, thank the Gods. He stood there in the bedroom doorway, flipping the cuffs of the flannel shirt's sleeves back, and watching her.

"Is it just me, or is that stuff as illegal as the hawk feather?"

She grinned, knowing sarcasm when she heard it. "It's sage. I'm smudging the place to get rid of negativity." She continued around the house, moving into the kitchen, back through the living room and into the bedroom before ending where she had begun. "You move counterclockwise when you're getting rid of things." She leaned close to the fireplace, and dropped the remaining piece of sage into the fire. "For the spirits. Thanks."

"You're an interesting woman, Selene." He sat on the sofa, took his bowl of stew from a coffee table that was made of one huge slab of a giant tree.

"I'm glad you think so."

She sank onto the sofa beside him, reaching for the apple she'd stashed in her bag. "Vegetarian," she said. "I found the beef stew in the kitchen."

"It has to beat hospital food." He took a bite, nodded. "Not bad. So what do you normally do after smudging the place with stinky smoke?"

"Refill it with positive energy."

"Aha. And how do you do that?"

"Lots of ways. Play music you love, fill the house with laughter, with joy, with friends. Or do something powerful and positive in the space you've cleansed. Like singing or dancing or—"

"Or sex," he said.

She met his eyes, held them. "How did you know that?"

"Lucky guess. Why, was I right?"

She had to look away. "Yeah. It's…probably the best way of all."

"Well, what do you know?" He ate in silence for a while. She tried to do the same, but her stomach was doing odd things inside her. She would like to get to know this man, to ask him about himself. Hell, it made sense, didn't it? Shouldn't she get to know him a little before taking him to bed? Shouldn't she learn something about him before she let herself fall head over heels in love with him?

Or was that lust? And what difference did it make, because she would certainly love him sooner or later, either way. He was her destiny.

But it felt kind of cheap to be this hot for him, even if he was her soul mate, when she knew nothing about him: where he was from, what he did for a living, what he liked, what he believed in. If he was her destiny, she ought to know those things. And so much more. But he couldn't answer those questions right now. In fact, he probably knew less about himself than she did. He knew nothing about his past. He was pretty sketchy on his present—wasn't even certain whose side Selene was truly on. And he knew nothing about his future.

She did. She knew all about that. He was hers. Forever.

"You're staring at me again."

Yeah, at his mouth this time. Imagining what it was going to be like the first time he kissed her. She told herself not to rush things. After all, he didn't know he was her fate. She didn't want him to think she was easy.

"Sorry." She returned her attention to her apple and made an effort to eat it, but gave up after only a few bites.

He set his bowl down. Empty. "So you're not hungry?"

"Too nerved up to eat, I guess."

"Yeah, I figured you might be wondering what the hell you got yourself into here, about now."

She frowned at him. "What do you mean?"

"Just that you must be realizing by now that you're up here in the middle of nowhere with a complete stranger. And that ought to scare you, if you have any sense."

"Well, I must not have any sense, then, because it doesn't."

"No? Well, just in case, Selene, I'll tell you what I can. I don't know much about myself, but I can promise you're safe with me. At least—I wouldn't hurt you. I don't feel the slightest inkling to do you any harm."

She nodded. "I know I'm safe with you."

He lifted his brows. "You do?"

"Yeah. I'm not stupid enough that I'd have brought you up here if I thought otherwise. You'll learn, in time, that I'm pretty...intuitive, Cory."

"And you trust that intuition, even when common sense disagrees?"

"Absolutely. It's never failed me yet." She took his empty bowl, and handed him her apple. "Here, finish this."

"No, I'm good."

"Okay." She took the bowl and half-eaten apple back into the kitchen. He got up and followed her, stood leaning in the doorway while she tossed the remnants of the apple into a garbage bag, carried the bowl to the sink.

"So what's got you so nervous, then?"

"I'm not sure yet," she said. And that was a lie, so she tried to backtrack and tell the truth. More of the truth, at least. "I imagine part of it is being hauled into the police station and questioned like a criminal last night. And part of it is having my family know I'm a Witch and my mother's reaction to that." She turned and leaned back on the sink. "It's odd, I've always been completely open about what I do. Just never told them that it had a name before. It's the word that's throwing them. *Witchcraft*. You'd think they could see that, wouldn't you? It's just a word. A widely misunderstood one."

"Uh-huh." He came to where she stood, reached past her to work the hand pump that was mounted to the sink until water flowed into it, icy cold. He was very close to her. His shoulder brushed hers, and she didn't move away. "So what sorts of things do you do? Besides dancing naked in the moonlight, I mean."

She watched him. He was washing the bowl now, in the cold water, using a bit of the dishwashing detergent that stood there on the sink. He didn't seem to mind that his side was touching hers, and she certainly didn't. "We don't usually do the nudity thing. It was just a lark."

"Hey, I'm not complaining." She smiled up at him, and for a moment, their eyes met and held. "You're a...beautiful woman, Selene."

"I'm glad you think so." She lowered her gaze, and the moment faded.

"So what else? Do you cast spells?"

"Sure, when it's called for."

"So if I misbehave, I could wake up on a lily pad with an appetite for flies?"

"No. We never do harm. That's the core tenet of the Craft." She glanced up to see he was surprised. "Didn't know that, did you? People think Witches are all about hexing and cursing. But it's absolutely the opposite. We cast spells for change, when that change serves the greater good."

"And never for selfish reasons?"

"Sure. We're human. But we always have to weigh our personal wants and needs against the greater good. If they conflict, we have to let it go."

"I see. That's a heavy burden. You ever get it wrong? Do something you think is for good that turns out to have been a mistake?"

"It happens. We have to be willing to accept the consequences. You know whatever you put out returns to you three-fold. Taking action for change is a risk. It's always a risk. You mess up, you reap the karma. If we mess up, we get messed up in return."

"Wow. That's a lot to think about for you, then, isn't it?"

"It becomes second nature. Besides, with great power comes great responsibility."

"That's from Spiderman, isn't it?"

She shot him a look. "You remember that, huh? I guess your brain hasn't been wiped entirely clean, then."

"Guess not." He took a towel from the rack, dried the bowl and handed it to her. She turned away from him to put it in the cupboard where she'd found it, though moving away from his warmth was the last thing she wanted to do. "So do you have a plan?" he asked.

"Tons of them."

"I'll bet. But I meant for tomorrow. Let's start there."

She nodded. "I think tomorrow we should go back to the falls. Take a look around those woods, if we can avoid the cops. See if we can backtrack a little, find where you were coming from, and maybe pick up a clue."

"Don't you think the police have already done that?"

"Sure. But they aren't me."

"They sure as hell aren't."

She let her eyes wander down his body, then stopped short at the white bandages around his waist, visible where his shirt hung, still unbuttoned. They were splotched with red. "Cory, you're bleeding"

He glanced down. "It's fine."

"No, it's not. I'm going to go see what this place has for first aid supplies. Something I probably should have thought of sooner. I could run out and find a drug store if—"

He crossed the room, put a hand on her shoulder. "It's fine. Use that intuition of yours, if you don't believe me."

She would, if she could quiet her mind long enough to hear it. "Are you in any pain?"

"No."

"Would you admit it if you were?"

He smiled a little. "Probably."

She thinned her lips. He was standing too close to her to enable her to think straight. "I'd feel better if you'd let me take a look at it."

"You can take a look at anything you want, Selene."

He was staring at her lips now, and she thought he was thinking about kissing her. And probably doubting whether it was wise to tangle this thing up with sex, when he wasn't even sure if he could trust her yet. She wanted him to kiss her. But it would lead to more, and he was in no condition for what she had in mind.

To save him having to make the decision, she made it for him, by putting her palms on his chest to keep him from coming any closer. And that was a huge mistake, because, damn, his skin felt good underneath her hands.

He swallowed hard. She felt his heart beating, strong and steady, and the warmth of his flesh against her palms, and she almost swayed closer.

He put his hands on her shoulders, maybe to steady her, or keep her at a distance, or maybe to pull her closer. Before he could do any of those things, she said, "You had surgery today." As if that were the topic under discussion.

"Minor surgery. A few stitches."

"A few stitches that are already bleeding through."

"Just a little."

"It'll be a lot more if we—" She broke off there, bit her lip because she'd damn near stated what was going unsaid here.

"If we what?"

The way he looked at her, the way his eyes just kept moving over her face, repeatedly, hungrily, and with an appreciation in them she couldn't help but notice, made her respond.

"You know what," she said. "We both know what. It's the real reason I'm so nervous tonight, and I think you know that, too. But it would be wise to take our time here, don't you think? You don't even know me yet."

He frowned just slightly, then nodded once. "I'm being a pig, huh? And after telling you how safe you were with me. And the truth is, you don't know me, either. I'm sorry, Selene. Chalk it up to the amnesia. I seem to have forgotten how not to come on like a cave man."

"No you haven't. The amnesia has nothing to do with…."
She waggled a forefinger between his chest and hers. "This."

"You're right." He drew a breath. "It's you, making me
forget my manners."

She smiled. "That's a sweet thing to say."

"Yeah, I'm a sweet guy. I think."

His little joke broke the tension that had built between
them, let her relax a little and breathe again. "I think so, too."

"Ah…like I said, you barely know me. I don't even
know myself."

"I know you plenty," she told him.

"That intuition again, huh?"

"Um-hmm. And just so we're clear on this, I'm not
saying no, Cory. That would be pointless. I'm just saying,
not yet. Okay?"

He nodded. "Okay. One question, though?"

"Sure."

"Why would it be pointless to say no?"

"Because this…" She repeated the finger motion, forefinger waving between them almost as if stirring the energies she
could feel there. "Is inevitable."

He looked surprised. "It is?"

"I knew that the minute you stumbled out of the woods and
fell at my feet."

He stared at her. She knew he was probably starting to
question her mental stability. Hell, he probably already had
been, given her claim of being a Witch, her wielding a dagger
over him, her dancing naked in a woody clearing. She took her
hands from his chest, finally, and, not without regret, lowered
them to her sides. "Don't look so nervous, Cory. I'm not going
to turn you into an obsession or become a stalker or anything
like that. And that's why we need to go slowly here. I want you
to know you can trust me. I want you to know who I am."

He still looked worried. "I'd kind of like to know who I
am, while we're at it."

"Oh, you will. I promise."

"Yeah? How can you be so sure?" He glanced at the room around them. "What if it never comes back?"

"Your memory? It will, Cory."

"But what if it doesn't?"

He was scared. It made him all the more attractive to her that he was willing to let her see that in him.

"If it doesn't, we'll start from square one. Hell, we can start right now. That is, right after I take a look at your belly. You game?"

He met her eyes and nodded.

He lay on his back on the big bed in the cabin's only bedroom. She'd insisted, so she could check the stitches in his belly and satisfy her curiosity. Or maybe she was just trying to drive him insane.

He wanted her. She knew it, and it was mutual. Why the hell did women always have to complicate things with all their emotional analysis and nitpicking? Why couldn't she or any other woman deal with this sort of thing in a simple straightforward way? Acknowledge the physical attraction went both ways and engage in a night of mutual mind-blowing pleasure.

But no. She was talking crazy, and he got the feeling she was seeing way more than was here—maybe concocting fantasies about predestination and soul mates and fate and that sort of garbage. Yeah, that was probably it—it would be right up her witchy little alley, wouldn't it?

And that meant he was going to have to watch his step. She wasn't the kind who would take sex casually. Apparently, he thought, he was. Crying shame.

Hell, what was wrong with him? He should have been watching his step anyway. And he supposed he was being a typical guy: more averse to having sex with her out of fear she might take it too seriously, than because she might have tried to kill him. That certainly told him something about himself, didn't it?

She was leaning over him now, looking at the little wound in his belly, checking the stitches the docs had put into it, shaking her head and frowning and bending closer. Her long hair brushed his skin way down low on his abdomen, and he thought if she didn't notice the swelling going on inside his jeans, she must be blind. But she wasn't blind, and he thought she knew exactly what she was doing.

Then she straightened and met his eyes. "I'm not trying to be a tease," she said.

"I didn't say you were." But he'd been thinking it. He experienced a surreal moment where he was sure she'd read his mind, and suddenly wondered if her delusions were for real. But he brushed the thought aside and told it not to dare return.

She stared into his eyes for a moment, then returned to her work, smearing some ointment onto a clean gauze square she'd found in the bathroom, pressing it to the wound and then taping it in place.

"So," she said a moment later, entirely out of the blue. "What's your favorite food?"

"Pizza."

She smiled. "That figures. What kind?"

He didn't answer though. He was too busy blinking in shock that he'd been able to come up with an instant answer to such a simple question.

"Cory?"

He shook himself, glanced at her. "How did I know that?"

"You know all kinds of things," she said. "You just have to stop looking so hard for them and let them come to the surface by themselves. You didn't stop to think about your answer. You just blurted it as soon as it popped into your mind. If you can keep doing that—answering without thinking first—you'll learn a lot about yourself."

She didn't bother wrapping the bandages around and around

his waist, as they had been before. When she finished, instead of being trussed up in layers of gauze, he bore a single clean, square patch, firmly fixed to his belly. It felt a lot better this way.

"So what kind?"

He frowned and tried to think of an answer. He considered and then discarded several possible toppings. Pepperoni was common, but didn't feel quite right. But who didn't like pepperoni? And there were other popular choices like mushrooms and onions and whatnot. But he didn't know what he would want on his own pizza.

She was right, he was thinking too hard. "I don't know," he finally said.

"I bet you like anchovies. You know, those salty little fish—"

"I definitely don't like anchovies."

She nodded. "Neither do I."

He sent her a puzzled frown.

"People react strongly to anchovies. You either love them or hate them. I figured if I threw them into the conversation you'd have an instant and honest reaction. And you did. You hate anchovies."

"Hate them."

"See how much you're learning about yourself?"

"I do." He was still lying on the bed, hands folded behind his head. "You're a smart woman, Selene. So what do you like on your pizza?"

"Broccoli, tomatoes, onions, peppers. I'm big into veggies. Oh, and I like pineapple sometimes, just to mix it up."

He nodded. "No meat?"

"I'm a vegetarian. Why? Does it sound empty to you without meat?"

"Yeah. And the idea of pineapple made me grimace, but the peppers and onions sounded right."

"See? We're gaining on it."

He'd been taking in the room, the knotty pine boards on

the walls, the wildlife prints, the rustic-looking dresser. But his gaze fell on her again when she went quiet, and he caught her staring pretty intensely at his chest.

She jerked her attention elsewhere as soon as she realized she'd been caught, but it was too late and she knew it.

It wasn't going to be easy to hold back, not if she wanted him as badly as she seemed to. And he hadn't decided that he would even try. He'd just have to be blunt with her about what it was. And what it wasn't. Her earlier comment that this thing between them was inevitable, that she'd felt it from the moment she'd seen him and that kind of romantic bullshit had him almost as worried as the idea that she might be trying to kill him.

And he supposed he'd have to be careful to make sure there were no sharp objects near the bed she might use to impale him.

"There are cots," he said, nodding at the folded and stacked pieces in the corner. "I'll take one of those for the night. Let you have the bed."

"I'm not the one with the stab wound in my belly."

"No, you're not. But I'm the guy."

She let her gaze slide down his chest. "Can't argue with you there."

"Didn't think you would." He got up then, crossed the room to take a cot from the folded stack, unfolded the thing and set it up on the floor near the bed, on the side nearest the door. His belly hurt, but not terribly. Bad enough that he might have winced once or twice, had there not been a gorgeous woman in the room.

She was taking blankets from a nearby chest and stacking them on the cot for him. She'd found a pillow, too. "There should be clothes in the dresser," she said. "Pajamas."

"I sleep in my—" He broke off there, thinking hard, trying to remember what he wore to bed, but there was only a big black hole.

"Oh, come on. Finish it," she said. "You sleep in your…."

"I think I was going to say shorts, but uh, I lost it."

"You stopped to think and chased it away. You need to work on shutting up your inner censor."

"Easier said than done. But I do agree with your point."

"So we'll work on it."

He nodded, arranged the blankets and pillow on his cot, and then, left with nothing much more to do, reached for the button of his jeans.

Her sharp, interested eyes followed his every movement. The way they flickered when focused on his lower abs and button fly let him know what she wanted. Why she was fighting it so hard, he didn't know. But he supposed he could wait, as long as he could keep her from getting too sappy about the whole thing.

He unbuttoned. He unzipped. Slow. Teasing her.

She licked her lips, then turned her head away. "I'm going to go get ready for bed."

"Okay."

"Be right back."

"Sure."

After that she left the room. He heard her moving around in the other room. Knew she was going through her backpack, probably finding whatever she'd brought to sleep in and putting it on. Or maybe locating some hidden weapon to use on him later. He heard the pump handle squeaking as she drew water, heard her brushing her teeth.

He managed to school his attention back to his own needs, but not without a hell of an effort. He zipped his jeans up again, put his borrowed shirt back on.

When he walked into the living room, she was wearing what she'd brought to sleep in: a ribbed pink tank top with a nightcap-clad teddy bear on the front, and a pair of very short pink shorts to match. The top didn't come down all the way to the bottoms, which snugged around her hips pretty low, leaving her middle enticingly bare. He tried telling himself he'd seen her wearing far less, but that didn't reduce the reaction any. And the silver ring in her belly button just about made him moan out loud. Damn, the woman was hot.

Long legs, unclothed. Bare feet that made him want to make her cute little toes curl up in sheer, unrestrained pleasure. He couldn't remember having sex before, but he knew he had, and he knew he liked it. He kind of had the feeling it was something he did well. Something he was good at. And he hoped that wasn't a bad case of wishful thinking. He couldn't wait to find out.

It took him a full minute even to notice that she'd pulled her silvery-blond angel's hair back into a ponytail and smeared some kind of white goop on her face.

He met her eyes. They peered out at him from that goop-covered face, and he grinned at her. "What is that, some kind of Witch's potion? The secret to eternal youth and beauty?"

"Yeah. It's made of toadstools, eye of newt and the testicles of a righteous man."

He lifted his brows, only half sure she was kidding.

"It's a soy-based moisturizing lotion with oatmeal, Cory. I bought it at Body-Bliss." She held up the bottle so he could see it clearly, then set it down and took up the washcloth she'd been holding, and gently washed most of the stuff away.

When she'd finished, a little dot of white remained on her cheek, and he reached up to press his fingertips there, a very slight caress. "Missed a spot," he said, letting his touch linger. She closed her eyes, and he doubted it was voluntary, but seeing it, that much of a physical, sensory reaction to so slight a touch, made him aware of how responsive she would be to other, more intimate contact.

He moved just a little closer, felt her breath stuttering out of her mouth, and touching his, and then he lost his nerve and backed away, let his hand fall to his side, regretting it with every cell in his body. "I'm heading to the outhouse. Be right back."

She opened her eyes, and it seemed to take her an extra

heartbeat to get her mind focused. "Right. Um, wait a sec. I have something you need."

Did she ever. He almost said it out loud, and decided against it even as she turned to rummage in her backpack. She pulled out a toothbrush, brand-new and still in its cellophane wrapper, and a tiny tube of toothpaste.

He took them. "Is this a hint that my breath is bad?"

"I haven't been close enough to know," she said.

"More's the pity." Damn, he should have censored that remark as well.

But she didn't react badly. In fact, she sent him a teasing smile with a twinkle in her eyes that said she agreed. "I buy them all the time, stick them here and there. Every bag, purse, backpack and suitcase I own probably has a new toothbrush lurking around in it somewhere. Pays to be prepared."

"You'd have made a great Boy Scout."

"Except that I'm a girl."

"I noticed." He held up the toothbrush. "Thanks, Selene. Go to bed. I'll be along soon."

"Okay."

He watched her all the way into the bedroom, then he shook his head slowly. Damn, he hoped she wasn't planning to try to kill him. At least, not with a knife.

Chapter 6

Chief Wheatly sat on the big sofa, mostly ignoring the mug of coffee Vidalia had insisted someone bring him, while other officers, Jimmy Corona and his long-time partner, fellow former Chicago cop Colby Benton among them, were upstairs, doing whatever it was cops did in cases like this. Vidalia didn't want or need to know any details. She trusted Jimmy. And Colby as well.

"And you're sure you don't know where Selene went?" the chief asked for the third time.

"Earl, you saw the note, same as I did. It didn't say where she went. Only that she wasn't leaving town and would call."

"And you believe that?" he asked.

Vidalia, who had been rocking in her favorite rocking chair at an agitated pace up until then, stopped rocking and lowered the ice pack from the back of her head to send him her patented Vi Brand death glare. "My daughter doesn't lie, Earl."

"Up until a day ago you didn't think she practiced Witch-craft either, Vi."

She turned the glare up a notch. He lowered his gaze. Maya came in from the kitchen with a cup of steaming tea, and Vi accepted it and resumed rocking. "You should be home with the twins," she muttered.

Maya sighed. "Kara's up there. They're fine."

"Still and all—" Vidalia stopped there as her son-in-law the cop—Kara's husband Jimmy—and her son-in-law the lawyer—Maya's husband, Caleb—came down the stairs, with Colby Benton close behind them. She sat up straighter in her chair. "Well? You find any clues up there?"

Jim said, "We lifted some prints, but they're probably not the intruder's."

"I told you, he was wearing gloves," she said.

"We had to check all the same, Vi." Jim glanced at Caleb and Colby. "I couldn't tell for sure if anything was missing, but I don't think so. It's more like the guy was looking for something specific."

The chief was on his feet now. "That's what I was afraid of."

"Why?" Vidalia said. "What do you think? Do you think this is connected to that stranger being stabbed out at the falls, Earl?"

Earl Wheatly averted his gaze, which told Vi a lot more than his words did. "We can't be sure of that. But it's a pos-sibility we ought to consider."

"Chief, we checked the outgoing calls log on Selene's phone. I've got the last number she dialed, about nine-thirty. It was to Tessa Monro."

"She's a friend of Selene's," Vidalia said.

The chief lifted his brows. "You know her, Vi?"

"Sure, as well as I know any of Selene's friends."

"And how well is that?"

She shrugged. "Nice girl, married to a nice young man name of Chet. Oh, such a sweet young pair. Just married last year. Selene was maid of honor at their wedding, matter of fact."

"I know her, slightly," Maya put in. "I agree with Mom, she's sweet."

"Any chance she's a Witch?"

Both women frowned at him.

"Well, it fits. After their little party busted up and Selene refused to tell us who all was out there with her, the first person she calls is this Tessa. Seems like she might have been involved."

"At the very least, she might know where Selene is hiding out," Jimmy said.

Nodding, the chief said, "Get an address and then take a run over there, Corona. See if she'll talk to you. And take Benton with you to get the husband out of earshot. If she is one of these Wicca types, she might be as secretive about it as Selene was."

Jimmy nodded, grabbed Colby and headed to the car.

Vidalia was still rocking, still holding an ice pack to the back of her head. But then she stopped all at once, and lifted her eyes to the chief's. "Earl, if this break-in is connected to that stabbing, then…that means it was the killer who was in my house tonight, doesn't it?"

"He's not a killer, Vi. That stranger didn't die and he's not going to."

"Well it wasn't Selene who broke in here, tonight. And it wasn't the stranger himself—he's in a hospital bed. So it would stand to reason—"

"Look, Vi, there's no reason to jump to conclusions here. We'll get to the bottom of this soon enough."

"Why would the killer come here? Why would he be going through Selene's room? How would he even know which room was hers?"

"The Samantha Stevens *Bewitched* poster on her wall might have been a clue," Maya muttered. But then she frowned at her husband. "But Mom has a point. What would that guy want here? What was he looking for?"

Caleb and the chief exchanged a quick look, and Vi knew they had notions, but they weren't about to share them.

"You don't have to tell me, boys. I'm not an idiot. If that killer came here, he was looking for witnesses to what he did to that stranger last night. And that means my daughter is in danger."

"We can't be sure of that, Vidalia," Caleb said softly.

But Vi wasn't listening. She got to her feet, and paced the room. "Selene likely brought all of this trouble on herself by tempting the devil the way she's been doing. Dabbling in Witchcraft of all things!"

"Mom—" Maya said.

"But that doesn't matter. My girl is in trouble, and you all know full well I'll stand against anyone—against Lucifer himself—to protect her."

"That's good, Mom. And I don't doubt it. Now I have just one question," Maya said.

"What's that, daughter?"

"You'd stand against the devil himself for Selene. But would you do something a whole lot easier? Like read a skinny little eighty-page book?" She held the book out to Vidalia as she spoke. The one Selene had left on the kitchen table with her note. "It would take you all of a half hour, I'll bet. Is she worth that much to you?"

Jimmy Corona and Colby Benton pulled into the driveway of the small Cape Cod home of Chet and Tessa Monro. It rested at the edge of town, and the lights were all turned off. Two vehicles rested in the driveway. They pulled their cruiser up alongside the curb and shut it off, then walked in tandem to the front door. Jimmy glanced around as they went. It was still dark outside, and they were probably going to startle the hell out of the young couple, showing up in the wee hours like this. But it had to be done.

They were almost to the door when they stopped short, startled by the sound of a telephone ringing inside. Then they glanced at each other, grinned and shook their heads. "That thing is louder than a fire alarm," Colby said.

"Hey, at least we don't have to be the ones to wake them up."

Colby nodded, and they moved along the sidewalk closer to the front door. But the phone was still ringing when they got there. No one had answered it.

"Who could sleep through that?" Colby asked.

Jimmy frowned at his best friend, looked at the door, saw the pry marks along the side. "No one, pal." He nudged the door with his foot, and it swung open without resistance. "Damn." He drew his sidearm and flashlight.

Colby did the same. They entered the house, guns ready, Jimmy going right, Colby left.

"Tessa? Chet?" Jimmy called. "Anyone here?"

No answer. The telephone stopped ringing—the caller had obviously given up. Jimmy made a mental note to check the call ID to see who it was later. He smelled something on the air, glanced at his partner to see if he smelled it, too, but Colby had his back to him, moving carefully through the house.

He slid along the hallway to where the bedrooms would be. Colby checked out the bathroom, and Jimmy moved farther, opened a door just as his brain identified the smells in the air. Gunpowder. And blood. Stronger here.

The bedroom door stood open, and he pushed it further, going in, light and gun first.

They lay in the bed, side by side, looking for all the world as if they were just sleeping. Except for the bullet holes in the blankets over their chests, and the blood dripping steadily from the mattress to the carpet below.

"Colby," Jimmy called. "In here."

Colby appeared in the doorway, a stack of books in his hands. He eyed the dead couple, swore under his breath.

"What's that you've got?" Jimmy asked.

"Found them in a woman's handbag, on a rack in the bathroom." He held them up. The books were on Witchcraft. "Looks like the chief was right. Tessa Monro was probably at the falls with Selene when it all went down."

Jimmy felt his heart go cold. If Selene had been home when the killer had been in her room, it could have been her found with a bullet hole in her head. He suppressed a shiver, and whispered, "We've gotta find my sister-in-law."

Selene lay in the bed, stiff and nervous and waiting for Cory to come back inside. It was silly to be this nervous. Not only because she had already decided not to let anything happen between them tonight. But above and beyond that was the fact that he was her soul mate. He was the man she was destined to love. So what was there to be nervous about?

And come to think of it, why wait at all? Why not just tug him into this bed with her when he came back inside and let nature take its course?

Because of his injury, she reminded herself.

His voice in her brain whispered, *a minor injury. A few stitches, no big deal.*

And she could be gentle with him. All she had to do was wait for him to come in, and peel back her covers, beckon him with a crook of her finger or maybe pat the empty spot in the bed beside her. And when he came to her, as he would, she could undo those jeans and push them down over his hips and she could finally see the rest of him, the parts she'd been fantasizing about all day. He would step out of the jeans, shrug off the borrowed shirt, lower himself into the bed beside her. She could just imagine the way it would feel to press her body tight to his as she ran her hands over his arms and shoulders, and that magnificent back.

She would kiss his neck, and his entire chest. She wanted to do that, just press her lips to every single place on his chest. She would push him down onto his back, to keep him still, so he wouldn't put any strain on the wound. And that way she could rain kisses on his belly, too. And maybe while he was lying there, she would have the courage to move her lips a little lower, explore things she had never ever tried before.

She wondered what his shape was, his size, and found herself curious and longing. Would he be hard already, or would she need to encourage things to get him to that point?

She wouldn't need any encouragement of that sort. She was wet and ready just from thinking about him. If only she could have him tonight.

When she had teased him long enough she would gently ease herself over him, straddle his body. He would lie still, and let her take him inside, and she would move over him, up and down him, taking him deeper every time. And harder. And faster, until…

"I'm back."

She opened her eyes and her mouth at the same time, made a sound that probably sounded startled and a little breathless. She was lying in the bed with her knees drawn up, and he was standing there in his jeans, the shirt unbuttoned and hanging open.

Do it, her mind told her. *Do it, just reach up there and grab his hand and tug him closer.*

"Do you have any aspirin or anything like that around here?" he asked.

She blinked and shook off the heat and the fantasies. "What? Aspirin?"

"Yeah. Or ibuprofen or whatever."

"You…you're in pain."

"A little."

She got hold of herself, flung her covers back and forgot about her own overheated libido. The man she loved was hurting. Her own needs could wait. "Lie down, Cory. I'll see what I can find."

It wasn't a lie, exactly. He *was* hurting, a little. But no more than he had been all along. It was just that when he came into the bedroom and caught a look at her, lying there with her arms wrapped around her waist, her eyes closed, her head tipped back, he'd known exactly what was going on inside her mind. He knew a woman deep into a sexual fantasy when he saw one. And then when he spoke, he'd heard the sound she made: half whimper, half moan. Those blue eyes opened; he saw what was in them.

Hunger. That woman wanted to eat him alive. And yeah, it shook him just a little. God, had any woman ever wanted him the way this one did? She was building his ego up to dizzying heights, and he wasn't vain enough to think every woman saw him this way. Even without a memory, he knew that wasn't even close to the case. She saw something more in him. Something he didn't even see in himself.

It made him feel powerful to be so desired. It was heady. And it was probably dangerous.

It threw him, too, and so he came up with the pain thing, knowing that would cool things off in a hurry. She wanted him, yes, but she seemed to care about him, too, for some odd reason. She wouldn't jump his bones if she thought he was in pain.

And why the hell was that a good thing? he wondered.

He made his way to the cot, and sat on its edge while she rummaged around the room. She went to the kitchen to broaden the scope of her search, and he told himself it had been a good move to distract her from thinking about sex tonight; a wise, smart, prudent thing to do, and the only correct course of action right now.

His body wasn't believing it, though.

"Couldn't find any pain reliever," she said, coming back into the room. "But I have a couple of solutions. Here's the first one."

She was holding a cup full of steaming liquid that smelled kind of rotten.

"Valerian root. I added mint and some honey to make it taste better. Trust me."

He took the cup from her, sipped just a little. It tasted

better than it smelled, which was a good thing. He took another sip. "You carry this shit around with you?"

"No, it's some Tessa had in a canister in the kitchen."

He nodded, confirming his earlier suspicion that this Tessa was one of the witches. "So, is this supposed to be good for pain?"

"Mostly it's good for tension, but if you relax the pain should ease. Couldn't hurt the memory any, either."

"Okay." He took another sip. "So what else have you got?"

"Reiki," she told him.

"Gezundheit.

She sent him a smirk. "It's a healing modality from Japan. Been practiced for centuries. I tried it on you in the hospital, remember? It seems to have worked pretty well so far."

"Well, it did *something* good," he said, heading for the cot.

"Not the cot, the bed. Cot's not big enough for this. I need room."

He lifted his brows. "Room for what? You getting into the bed with me, Selene?"

"Yeah. I need to be able to put my hands on you."

He almost closed his eyes and groaned aloud. Maybe she was right and this thing was inevitable. Maybe he should just stop fighting it. Hell, he was only human. He shrugged off the shirt, took off the jeans, waiting for her to object, but she never did. Then he got into the bed.

He pulled back the covers, then lay on his back. He started to pull the covers up over him, but she covered his hand with her own, stopping him. "Leave them off."

"All the better to see me?" he asked.

"All the better to touch you."

"You're killing me, Selene."

"No. I'm healing you. Just close your eyes and relax."

He closed his eyes, but he didn't relax. Not by a long shot. Especially not when she got onto the bed, making it move with her weight as she shifted herself around until she was sliding her ass in between the pillow and the head of the bed.

"Lift up a little," she instructed.

He almost asked if he shouldn't roll over first, but bit his tongue, and let her slip underneath him until his head was resting in her lap, and her legs stretched out along either side of him. Her hands lay across his head, warm and comforting as a wool cap in the winter time.

"What do I have to do?" he asked.

"You don't have to do anything. Just relax. Let your mind rest."

"And while I'm resting, what are you going to do?"

"I'm already doing it."

He popped his eyes open. She was upside down, from his point of view, her head bending slightly forward so her spun-silver hair hung down close to his face, and her pale spooky blue eyes were almost lazy as they mated with his. Half closed, utterly calm, gently smiling eyes.

His head registered something, and he realized it was heat—not the sexual kind, though that was still simmering as well—and it made him frown. "Are your hands always this hot?"

"Not always."

"So why are they now?"

"Because your head needs healing. Relax."

"You, um….you're sure you know what you're doing, right?"

She smiled a little wider, held his gaze. "The beauty of Reiki is that you can't mess it up. I'm just a channel for the energy. It knows what to do, where it's needed, how to work. I just plug you into it and let it do its thing. Understand?"

"Not really." But he didn't care. It felt *good.* As if someone had put a hot pack across his forehead. He'd had a slight headache. Tension, stress, whatever, but it was fading fast.

She held her hands there for a long while. He noticed they stopped being as hot, seemed to cool a bit, and that's when she moved them to a new spot. She laid them over his face for awhile, but they didn't get hot there. Then she let them rest on his neck, and then on his shoulders, where they got pretty warm again. Sometimes she left them a long time, and other times only for a few minutes.

"I'm going to move now," she said, her voice deeper than before, soft and almost hypnotic. And he was *feeling* kind of hypnotized, come to think of it. "Just relax."

She slid out from beneath his head, and lowered it gently onto the pillow. Then she moved around beside him, and finally blew his relaxed state entirely by straddling him. None of her weight was on him, though. She supported it with a knee on either side.

"Easy now. This is just the most efficient way to get to you."

"Right. And you do this with all your…dare I say 'patients'?"

"No, I don't do this with everyone. But there's no point in being shy with you, is there, Cory?"

"Isn't there?"

"None whatsoever."

He was about to ask why the hell not, but she was pressing those warm, warm hands to his chest now, skin on bare skin. And he liked that. He just wished she would rub a little, rather than simply leaving her palms still that way. And yet it tingled and got warm where she touched him, and he tried to just let his mind go still and run with this thing.

Eventually she moved her hands lower, resting them on his abs, covering the knife wound this time. And that hand got really hot. So hot it almost burned him.

"Wow."

"Yeah," she said. "The more you need healing, the more energy moves through. I expected it here. But it was just as bad around your head, and that threw me."

"Why?"

"Because I don't know what's wrong up there."

"The amnesia?"

She closed her eyes. "But why do you have amnesia? Jimmy said the doctors suspected you'd been drugged. Did they ever say for sure?"

"No." It took her reminder to drive it home to him anew, that niggling feeling that there was something more wrong with him than a knife wound in his belly. He drew a deep breath. Her hands were hot again, but no longer burning. "They ran a bunch of tests on me at the hospital, but I left before I ever heard any results."

"I see."

Her hands grew cooler. She moved them away, and then shifted them lower, toward his groin. But before she pressed her palms to him there, he caught her wrists, stopping her.

She met his eyes, hers no longer relaxed but startled.

"I'm only human, Selene. If you don't want to have sex with me, then back off, okay? It's not nice to torture a guy like this."

She blinked rapidly, and her cheeks heated. But she held his eyes, though he thought she really would have rather looked anywhere else.

"It really is one of the hand positions. I just…wasn't thinking."

"And I can't seem to stop thinking."

Her brows drew together. "It's not that I don't want to. Please don't think that."

He tipped his head to one side. "I don't know, Selene. I mean, how am I supposed to think anything else?" He knew better. Knew she wanted him. He knew why he was holding back, though he was on the brink of changing his mind. He wanted to hear her tell him why she was.

"It's….complicated."

"It's simple. Beautifully, blissfully simple, Selene. We're two adults, without a reason in the world to deny ourselves a night of pleasure. I want you."

"You do?"

"So much my eyes are crossing."

She smiled, relaxing a little, he thought.

"So if you want me, too, then what the hell are we waiting for?" he asked.

She thought and thought. He could see her searching her mind for a reason, any reason, and she finally caught hold of the easiest one. "Your wound—"

"Is a very convenient excuse. But not a reason. Not really. You know that, Selene. You were lying there thinking of ways you could take me without hurting me when I walked in here a while ago."

She shot him a look, then averted her eyes quickly. "It showed?"

"Yeah. It showed. Unless I'm totally misreading you. Unless you really don't want me at all and I'm just imagining all of this chemistry I feel bubbling up between us and—"

"Shut up."

He shut up.

She sat there on the edge of the bed, mulling and pondering. Then she turned to him. "I've never done this sort of thing before."

"Had sex?"

She rolled her eyes at him. "With a man I just met. It's not me."

"But it's different with us, right? You said it was inevitable. You said—"

"Don't pretend you believe any of that. I know you think I'm flaky."

He shrugged. "You believe it. Does it really matter if I'm skeptical right now? If you're right, I'll find out sooner or later, won't I?"

She nodded. "You…we haven't even…kissed. Yet."

He smiled slowly, and reached up for her, slid his hands around her back until they rested between her shoulder blades, and drew her down until her chest was only an inch from his, and her mouth hovered a breath away. "I'm about to fix that."

"Okay."

He pulled her just a little further. Their mouths met, and some kind of explosion went off inside him. It wasn't intentional. It wasn't planned. He'd intended to kiss her gently, get a little bolder, a little deeper as he went along, but definitely take his time and seduce her mouth into full surrender.

It didn't happen that way. He felt her lips under his and then felt something go "bam." And there wasn't any thought after that. He was twining his arms around her and ravaging her mouth while his hips arched into her to tell her what he wanted. His heart pounded so hard it made his teeth rattle. His skin got damp and he was shaking. And to say he was hard for her didn't come close. He was throbbing. For her.

More. He needed more. He needed all of her.

She jerked herself up and away from him all at once. Hair in her eyes, lips wet and parted, eyes glassy. Panting. And her nipples were hard and straining into the tiny pink tank top. He stared and wanted to touch. Pinch. Taste. Nip.

"What the hell was that?" she panted.

"You're the Witch, babe. You tell me."

She shot him a look that made him regret the words. "You think I put some kind of…sex spell on you?"

"I was kidding."

"Well I didn't! I don't work that way."

"I told you, I was kidding." Although, now that he thought about it, it bore a little more thinking. She did claim to be a Witch. And he was pretty sure that if he'd ever experienced that kind of reaction from kissing a woman before, he'd have remembered it.

Then again, maybe he wouldn't.

And he didn't believe in Witchcraft anyway. At least, he didn't think so.

"I didn't expect that," she said. Her voice was a whisper. And she seemed pretty in awe over the power of this thing between them.

"I didn't either. You want to do it again?"

She looked at him, and he knew she was about to say yes, knew it right to his toes, but then her eyes slid lower on his belly and stayed there, on the wound. "You're bleeding again." She shook her head. "And no matter how gentle I try to be, with this kind of dynamite between us, I don't think it's going to work."

She slid into the bed beside him, and pulled the covers up. "We're going to have to settle for snuggling tonight." Rolling onto her side, she lay one arm over his waist, and rested her head on his shoulder.

She was kidding, right? She *had* to be kidding.

But no. If anything she snuggled closer, and he felt her body relax, felt her drift off into sleep and heard her breathing pattern change.

She wasn't kidding. She was killing him.

He was surely going to die before morning.

He woke to a round of delicious smells wafting through the cabin. Bacon and coffee were foremost among them, and they tickled him awake as they wriggled from his nostrils to his brain, and triggered his stomach to growl.

He rolled to one side and opened his eyes.

She was lying on her side, facing him, smiling. "Morning," she said.

He was smiling back before he thought better of it. She was getting entirely too many notions about him. And maybe that meant she wasn't out to kill him, but he had to wonder if this wasn't worse. "Morning," he said. And in spite of himself, it came out sounding sexy and romantic.

"I made breakfast."

"From here? Must be one of those Witchcraft things, huh?"

Her smile widened. White teeth. Full, wet lips. Damn she looked good in the morning. "I got up and washed up and cooked. You were still sleeping, so I decided to lie beside you and wait for you to wake up."

"So you've been lying there watching me sleep for ... how long?"

"A while. Not long enough for the food to get cold, though."

"Well, thank God for that."

She bounded out of the bed, and sort of bounced out of the room. That spring in her step, the way her gleaming angel-blond hair swung when she moved, the sway of those hips.... Damn, he was hard again and actively fighting the urge to lunge from the bed, grab her by the waist and haul her right back into it with him.

She'd washed up. Her breath smelled minty fresh, and her face was scrubbed clean. No makeup. She wore jeans and a pale, baby-blue T-shirt. That gave her the edge over him, he thought. He probably had morning breath and stubble.

He'd barely completed the thought and convinced himself to get up out of bed, when she returned with a wash basin in hand, sloshing water all the way. She set it on the nightstand, where a clean washcloth, towel and shaving gear waited. Beside that was a glass of water, his toothbrush and a tube of paste.

He glanced up at her. "You really have to get over this habit of waiting on me."

"Why?"

"Because I'm not that badly injured."

"So?"

He licked his lips, tried again. "I prefer to feel like I'm pulling my weight. Doing my share."

"Good. I'll let you wait on me later."

"Couldn't we both just sort of—wait on ourselves?"

She blinked and tilted her head to one side, almost as if his words didn't compute. Then she shrugged. "I was going to offer to shave you. Always wanted to try that. But um…you go ahead. Wait on yourself. Be quick, though. I'll have breakfast on the table in five minutes."

"Okay." So much for not waiting on him. Hell. He wondered why it bothered him so much and decided it probably was a clue to his personality. He must be an independent prick. Who else would be ungrateful for this kind of attention from a woman who looked like this one?

He made quick work of washing up, ran the razor over his face, and brushed his teeth. Then he toweled down, dressed and joined her in the kitchen, where she'd filled his plate and poured his coffee.

"Taste," she said, nodding at the cup.

He tasted, grimaced. "Needs cream."

Smiling, she leaned over him, breast brushing his shoulder, and poured creamer into his mug. "Gas-powered fridge. Everything was just stocked last week, Tessa said, so—there, try it now."

He sipped again, nodded. "Good. Perfect." She was acting like a wife. A newly minted, fresh-from-the-altar bride. And it was chafing him under the collar like an overly starched shirt.

His plate had three strips of bacon, two eggs over easy, some golden-brown buttered toast. He reached for the salt shaker, and she beat him to it, grabbing it first and handing it to him.

Instead of taking it, he stared up at her. "Selene?"

"Yeah?"

"Sit down and eat your breakfast."

She blinked, then averted her eyes and looked a little sheepish. "Sorry," she said, sinking into her own chair. "I'm the youngest in my family. Everyone tends to try to take care of me, you know? I guess the opportunity to take care of someone else for a change is a little too much fun."

He thought there was more to it than that, but he didn't say so. "It's not that I don't appreciate it."

"No, I know that. You just need more time to get used to it."

The comment took him aback, but he chose to ignore it, and instead dug into the meal.

"Good?" she asked when his plate was half empty.

"Great. The bacon's a little…different."

"That's because it's not bacon. It's Fakin' Bacon. One hundred percent meat-free. Hard to tell the difference, huh?"

He frowned at her, and took another bite of the food in question, chewed and swallowed. "That's not meat?"

"Nope. Good isn't it? Tessa's a vegan. I figured there had to be a few vegan-friendly foods here."

"Does that mean she has pointy ears and no emotions?"

"No. It means she's a vegetarian like me, but one who not only doesn't eat meat, but any other animal products. Like dairy and eggs and honey."

"Wow, that's extreme." He took another bite of the phony bacon. "It's pretty damn good. Better than I would have expected."

"Even better when you consider that no animals had to die to provide us with it, and that it's only got a tenth of the fat and calories, and no cholesterol at all."

"Healthy as hell, huh? So how come you're not eating any?"

"Because I prefer oatmeal." She nodded at own plate and bowl. The bowl held oatmeal, and the plate, half a slice of toast. She was eating the other half, with jelly on it.

"So do you have a plan for the day?" he asked her.

"After breakfast, I need to drive to the nearest pay phone. The cell's got basically no signal. I have to let my mother know where I am, or she'll worry herself sick."

"I'll go with you, if that's okay with you."

She glanced at him. "Of course it is." Then she studied him a moment, and tipped her head to one side. "You don't trust me, even now, do you?"

"Who said I didn't trust you?"

"You did. Just now. Do you think I'm going to sneak off to meet with whoever's trying to kill you, or that I'm going to call him and tell him where to find you?"

He licked his lips. "It crossed my mind." Though he realized he was more and more convinced she was as innocent as she claimed to be. Still, telling her that would be a mistake. At least it gave him a viable reason to keep her at arm's length.

"Damn. You're a tough nut to crack, aren't you? I wonder if you were always this cynical or if it's just a side effect of the amnesia."

"Wish I knew."

She shrugged. "Guess time will tell, huh?"

He didn't want to say that he doubted there would be time. Not with her, at least. If he ever remembered his past, his life, he was pretty sure he would want to get back to it. And she'd pretty much convinced him that his former life wasn't here in Big Falls, Oklahoma.

He finished his breakfast, and tried not to watch her as she finished hers. But he couldn't help but watch her. Every time those white teeth closed on a bit of the toast, every time that pink little tongue darted out to lick the crumbs from her luscious lips, every time her throat moved when she swallowed, his attention was riveted.

He wondered just how long he'd been without sex, and thought it must be a very long time, if watching a woman eat toast could get him this hot.

Finally, she leaned back in her chair to sip her coffee. He took the opportunity to jump up and clear the table. She started to get up, too, and he met her eyes, shook his head sternly. "No way. You sit there. It's my turn."

She sank back, smiling softly and watching him as he washed the dishes.

Cory could feel her eyes on him, watching his every move. He hated that he was starting to trust her. Even to like her. Damn, if he couldn't keep some distance and perspective, he was liable to dig himself into a hole too deep to get out again. And keeping his distance was going to be damn tough when he fully intended to have intense, incredible, blood-boiling sex with her. Repeatedly.

Chapter 7

Selene got into the passenger side of her sister's new station wagon, just to see what Cory's reaction would be. He glanced at her through the window, shrugged his incredible shoulders—Goddess, why couldn't she stop noticing his body?—and got behind the wheel. Selene had the keys in the switch and the engine running before he'd even closed his door. She didn't want him taking time to think about it.

And he didn't. He backed the wagon up, shifted into Drive, and eased the car onto the dirt track that passed for a road, heading back the way they'd come. "You didn't feel like driving?"

She didn't answer right away, just watched him maneuver the car around a smattering of potholes, and take a hairpin curve with long-practiced ease. "I just wanted to see if you had a license back in your old life."

As soon as the words were out, he jerked the wheel and the car swerved.

"Knock it off," she said. "You know how to drive. You handle the car like a pro."

He glanced at her, got the vehicle under control with little more than that slight veering off course. "For a second it hit me that I might not. That was kind of risky, wasn't it? What if I didn't know how to drive? I could have put us into a ditch."

"If you didn't know how to drive, you would have got behind the wheel and felt awkward and confused. You wouldn't have just started driving as if it were second nature."

"You sure about that?"

"No. But it seems logical. Besides, I cast a protective ball of energy around the car to keep us safe, just in case."

He reacted to that remark with a slight raising of his eyebrows, and nothing more. "You're a little bit impulsive, aren't you?"

She smiled in his direction. Did she dare take that question as a sign he was interested in getting to know her? "You're just noticing that, huh?"

"It seems to be one of the patterns I see emerging."

"Yeah? You notice any other patterns?"

He nodded. "You're enthusiastic. You're optimistic. And friendly."

"Not bad for a one-night acquaintance."

"I wish I knew as much about me." He reached the bottom of the dirt track, where it spilled onto a paved road. "Which way?"

"Left. Down to the main road, then right. There's a convenience store with a pay phone about three miles down."

He took the turn, and drove a bit faster.

"And I think I do know as much about you, you know."

"Yeah? Hell, you've been batting a thousand so far. Go for it."

"Well, I guess I think you're a bit of a...a player."

"A *player?*" He sounded offended.

"I don't mean that in a bad way."

"I didn't know there was a good way."

She shook her head hard and started over. "Okay, maybe that's the wrong word. What I mean is, you seem really interested in sex. But completely uninterested in...romance."

"If by romance you mean commitment, I think you might be right."

"I guess that's what I mean. I wonder if you've always been that way."

"I have no idea. But it seems to come pretty naturally."

"You'll get over it, though."

He lifted his brows and stared at her. "I will?"

"Sure. When a person meets his soul mate, all that resistance and fear just melts away."

"It does?"

"Sure it does. You'll see."

He frowned at her, taking his attention off the road.

"There's the store, right there. See the pay phone out front?"

He jerked his attention back to the task at hand and pulled into the store's parking lot, swerving close to the phone booth. He put the car into Park and shut off the engine, but didn't open the door right away. Instead he sat there for a minute, staring at his hands on the wheel.

"Something wrong, Cory?"

Lifting his head, he met her eyes, and his were narrow and probing. "Yeah. I just uh, was wondering—you seem to be implying that...um...I've met my soul mate. I mean, is that what you meant?"

"Yeah. That's what I meant." She couldn't help but smile, and damn, she knew she was probably scaring the hell out of him, but she honestly didn't believe in beating around the bush. He might as well know the truth. She'd grown so frustrated in trying to guess his feelings—if he even had any feelings—for her, that she was no longer capable of keeping quiet about her own.

"So you think that you...and I..."

"We're destined for each other, Cory. It's as simple as that."

He puckered his lips and blew a sigh, and his eyes looked worried.

"Oh, come on, think about it," she said. "Do you know how big those woods around the falls are? It's a thirty-thousand-acre forest, Cory. What are the odds you would find your way straight to me when you could have gone a hundred other directions? What are the odds on that knife wound leaving you with just enough strength to make it to my side before you collapsed? What are the odds against all of that happening on the one night in the month when I was even out there?"

He gnawed his lip. "I take it you don't believe in coincidence?"

"Synchronicity. Not coincidence. I was asking the universe to be sure and send me a sign to tell me when the man I was meant to love forever came into my life. And the girls were joking about what the sign would be. One said you'd fall at my feet, another that you would die without me. Tessa said there would be a fork-tailed comet to tell me it was you. Well, you fell at my feet, Cory, and you would have died without me. And I saw the comet. I saw it."

"Selene, you're really over the top with all this."

"You ran out of the hospital and right in front of my car last night. How do you explain that?"

"I don't."

She sighed, because she wasn't getting the reaction she had hoped for from him. Hell, nothing she had said or done to him since the day they'd met had elicited a reaction she would have hoped for. Instead of softening up and pulling her to him or telling her he felt the same, he just looked kind of panicky. "I'm scaring you, huh?" she asked.

He lifted his brows and nodded. "Yeah. You might say that."

"Don't be scared, Cory. I'm not gonna pursue you or try to guilt you into marrying me after we have sex tonight. I'm not wired like that. I'm totally into living in the moment, and milking every bit of life for all the joy you can get out of it. If I'm right, and we're meant to be, you'll feel it, too, and you'll let me know. If I'm wrong, then we'll just enjoy this for what it is. No pressure. No expectations. No regrets. Okay?"

He blinked.

"Okay?"

"Uh. Sorry. I kind of lost the thread after you said we were going to have sex tonight."

She searched his eyes, knew he was teasing her, and punched him lightly in the shoulder. "Moron."

"Thanks for—reassuring me, I guess. I just hope you're not saying what you think I want to hear. Because…I *really* want to have sex with you."

She went warm right to her toes. "Me, too."

"But I don't want any—strings. It can't mean anything."

A little pinprick of pain stabbed her in the heart. She ignored it, denied it, kept her chin high. "It'll mean something, Cory. To me. But I can handle it not meaning anything to you. I'm a grown-up. I wish it were different, but, stupid as it probably is, I want you either way."

Selene opened her car door, and dipped into her backpack for some change, then went to the pay phone. Maybe, if nothing else, he might be starting to trust her, she thought. But no, that wasn't the case either. At least, he didn't trust her enough not to get out of the car and stand close enough to listen to her conversation.

It chafed, but it turned out to be a good thing.

She dialed her home number, but her mother didn't answer. Maya did.

"Maya? What are you doing there?"

"Selene. Oh, thank God, Selene. Honey, you've *got* to come home."

"What's wrong?" Her blood seemed to slow and chill in her veins, as a sense of dread washed through her. "Where's Mom?"

"Lying in bed with an ice pack on her head. Selene, a man

broke in here last night. Mom interrupted him and he knocked her down the stairs."

"*What?* Is she all right?"

A hand lowered on Selene's shoulder, and she turned to see Cory staring at her, a worried look on his face and his eyes full of questions. She covered the mouthpiece with a hand. "Someone broke into the house and knocked my mother down the stairs last night," she said, filling him in. Then she reached up to cup his nape, and drew his head down beside hers, while tipping the phone slightly to allow him to listen in.

"Is she okay?" she asked.

"Yeah, she's fine, just mad as hell and worried about you. Selene, whatever the guy wanted, he apparently thought he'd find it in your bedroom. That's where he was rummaging around."

"Did he take anything?"

"Not that we could see. But...oh, God, Selene, I don't know how to tell you this."

"What?"

"Jimmy checked your outgoing calls log on your phone, thinking that if he knew who you'd called he might have a clue where to find you. The last call you made was to your friend, Tessa. So he drove over there. Him and Colby.

She didn't like the sound of Maya's voice. "Tessa has nothing to do with this, Maya. Don't let anyone drag her into this."

Maya didn't reply. A long beat went by.

"Maya?"

"Tessa's dead, Selene."

She thought she might have whispered the word *no,* but she wasn't sure. There was a thundering tempo pounding in her brain, and a rush of iciness rising through her body.

"She and Chet were murdered last night. Someone shot them as they lay sleeping in their own bed. Jimmy thinks it's all related."

Selene's eyes were clouding now, welling with tears that burned and blurred her vision. "Tessa," she whispered.

"Selene, you have to come home. If this has anything to do with that man in the woods, that stabbing—"

"Why...why would it?" she managed.

"Was Tessa one of the women in the woods with you that night?"

She didn't answer but the gasp might have given her away.

"They found books on Witchcraft in her house, Selene. It's too late to try to protect her now. But you don't have to tell me. Just know this. Jimmy thinks that whoever stabbed that stranger in the woods might be systematically trying to track down any witnesses who might have seen him. Meaning you and those other women who were with you. Do you see that now? You *have* to come home, where we can protect you."

"No," she whispered. "I have to warn the others. I have to tell them."

"Selene—"

"I'm safe, Maya. Don't worry. Tell Mamma I'm sorry."

"Selene, don't you *dare* hang up! There's more you don't know. That man, the stabbing victim, someone tried to kill him in the hospital, and now he's vanished. No one knows where he is."

She glanced up and into Cory's eyes, though his image swam because of the tears in her own. "He's with me."

"*What?* Why?"

"Because he's supposed to be," she said. He heard it, flicked his gaze away momentarily. Forget that, she didn't even care. "We're going to get to the bottom of this. And no one else is going to die, Maya. Tell Mamma that I'm safe. I'm not alone, and I'm safe, and I'm sorry for all of this. Tell her I'll be in touch."

She turned and tried to put the phone onto the hook, but missed. Warm, strong hands closed over hers, taking it from her, hanging it up.

"I'm sorry, Selene," he whispered. "I'm so sorry about your friend."

"I can't believe she's dead." She could still see Tessa, dancing under the moonlight, wearing nothing but a sarong skirt knotted at her slender waist. She could see her wide smile and her shining eyes, and hear her voice chanting the names of the Goddess. "I love her."

Cory pulled her into his arms, and even though she knew he was probably regretting doing it, that he was only holding her because he felt he had to, given the circumstances, she let him. It hurt. It hurt losing Tessa. And it hurt having this man hold her as if he cared when he probably didn't. She'd said she could deal with it—with him not giving a damn about her, not feeling anything for her at all. But she'd lied. Deep down, she wanted him to love her.

God, how she wanted it. But it didn't matter, not now. Tessa mattered. And Chet. Two lives snuffed out before their time. How could she even think about her own problems at a time like this?

She closed her eyes, and let her tears soak into Cory's shirt at the shoulder. She felt his strength surrounding her and tried to absorb some of it into herself. When the sobs began to wrack her body, he held her even tighter. But eventually, he lifted his head, and whispered, "People are starting to notice us. We should get out of here."

She nodded, her face moving against his shirt. "This time I really do need you to drive."

"All right." He took her to her side, opened her door, and helped her get in. Then he went to the driver's side and got behind the wheel. "Where to? Back to the cabin?"

She couldn't seem to stop the flow of tears, but she nodded anyway. "But not for long. They know I called Tessa before I took off. It won't be long before they find out her husband had a cabin and come looking for me there. We should pack up some supplies and get out of there and warn my friends."

He nodded. "And then what?"

"Then we're going back into those woods. And we're going to find anything that might need finding there. Anything the police might have missed. Anything that will lead us to the sonofabitch who stabbed you and murdered my best friend."

"And then?"

She lifted her head, stabbed his eyes with hers. "And then he's going to find out what a huge mistake it is to piss off a Witch."

"Damn. Remind me to make a note of that."

"I'm not kidding, Cory."

"I don't think for one minute that you're kidding Selene. Not when your eyes are practically burning holes in my skull."

She turned and stared straight ahead, visualizing her friend's killer in her mind's eyes, and began to chant;

> I invoke the Law of Three
> What you did returns to thee
> I invoke the Law of Old
> Return the pain to you threefold
> I invoke Diana's Wrath
> Disaster rains upon your path
> I invoke the Dark God's Sword
> Sever now your silver cord
> I become the hand of doom
> Murderer, you'll meet me soon
> With good to all, except for thee,
> And by my will, so mote it be!

Her chant sent chills racing up and down Cory's spine. He literally shivered in the car. It wasn't just what she said, but the way she said it. The icy-cold, dead-calm tone of her voice. And the steely, faraway look in her eyes—as if she were staring into the face of the man she addressed with her curse. As if he could hear her.

Hell, maybe he could.

Cory reminded himself that he didn't believe in Witchcraft. Or at least, he was pretty sure he didn't. But right now, he thought, he would hate like hell to be on the receiving end of whatever kind of magic she was working. Because he had a feeling it was going to *do* something. And he didn't think it would be good.

Selene was moving at warp speed through the tiny cabin, gathering items up and shoving them at him while he stuffed them into the car. A pair of sleeping bags she'd found in the closet. An armload of Chet's clothing for him. Her backpack and a bag of food from the kitchen. A twelve-pack of bottled water. A pair of walkie-talkies. He loaded it all and came back for more.

She stood motionless in the middle of the living room, a pair of flashlights in one hand and binoculars in the other, her eyes wide and fixed on nothing.

"Selene?"

She blinked out of her stupor, shook herself. "Go. Go, go now!" And before she finished speaking she was running for the door.

He didn't have time to do more than follow and dive into the passenger seat even as she was slamming the car into gear. The tires were spinning before he got his door closed, and then they were in motion.

"What's wrong?" he shouted.

"They're coming." At the end of the driveway he expected her to turn left, and head back down the dirt road as they had earlier. But she didn't. She veered right instead and took off as if the devil were behind her. She sped over the dirt road, heading uphill, swooping around sharp curves as they moved higher. And then she jerked the car into a bare spot on the shoulder, yanked the binoculars off the seat, and turned to aim them through the side window.

He followed her eyes and saw the cabin spread out below

them, giving them a perfect view. A second later, she handed the binoculars to him.

Frowning, he took them and looked. "I'm not sure what I'm looking for … holy hell." As he focused on the cabin, he saw two vehicles skidding to a stop in its driveway. A red sports car and a green Jeep. Men got out of the cars—he counted five of them—all of them carrying weapons. Shotguns, he thought. They fanned out, surrounding the place and moving in.

His shoulder slammed against the seat as she jerked the car into motion again, then he lowered the binoculars and turned to face forward. "How did you know?" he asked without looking at her.

"I don't know. I just did."

He turned to stare at her as she drove. Her face was intense, her entire being, focused. "Where are we going?"

"Away."

"From here?"

"From everything."

"Don't you think we should call someone?"

"No signal from here. Check if you want."

He didn't bother, because he was beginning to believe her. To trust her. More than that, he was beginning to believe she really had…something.

He reached around her, then, to fasten her seatbelt, which she hadn't taken time to do herself. When he did that, she sent him a look that was so tender he knew she'd read way more into the act than he'd intended. He didn't want her to get herself killed. Hell, that didn't mean he was buying into her soul-mate delusions. Sighing, he buckled his own and settled in for the ride. She didn't slow down for miles, but eventually she seemed to relax, though she still kept jerking her gaze between the rearview mirror and the road ahead. He had no idea where the hell they were. She took winding back road after winding back road, twisting, turning log trails that cut from one to the next. And then, finally, she pulled the car right up to a barn in the middle of nowhere that looked on the verge of collapse. Its paint was long gone, its boards a deep shade of aging gray. Its theme was broken boards and half a sagging roof. The other half had collapsed. The door, or what had once been a door, was barely hanging from its rusted track.

She stopped there and looked at him for the first time since he'd fastened her seatbelt for her. "We can stash the car in there. No one comes here. It won't be spotted."

"And then what?"

"We hike to those woods where you were attacked." She pointed. "This road borders the woods that are north of the falls. Other roads cut down to the eastern and western sides of the trees. So we check these out. See what we can find out here."

"You think it's safe?"

"No."

He frowned at her. She held his gaze. "But I don't think anywhere is safe for us right now. And it won't be. Not until we solve this thing."

Lowering his head, he frowned. "You know, Selene, it's me these guys are after."

"Not if Jimmy's theory is true."

"Jimmy. Your sister mentioned him on the phone. He's a cop, right?"

"And my brother-in-law. He thinks these guys are looking to eliminate any eye-witnesses to that attack on you. He thinks they believe me to be one of them. And my friends, the women who were with me in the woods that night, they're in danger, too. As soon as we finish here, we have to get to where we have a signal and phone them. Warn them. I'm in this, Cory. And so are they. Nothing to be done about that."

He was quiet for a moment. "I'm sorry. I really am."

It surprised him when she touched his chin, lifting his head until he met her eyes again. "It's kind of pointless to apologize, Cory. This was fated."

"I don't believe in fate."

"Well, I predict that before this is over, you will." She was beginning to doubt her own words, though. If he were going to feel anything for her, ever, wouldn't he have started to by now?

"Do you think we should go now, find a spot with a signal and call your friends first?"

"It does seem like the logical thing to do, but my gut is telling me this has to come first."

"You always trust your gut?"

"Always." Until now, she thought. He was making her begin to doubt herself for the first time. "Now let's see if we can get that barn door moved, okay?"

He nodded and got out of the car. Damn, he hated that she was still so convinced there was some universal force at work, throwing them together. Women and their romantic notions. He reminded himself of what she'd told him earlier. That she wasn't going to get all obsessed about him, that they should enjoy whatever happened between them for what it was, and let the chips fall where they would. And that they were going to have sex tonight.

That was, of course, before she'd learned about the murders of her best friends. Maybe that would cancel it out. Probably, he decided. She wouldn't feel like having sex when she was clearly in mourning, much less scared half out of her mind that she would be the next victim. Though she seemed far more concerned about her friends' safety than her own.

He got out of the car, and so did she. They moved to the barn door, which was hanging by one rusted roller. "I think if we pick up this side we can—yeah, that's it." She helped him lift the door and they pushed and shoved the stubborn thing open until there was enough room to allow the car to pass. It wasn't easy, but she did her share. She was stronger than she looked.

They went inside the dark barn to make sure nothing was in

the way. Old hay was scattered on the floor, and the air smelled musty and stale. As if it hadn't seen the sun in a very long time.

"Looks good," he said.

She nodded and went back to get the car, then drove it inside while he waited there. She flicked the headlights on when she got to the barn door, pulled in slowly as he kept watch for any hazards. He signaled her when she'd cleared the doorway, and she cut the engine, shut off the lights, but didn't get out of the car. When he glanced inside to see why, she was removing clothes from her backpack, and putting other items into it. A couple of the water bottles, the flashlights and some other things.

Then she got out, slung it over her shoulder, and headed for the door. They managed to close it again with no little effort. Selene handed him her backpack, then snapped a branch off a nearby evergreen, and whispered a thank you—to the tree, he thought.

"What's that for?"

"Covering our tracks. We flattened the grass out here when we drove in." She used the branch to sweep through the flattened grass, fluffing it again as best she could. She was thorough, and she was good.

When she finished she tossed the limb into a thick pile of brush, and reached for the backpack.

"I'll carry it," he said. "So we're within walking distance of the falls, then?"

"Yeah. If you're used to walking."

"I am." He said it without forethought, and then wondered why. She only smiled knowingly, and led the way. He was surprised again when they emerged from the thick woods onto yet another dirt road.

"This doesn't look like the falls," he said.

"It's not. But this road borders the stand of forest that ends at the falls, about three miles that way. The woods are triangle-shaped. The road near the falls forms the base, and this is the left side. Another road angles back to the falls road, five miles south."

"So you figured we'd walk the boundary first."

She nodded. "You're from out of town. You must have been in a vehicle at some point and you couldn't very well drive the car into the woods."

"If it were sitting along the roadside, somewhere, the cops probably would have found it by now."

"Probably. But I'm better at finding things than most people are. I'll see things—sense things—they might have missed. Trust me on this."

He did trust her. More and more with every moment that passed.

"Before we go on, I need to do something," she said. "If you can bear with me for a few minutes."

He frowned, gave her a nod of assent, took a seat on a nearby tree stump. Selene came behind him and took something from the backpack. A pouch on a string. "What is that?" he asked.

"It was Tessa's. She left in such a hurry that night, she forgot it. The police got most of the things left behind, but this...I don't know. Somehow they missed it. I grabbed it before they took me in for questioning. I guess now I know why."

"I don't."

She sighed, gave him a soft smile, and turned to walk a few steps away into the woods. Then she stood in absolute silence for a long, long time. Her eyes were closed, her body still, the pouch cupped in her hands and held close to her heart. He watched the wind moving through her gleaming silvery blond hair. He thought he saw her lips moving now and then, but he couldn't hear anything she said, and knew it was private. Eventually, she knelt down, and using her hands, scooped away some topsoil and mulch. She brought the pouch to her lips and held it to them for a long moment. Then she placed it into the hole she'd made, covered it reverently, and patted the filler down.

He expected her to get up again, to tell him she was
finished. When she didn't, he went to her, knelt beside her and
put his hands on her shoulders. "You okay?"

She shook her head side to side.

"You going to be?"

"Yeah."

"I'm sorry I got your friend killed."

"You didn't, Cory. The man who shot her did that."

She started to get up, and when she lifted her face, he saw the
tears on her cheeks. It drew a reaction out of him, one he didn't
expect. A sharp pain lanced through his chest, and his stomach
knotted up, just briefly. Hell. If he didn't know better, he might
think he was starting to care about this odd little creature.

"Goodbye, Tessa," she whispered.

Something skittered, and drew his gaze sharp and fast.
But it was just a squirrel, fat and gray, scrambling through the
undergrowth with its lush tail sailing behind it. As he watched,
it paused and turned to look back at them, chattered loudly,
then turned again and darted away, out of sight, leaving only
silence in its wake.

He looked at Selene again. She was staring at where the
squirrel had been, tears streaming. "She's okay," she whispered.

"Huh?"

"Tessa. Squirrel was her personal totem. He was letting us
know that she's okay." She turned toward him, but her knees
buckled a little, and he instinctively gripped her around the
waist to keep her from falling. He wound up standing face to
face with her, his hands on her waist, her eyes wide and wet
and full of pain, staring up into his.

And the next thing he knew he was kissing her. Just that
quick. Just that sudden. He was kissing her, drawn to her as
if she were gravity itself. She moaned, twined her arms
around his neck and opened her mouth wide beneath his. Her
body arched into him, and he pressed back, even though he
was so much taller he was pushing into her belly. She pushed,

too, rubbing her center against his thigh, her body silently asking for more. And she held him so hard he felt her desperation, her heat, and her hunger. Everything in him wanted to fill every last one of those needs, and then some.

And then she was sliding her mouth from beneath his and resting her head on his chest, and panting. "I want you so much, Cory."

"That's good to know."

"But I can't focus on what I want, not now. We have work to do. And I think my friends' lives—and our lives—depend on it."

Right then, he felt as though *his* life depended on having her, naked and writhing underneath him. And he was pretty amazed that he felt that way, given everything else that was going on. He knew she was right. So he took a deep breath, and told himself he *would* have her. Clearly he'd been wrong earlier when he'd thought her grief would delay their mutual gratification. Instead it seemed to intensify her need.

He had to stop thinking along those lines, though, or they would never get anything done. Reluctantly, he let one arm fall away, but kept the other around her shoulders and held her tight to his side as they returned to the dirt road and began walking.

Chapter 8

She walked beside him along the winding dirt road's edge, close enough to the dense forest that they could scramble out of sight should anyone come along. Her senses were attuned, alert, her chakra centers wide open. She wanted to feel everything, sense any danger, any clue. Like a doe during hunting season, she moved with every sense at high focus, eyes wide and constantly darting, almost scenting the air with every breath.

But that made for a bad situation when she was walking with this particular man. Because having her senses so open, so receptive, made everything about him even more apparent to her, and more irresistibly arousing. How tall he was; she loved his height, even though it made kissing him awkward as hell. She had to stand on tiptoe, and balancing became precarious—particularly when having his mouth on hers made her head spin. She loved kissing him. Her head only came up to his shoulders. Damn, he was tall. To her. Maybe six one, six two.

She loved six one, six two, she decided. When he held her she felt small. Protected. And yeah, that wasn't a very ERA type of thing to find attractive. But she did. She liked that he made her feel small and delicate, while he seemed big and strong as he held her. Never mind that it wasn't PC. It was hot.

She noticed everything about him, and she tried to fight it too hard, because it kept her from focusing on the pain gnawing at her heart over her friend's death. And it didn't distract her enough that she thought she would miss anything she needed to find. So she indulged herself just a little. She watched the way his body moved, how comfortable he seemed in it, the easy way he walked, and how close he stayed to her.

She'd wondered, for a moment, if it really was so one-sided, this burning attraction. Okay, she knew he wanted her sexually, but was there anything more? He walked so close he had to brush up against her side now and then, and every once in a while he put a hand to the small of her back as if to steady her or help her along. He looked down at her often, and sometimes when he did, if she glanced up quickly enough, she would catch this look in his eyes that was almost…dreamy. Kind of a bedroom look, but also one that seemed to border on awestruck or even adoring.

Maybe she was reading too much into that look. But when she'd first glimpsed it, it had made her suck in a gasp of surprise. For a guy who wasn't into romance, he sure as hell could melt her heart with those eyes of his. Was there a chance that maybe he cared, just a little? Or was it only wishful thinking on her part?

She wanted him, and there was an urgency about it that she was sure had something to do with the death of her friend. Grieving over death made her want to embrace life with everything in her. And sex with him would surround her in the very essence of life. Tessa would totally understand that. Would cheer her for it, she knew that.

"Hey, look at this," he said.

She was staring at him, and he was staring at something

else, slightly ahead of them and apparently at ground level. His face was shadowed with beard, and it was so incredibly sexy she couldn't stop checking it out. The skin beneath the dark bristles. She imagined running her palms over it. Her cheeks over it. Her lips.

"Selene?"

He was looking at her now, rather than toward whatever discovery he'd made. She blinked and tried to shake away her distraction. "Sorry. I was just … thinking."

"About Tessa?"

"In a way. She and Chet wasted a lot of time. And it turned out to be time they didn't have."

"I'm sorry to hear that."

She shook her head. "It's important not to waste time, don't you think? I mean, none of us know how much we have. We should be milking every second of life for every drop of happiness we can. Shouldn't we?"

"Yeah. Unless killers are after us and our lives depend on finding out what's going on. In which case, milking life for a bucket of joy gets second billing."

She thinned her lips, lowered her head. "What is it you see?"

"Tire tracks. There, look."

She looked. There were curving marks in the road where a car had apparently lost control. She frowned, moving closer. "Tire tracks, to here, as he started to lose it, then skid marks from here on."

He nodded in agreement as the two of them walked the length of the tracks, bent over and squinting at the road. "The car ended up over here—look at this."

She saw the broken brush, berry briars and saplings crushed, and tire tracks in the soft earth. There were places closer to the road that were all dug up, and there were clear drag marks. There was also a set of neat tire tracks a few yards behind the spot where the first car must have veered off the road. As if someone had pulled over behind it.

"The car was here, but it looks like someone pulled it out," she said.

"Could be the police found it and towed it in."

"I can find out later. Come on." She reached for his hand and when he closed it around hers, she shivered for a minute. Goddess, that the man could make her shiver just by touching her. It was freaking unreal.

"Where we going?" he asked.

"Look, are you putting this together? What are you seeing here?"

"A car went off the road. Someone pulled it out."

"A car went off the road. Another car was behind it, can't tell how far, but when it went off the road, the second car pulled over here." She pointed. "And that looks to me like a footprint. Whoever was in the second car got out and headed into the woods."

He was getting it now, she could see it in his face. "Going after whoever was in the first car?"

"Let's check." They stepped over and around brush, to where the tracks of the first car ended in a rutted spot. "Looks like he spun the tires here, and just dug himself in deeper," she said.

"Yeah, and then he got out of the car." He was bending near where she guessed the driver's door would have been. "I've got footprints over here."

She knelt beside him. "Cory?"

"Hmm?"

"Stand up."

He did. She nodded. "Now, take two steps backward." He frowned at her, but she said, "Just do it. Trust me." So he did. And then she bent close to the footprint he'd left in the moist forest floor, and crooked a finger at him for him to come join her. He did. "Take a look," she said. "This is the footprint made by whoever was driving that car. And this is the one you just made."

He looked from one to the other. "They're the same."

"Yeah. *You* were driving the car that went off the road. And I'm betting the killer or killers were behind you even then, which is why you got out and ran into the woods." She straightened.

So did he, and as she moved across the flattened grass where the car had once rested, looking for clues, he stood there, staring in the woods. The strain on his face was clear. He was trying to force a memory.

Then she glanced down, and sucked in a breath. "Cory?"

"Yeah?"

"You weren't alone."

"I know. I was being chased, apparently."

"I mean in the car. You weren't alone in the car. You had a passenger. He got out and ran, too."

"What?" He joined her where she was, knelt and saw the second set of footprints, very similar to those he'd made, though smaller than his own shoe. Then he rose fast, and stared into the woods. "There was someone else with me. Did he get away? Or is he—"

"I don't know. Maybe the police found him by now, or maybe he got away on his own. But we'll find out."

"Yeah, listen, you head this way, I'll go east. We'll make a loop, about fifty yards wide, then close it in slowly until we pick up a trail." He tipped his head up. "I hope we have enough daylight left."

"We do. Because I have a faster way."

He shifted his gaze to hers. She went up to a tree, touched its trunk, spoke to it silently, and then snapped a small forked branch from a larger limb.

"What's that for?"

"It's a dousing rod. You've heard of them?"

His brows arched. She loved watching the expressions as they moved across his face. He was so incredibly attractive to her. "Isn't that what some old-timers use to find water?" he asked.

"Or oil or minerals. Or anything else you can think of. You want to find something, you just feel for its energy with a little help from nature. It's all the same."

"Oh, come on, Selene. This is no time for your Witchcraft stuff. Let's just start searching."

She tried to stifle the hurt. Told herself he was upset, being back here—it was probably stirring things up in his subconscious. "That's exactly what I'm doing."

Frustrated, he sighed, and headed deeper in the woods. She rolled her eyes, thought it was probably a good thing she was seeing that the man actually *did* have a few flaws. Everyone had flaws, and it wasn't healthy to see him as flawless. Hell, she already cared far more about him than he did about her, putting her in a position she'd sworn she would never be in. Almost at his mercy, craving any crumb of affection he might drop.

This was a step in the right direction. She might as well identify his flaws and figure out how tough they would be to live with, before she got herself too entangled. He might be her soul mate, the man she was destined to be with. But there was still free choice. She could turn away.

Yeah, like I could stop breathing. Just as easy.

She could decide to be with someone else, someone easier but less perfect for her.

As if I could ever want anyone else like this. I know damn well I'll never feel for any other man the way I feel for him.

Or she could decide to be with no one at all.

Yeah, that's more likely. It's him or no one. Because he's the only one I'll ever want.

Either way, she might as well have all the information before making the call.

He was a skeptic. He didn't believe in her powers, not really. Why did that hurt so much? How had she let him gain the power to hurt her so very, very deeply?

Still, it was good to know all of that up front.

She took a deep breath and closed her eyes, then drew energy up from the Earth, feeling it filling her body, her arms, her hands, and the branch in her hands. She held the forked end, one slender length in each palm. The two formed a V, meeting and blending into a single length of wood that pointed away from her body.

"I am your sister, beautiful tree of apple, and I ask for your help. Find what needs to be found. Guide me, let me feel through you. Feel the energy. Find what needs to be found."

She stood there, silent, and attentive. But she felt nothing. So she turned, holding the branch loosely in her hands, so that the pointed end swung a bit and pointed mostly groundward. But as she turned further, her hands began to grow warm. And the end of the branch twitched, and then pulled. The single end rose, slowly, pointing her in the right direction.

"Thank you sister apple tree. Just a little more."

Selene began moving in that direction. Then she stopped at the spatter she saw dotting leaves and grass, and the feeling on the air and the scent of human blood.

"Cory!" she called.

There was a pause, then he came crashing through the brush to where she stood, still holding her stick, her focus on it. "There's blood here," she said without looking away from the stick.

"Holy—"

"It might be your own," she warned. "But—"

"No. My tracks go off in another direction. Look, there's a print. Too small to be mine."

She nodded, gazing at the branch she held. "Where is he?" she asked the stick.

"Sister apple, help me find him." As she spoke she turned, slightly left, then slightly right, then a little farther, and then she stopped as the single end of the branch rose on its own, pointing her in a clear direction.

"Crap," Cory went on. "Did that thing just move all by itself?"

"Energy moved it." She traipsed through the brush and briars and amid the saplings and trees, heading in the direction her stick had pointed.

"What energy?" he asked, following her.

She stopped, and stood staring at the body on the ground. She could see why the police hadn't found him. He was deep in the woods, and there was brush surrounding him. "His," she said.

It was a young man, his dirty-blond hair cropped short; as short as Cory's. And that wasn't, she realized slowly, where the resemblance ended. He had a blood-soaked shirt over his chest, and he was deathly white and deadly still.

"Oh my God." Cory fell to his knees, hands going to the body's shoulders as he stared at its deathlike face. "Oh my God, Casey!"

Selene frowned. "You know—you remember him?"

He looked up, his eyes wet and utterly stricken. "He's my kid brother."

"You ... you do remember."

"Just that. Nothing more. That and—that I promised our mother I'd take care of him. And damn, look at this. Just look at his. Casey...."

She knelt beside him as he lowered his head, probably to hide the tears that were streaming down it now, or to try his best to silence the sobs racking his glorious back and shoulders with every breath he drew.

"I'm sorry, Cory. I'm so—" As she spoke, she touched the face of the young man on the ground, and then she went still. "Casey?" she asked.

Cory stopped sobbing and lifted his head. "Selene, what—?"

"He's still warm." She was moving her hand now, sliding her fingers over his throat, and then bending to press her ear to his chest. She sat up fast. "He's alive, Cory."

* * *

Even as he scrambled closer to his brother, Selene was yanking one of the walkie-talkies from the backpack he wore. She switched it on, switched the channels.

"Channel nine," he muttered as he bent over his brother, noting the blood-soaked shirt Casey wore. "Police monitor that one." He tore the shirt open. "I think he's been shot, Selene."

She was keying the mike as he spoke. "This is an emergency transmission. Can anyone hear me?"

It wasn't long before a familiar voice—Jimmy's voice—came back, loud and clear over the speaker. "Is this who I think it is?"

"No names. We don't know who might be listening in. Listen, I've got a badly injured man, looks like a gunshot wound, just inside the falls woods, off North Road where I assume you guys already found the car. Am I right on that?"

"Affirmative. But we searched those woods."

"He's pretty well hidden. I'm going to mark the spot with a strips of white cloth. You'll need advanced life support, EMTs and you're going to want to comb the area for trace evidence."

"We'll be there in five. *Wait* for us."

"Can't."

"Your family—"

"I'm switching off, Jimmy. Hurry, okay?"

Before he could reply she switched off the power. Then her hand was closing on Cory's arm. "Come on. They'll be here soon."

"I *can't* leave him." He had shrugged off his borrowed jacket, draped it over his brother's torso. And as she tugged at him, he was lifting Casey's feet up, elevating them with help from a nearby fallen log.

"We won't leave him. We'll hide nearby, close enough to keep an eye on him until he's safely in the ambulance."

He spun around to face her. "And then what? Leave him

in the hospital so this asshole can sneak in and finish him off, just like he tried to do to me? No way."

"They know these guys are going to try that, now, Cory. They'll take precautions. He'll be safe."

"And what if he's not?" He was glaring at her, snapping, almost shouting. He didn't realize it until he glimpsed the wounded look in her eyes.

She didn't snap back, though. Instead she put a hand on his shoulder. "What else are we gonna do, Cory? We can't fix a gunshot wound. Not even me. We can't pack him out of here on our backs. It would take too long, and he's already been out here almost twenty-four hours. He needs help, more help than we can give him. You've done everything you can for him for right now. He's warm, his legs are elevated, he's not bleeding. They'll be here soon, I promise."

"Couldn't you—you know, do that Reiki stuff on him?"

"I can. And I can do it from a distance."

"You can?"

"I wouldn't lie to you, Cory. There's a symbol specifically for distance healing. Trust me."

He lowered his eyes.

"This is his best chance, Cory. If it were one of my sisters lying there, I swear to you, this is what I would do for her."

Blinking away hot tears, he lifted his gaze to hers again, nodded once. "I know you're right."

"Okay. Now, don't bite my head off, but before we duck into some nearby cover, we need to go through his pockets."

"What the hell for?"

"Well, you remember him enough to know he's your brother, right?"

"Yeah."

"Enough to know what the two of you were doing out here in this forest? Who was after you, or why?"

He closed his eyes, shook his head side to side. "No."

"Then maybe something in his pockets will tell us."

He refocused, staring down at his fallen brother, who was breathing so shallowly it was barely visible.

"I'll do it." She shouldered past him, and bent over his brother, carefully going through his pockets. "No wallet, same as you," she said aloud. But there were a set of keys, some nail clippers, loose change, and a pocket-sized planning calendar. "Not a big haul, but—"

He put a hand on her arm. "Listen."

She listened; he could see she heard sirens in the distance, getting louder, closer. "Damn, that was fast. Come on, this way. And try to step lightly. We don't want to leave them a clear trail."

He went where she led, confident in her ability and her knowledge of these woods. Amazed that he was so sure of it, when he was sure of nothing else. But he was, and he wasn't proven wrong. She led them no more than fifty yards away, into the shadow of the root plate of an upturned tree. Tangled roots, soil and weeds formed a natural cave, and they crawled into it, pulling brush behind them until he was sure they were invisible.

"You spend a lot of time in the woods, don't you?" he asked.

"Yeah. And so do you."

"You think?"

She nodded. "You walk without breaking twigs or crushing plants as if it's an automatic thing. You probably don't even know you're doing it. And you don't grab onto trees and saplings as you pass, the way less experienced people would. Why is that?"

"You leave scent wherever you touch. Any animal that regularly passes this way would change his course. We don't want to interfere with them like that."

"We?"

He blinked, then frowned. "I don't know, Selene. You're right, that meant something, but I don't know. It just came out."

"Yeah, like something you've talked about before."

"Here they come."

They crouched there, side by side. When the sirens stopped, and the men fanned into the forest, he could hear them in the distance, crashing through the undergrowth. Closer, he could hear only her breathing. Gentle, shallow breaths, designed he was certain for silence. In and out and in again. She was sitting on her knees, bent slightly forward, straining to watch. He was sitting flat, knees bent up in front of him, watching via an opening in the brush as men surrounded his kid brother.

He did remember some things. Kid things. Swinging from a rope and dropping into a water hole. He could see Casey clear as day, skinny and freckled in cut-off denim shorts, with a blood blister under one toenail. He could hear, just as if the voice were real and present, his mother telling him over and over, *You take care of your baby brother, Cory. I'm counting on you.*

I will, Mom.

Selene sent him a sharp look, then a questioning one.

He hadn't been aware he'd spoken the words aloud. But he knew they meant something. He knew by the contracting of his heart and the way his stomach was knotting up. "I promised our mother I'd take care of him," he whispered, because it was too much to keep in. It refused to stay in.

Her brows rose, and then she was kissing him. Her arms sliding around his neck, her mouth caressing his with a gentleness that seemed designed to heal. Or comfort. If a kiss could do either of those things, and at the moment he rather thought it could.

Then she released him, and sat back on her heels to dip into a pocket. He didn't even dare to think what she might be doing. Knowing her, she was going to pull out a magic wand or something, give it a flick and send a spiral of pink glitter wafting out to Casey, at which point he'd spring to his feet and dance a jig.

No. She pulled out a chain with a crystal prism hanging

from one end. Holding it carefully, she brought it close to her, kissed it, and then whispered to it, "Tell me if Casey is going to survive this. Yes or no?"

"How can I tell you something like that when I—"

"Not you," Selene interrupted. "The pendulum." And with that she let the thing dangle, holding only the very end, and steadying it with her other hand until it hung motionless.

She stared at the stone, and he couldn't help but stare, too. It began to move, so slightly at first that he wasn't sure it was moving at all. But it was. It swung, slowly, forming a circle that grew larger and wider, until Selene gave the chain a tug, neatly snapping the crystal upward and catching it in her palm.

"What was that?" he asked.

"That was a yes. A very definite yes. He's going to live, Cory."

He met her eyes, and wondered how she could be so sure of her alleged powers, when he doubted.

"Hey, I found him, didn't I?" she asked.

She had, at that. He nodded, and turned his gaze back to the woods, to see the paramedics lifting Casey on a stretcher, and carrying him back toward the ambulance that waited on the nearby dirt road. The ambulance's siren came to life, and then began to fade. But the police were still scattered around the area, one of them even now stringing yellow tape from tree to tree.

"Let's get out of here. We've got a lot to do," Selene whispered.

"How? There are a dozen cops out there."

She tilted her head. "This way." Then she turned onto her hands and knees, and began crawling deeper into the darkness.

And even in his grief and worry over his brother, he noticed the small, round butt wriggling away from him. He swore under his breath, and did what any red-blooded male would have done. He followed her.

Chapter 9

Selene drove, because this time it was Cory who was emotionally overwhelmed. She could see it in the slump of his shoulders, the tightness of his jaw and the frown lines between his brows. He was scared to death for his brother. That he cared so much, that he took so seriously a promise he'd made to his mother, those things told her a lot about him. Not that she'd needed to know more than she already did. Her soul already knew his. Her heart had recognized him on sight. He was the man she was fated to love, and she knew better than to question something that felt so true. So real.

Maybe they wouldn't be together forever. Maybe he would never feel the same way about her. Maybe she'd misread all of that. After all, just because he was the one her heart had waited for, didn't mean it was going to end well.

"I wish things could have been different," she said as she guided the station wagon down a back road to pick up the main highway and an area with cell reception. "I wish we could have met like two normal people, taken time to get to know each other without all the negativity messing things up."

"Negativity."

"Yeah."

"You mean, like people trying to kill us, your friends being murdered and in danger, my brother being shot and left for dead."

"Exactly."

He shook his head. "*Negativity* is a pretty mild term for all that."

"Still…."

"Yeah. I know what you mean."

She shrugged. "But maybe you never would have noticed me if we'd met over coffee, or at the Corral, or—"

"The Corral?"

She glanced his way and smiled. "I forgot, you don't anything about me, do you? Sometimes, it feels like we're old friends—like you know me really well. I keep forgetting. The OK Corral is a saloon in town. It's our family business."

"You own a saloon?"

"My mom, technically. But we all help out."

"All of you? And how many would that be?"

It was nice that her chatter seemed to be distracting him a little bit from his own worry. She wanted to make things better for him. She wanted to make everything in his life right for him. "There's my mom, my four sisters, and me."

"Five girls in one family. Hmm. They all look like you?"

"We bear some pretty striking resemblances, I think. But uh, if you're thinking what I think you are, forget it. I'm the only one who's not married."

He smiled, not admitting a thing. "So you're the youngest, then?"

She nodded. "And you're the oldest?"

"Yeah. It's just me and Casey. Mom passed two years ago,

and Dad—" he broke off there, shot her a look and shook his head. "How the hell do you *do* that?"

"Get you to remember things you thought you couldn't remember?" She shrugged. "I don't know. I'm just glad I can. What were you going to say. Your dad…?"

"He lives alone, drinks himself to sleep every night and wants little to do with anyone else. Been that way since she died." He sighed deeply. "He loved her so damn much. Too much, really. She felt smothered most of her life. I mean, Casey and I could see that, but she couldn't tell Dad. It would have killed him. The man was entirely dependent on her. There was nothing else in his life. He didn't give a damn about his sons, even."

He blinked, shook his head slowly. "Wow. Where did all that come from?"

"It's all coming back. You give it another day or two and you'll be as good as new." She thought maybe she'd just had her first clear glimpse at his emotional composition. He didn't ever want to love the way his father had.

"So tell me more about your dad. You and Casey—you haven't given up on him."

"No. We keep trying."

She nodded knowingly. "I figured as much." Then she steered the car into a pull-off. "See if we have a signal here."

He tugged the cell phone out, and turned it on. Then waited, watching the screen. "What made you figure as much?" he asked.

She shrugged. "You're a caring person."

"And you know that because…?"

"I just do. Signal?"

"Yep." He handed her the phone and she saw two bars in the panel. "Perfect." She began making her calls.

He watched as she disconnected, watched her eyes, which had grown more damp with every conversation. It was clear to him that she loved the women of her circle in a way that went beyond friendship. Maybe even beyond sisterhood.

"Helena's devastated and terrified. I think she's going to take a leave of absence from her job and leave town for awhile."

"She doesn't trust the Big Falls police to protect her?" he asked.

She wasn't really looking at him, was somewhere else, with her friends probably. "It's not so much that. She's a kindergarten teacher. I'm not sure she'd be likely to keep her job if it came out that she was a Witch, much less that she was somehow entangled in a murder investigation." She lowered her eyes, staring at the ground. "Goddess, keep her safe."

"You gave her good advice, Selene. Told her to leave town by car, rather than using any public transportation, told her not to tell anyone where she was going, and to take enough cash so she doesn't have to use her credit cards. To pick up a prepaid phone card from a discount store and use that to contact you, so it can't be traced back to her."

He frowned a little, and she finally looked at him. "What?"

"You just seem…to know a lot about covering your trail."

"Not because I've ever had to. My sister Melusine is a private investigator, married to another P.I., one of the best in the country. My sister Maya is married to a lawyer whose dad is a retired senator. My sister Kara is married to a cop. You pick things up."

"What about the other sister? That's only three."

"Hmm, you have been paying attention, haven't you?"

"Absolutely."

"The other sister is Edie. Retired model, current photographer. Married to Wade Armstrong, who owns two successful auto shops."

"So are you an expert on auto repair and photography, as well as eluding the police?"

She tipped her head to one side, searching his face. "You're not still suspicious of me, are you Cory?"

He shrugged. "Less and less, to be honest. But then…little niggling doubts crop up every now and then." He waited for her reaction—hurt or anger or at least irritation—to show up in her face. But it didn't. Instead she seemed to mull his words over. She seemed thoughtful, focused.

"Sorry," he said. "That must seem pretty ungrateful, after all you've done for me."

"No, it just seems cautious. Given your lack of memory, it's even logical. I mean, I don't like it, but I think it'll pass. And I guess I have to appreciate the honesty."

He lifted his brows. "That's all very rational. Now tell me how you really feel."

She stared at him for a long moment, then sighed. "Okay. I want to smack you upside the head and ask you what it's going to take to convince you I'm on your side here."

"And your feelings are hurt."

"Well, sure they are. I'm trying to be patient with you, Cory, but damn."

"I'm sorry."

She nodded. "I know."

She did know. He appreciated her honesty, too, and it bugged him that he'd hurt her feelings. And part of him was smacking himself upside the head, and asking just how stupid he must be to keep doubting her, even a little bit. His gut trusted her. It was his head giving him trouble.

Time to readjust the subject. "You told me about Helena. What about the other two? Marcy and Erica, right?"

"Marcy's going to the police, going to cooperate fully and hope they can protect her and her boys."

"She trusts them, then?"

"I think it's more that she's angry. She loved Tessa. She wants vengeance. Knowing Marcy, she's probably hoping the killer will come after her so she can have a shot at making him pay. She's got a temper on her like…like my sister Mel."

"And Erica?" he prompted when she drifted off into silence again.

"There's the rub. With all that's happened, I totally forgot. Erica's out of town. She doesn't know about anything that's happened since the night I found you. Not the break-in at my house, not … Tessa and Chet. Nothing."

"And you can't reach her?"

"We *have* to reach her. She has to know she's in danger. But we can't reach her by phone. She's at a Pagan festival at a campground in Texas. She told me she'd be completely cut off. I tried her cell, but no luck."

"Doesn't this campground have an office?"

"Yeah, but they won't admit she's there even if we call and ask for her."

"Not even if you tell them it's an emergency?"

She shook her head slowly. "It's owned by Witches. They know how important anonymity is to some of us, and they also know the lengths some people will go to, to uncover our secrets. They protect their guests."

He nodded slowly, and it came a little clearer to him the risk some of these so-called Witches had to take to practice their faith. It really didn't make a lot of sense, in the twenty-first century, in an enlightened society. But he thought it was real.

"Suppose the police contacted them. Would they get a message to her then?"

"That would mean telling the police she was one of my coven, and telling them where she was."

"And you're not willing to do that."

"Her father is the local minister, Cory. I can't do that. It's not my secret to tell. I gave my word, took an oath—"

"Okay, okay. Understood." And it hit him again that a woman who took her promises as seriously as Selene did was probably a woman he could trust a hundred percent. His niggling doubts were fading fast. "So what are we going to do? What do you want to do?"

"We have to go down there. We have to find her ourselves, warn her."

"But if they're that careful about their guests, isn't it a pretty sure bet she's safe?"

"Maybe. At least until she leaves, and walks right back into town without even knowing she's at risk. Besides, Cory, it's her life. She has a right to know it's in danger, and make her own decisions about how best to proceed."

"You Witches are real big on that aren't you?" She lifted her brows and he went on. "You know, your right to have all the information and make your own decisions, and all?"

"Personal responsibility," she said. "We make our choices, and accept the consequences. The karma. We don't blame circumstances or our childhoods or the devil for what we do. It's all on us. And it's important to us."

He nodded. "You told the police you wouldn't leave town."

"Yeah. But Erica's safety is more important, don't you think?"

"So you're choosing the lesser of two evils?"

"I think of it as choosing the greater good."

He nodded, but thought it was just semantics. "So then, we're going to Texas?"

"I'm going to Texas. You don't have to come with me. You don't owe me anything, Cory. There's nothing keeping you with me."

He kind of thought there was, but he wasn't sure what, or why or…hell, he liked the woman. He wanted to make sure she was safe. And no matter what she said, he *did* owe her. He didn't say any of that out loud, though. He just said, "I want to go with you."

She smiled, a sad, half smile dulled by grief, but it brightened her face a little. He saw a lot in that smile. More than just gladness. He saw relief, and maybe some nervousness, too.

"If that's okay with you," he added, even though he could tell by her face that it was.

"More than okay," she said. "Way more."

* * *

They drove until neither of them could stay awake any longer, then pulled into a motel that looked cheap enough not to be too fussy about ID, not that he would have had any, anyway. Selene went into the office alone, paid cash in advance for a room, one room. And she supposed she could have blamed that on wanting to save the cash she had for any other expenses they would encounter on the road. But she wouldn't have booked separate rooms even if she'd had barrels of money, and she wondered if he knew it.

When she came back out, he had parked the car, and was standing near it, waiting for her. She looked at him, and her eyes got stuck for a minute. Damn, she loved looking at him. His bedroom eyes were particularly sultry tonight, probably because he was exhausted.

She went to where he stood, held up the key. "Number seventeen. It's around back."

He nodded. "You want to move the car closer to the room?"

"No, this is fine. I registered with a made-up plate number. They didn't bother checking but if it's parked outside the room, someone might notice. Though I doubt it."

She led the way and he fell into step beside her, surprising her when he took the key from her with one hand, and took her elbow in the other. "Seventeen. Right here," he said, and he unlocked the door. He held it open while she walked inside.

He hadn't said a word about her getting one room rather than two. And he didn't mention the great big king-size bed that took up most of the space inside it, either. He noticed it, though. She saw him noticing. He stood in the open doorway and his gaze stayed on that bed for a long time. Then he finally walked into the room, tossed the key on the dresser, closed the door, and turned the lock.

"You, um, hungry?" he asked. "It's been awhile since we stopped for a snack."

"No, I'm good. Kind of eager for a shower, though."

"You go ahead," he said. "I'll grab our stuff out of the car. Maybe snag a couple of colas from the machine outside."

"Make mine diet."

"Got it."

He headed out, and she went straight to the shower. She took her time, made it long and hot and thorough, the way she hoped he would be later on. She smiled at that thought, and wondered how it would be, their first time together. Guilt niggled at her, down deep. Guilt that she could be thinking about him, about sex, when one of her best friends was dead and three others were in danger, and when his brother was clinging to life in a hospital and was probably in danger as well.

But she needed this. She needed relief, release. Sex. With him. And she knew she'd done all she could do today. There was nothing else that could be accomplished until they'd rested.

Besides, sex could generate energy as no other act could. She'd use that to strengthen their chances.

She needed him tonight. No question. She hoped he wasn't going to make her come right out and ask. She hoped he knew, that he could read her. Then she shrugged and decided she wasn't going to leave any room for him to doubt.

Her own doubts, though, those were harder to silence. She felt a little cheap, being so willing and so ready to jump into bed with a man who probably could care less about her. It would be meaningless to him, he'd told her as much.

But not to her. And this might be the only chance she ever had to be with him, to be with the man who was her destiny. How could she possibly pass that up? It was stupid and self-destructive to care this much when he cared so little. But knowing that didn't change it. She couldn't help the way she felt.

She heard him when he came back in, but finished at her leisure, figuring it would be good to make him wait a little. Anticipation and all that. When she finally finished, she stepped out of the shower, dried off and wrapped a towel around her, under her arms. Then she stepped out of the bathroom.

He was sitting on the edge of the bed. The TV was on, but he wasn't looking at it. He was looking at her. And she was pretty sure he was thinking about taking that towel off her.

She ran a self-conscious hand through her hair and smiled. "No comb or brush in there."

"Your bag is here."

"Yeah." She didn't go to it though.

He said, "I, um—I guess I'll hit the shower myself now." He got to his feet, walked past her to the bathroom door.

"Don't be long, okay? And watch your stitches!"

He stopped there, with his back to her, and she saw the way his head came up and his spine went a little tighter. "Five minutes," he told her. "Ten at the most, but, uh, I'll shoot for five."

"I'll time you."

He glanced over his shoulder at her, and there was fire in his eyes when they met hers. Oh, yes. He got the message, loud and clear. She lowered her eyes and turned away, embarrassed and nervous as hell. But mostly, she was just turned on, right to her toes.

Chapter 10

Don't be long.

Did that mean what he thought it meant? Part of him hoped like hell it did, and part of him was sure having sex with her would be a huge mistake. She had ideas. Romantic notions about soul mates and love at first sight and predestination, all rattling around inside that gorgeous head of hers.

Sure, she *said* it wouldn't matter. That they could just enjoy each other and see where things led. But she only said that because she thought she knew where they were leading. To some kind of happily-ever-after scenario that probably included a cat and a picket fence and a white wedding.

Hell.

Part of him wanted to climb out the bathroom window and vanish until morning.

It wasn't a big enough part of him, though. The rest of him was clamoring for her, and he didn't think he had it in him to deny himself the pleasure. And he would make sure it was mutual.

He ought to be too sick with worry for his brother to be able to so much as think about sex. But for some reason, he'd believed her when she'd told him Casey would be all right. Way down deep where logic couldn't reach, he believed her.

He took his shower in record time, using the hotel-issue soap and shampoo she'd left in the tub for him. His five minutes were probably closer to three, but he took up the extra ones by brushing his teeth and checking himself out in the mirror. And then he stood there, naked, thinking he probably ought to put something on. Marching in there buck-naked would seem pretty damned presumptive, wouldn't it? And maybe a little arrogant.

Okay. All right. He slid his shorts back on, and was shocked that his hand was shaking a little when he gripped the doorknob.

Hell, you'd think he was a trembling virgin. He wasn't. He was certain he wasn't. But this was big, major, and he didn't fully understand why.

He got a grip on himself, stiffened his spine, and opened the door.

She lay on her side, facing him with a sheet over her. Her bare arms were out. One unclothed leg was also exposed, clear to the hip, bent a little at the knee and looking sexy as hell. He didn't see a stitch of clothing anywhere and he was pretty sure she wasn't wearing any, though her torso was undercover.

"So are you gonna stand there staring at me, or get in here with me, Cory?"

As if it was ever a question. He moved closer, and reaching out to take the sheet in his hand, he tugged it slowly off her. All the way off her.

Naked. Completely, gloriously, beautifully naked.

A shudder worked through him. It started in his groin and split like a forked lightening bolt, shooting up his spine and all the way to his toes. He swore softly, but didn't move. And he couldn't seem to make his eyes return to hers. They were everywhere except on her face, and they were stubbornly refusing to obey his mental commands to stop staring at her round, soft breasts, the curve of her waist, and the smooth rise of her hip.

"Hey."

The sound of her voice gave him the nudge he needed. He slid his gaze back up to hers. Slowly.

"Are you having second thoughts or what?"

"Uh-uh." Well, that was eloquent. Hell, what was wrong with him?

"So why don't you get in here? It's kind of chilly without the covers."

His eyes shot right back to her breasts again. "I can see that."

She released a breath. It was soft and a little raspy, and it rubbed his senses until they tingled. Then she reached up, hooked her forefinger over the front of his bulging shorts, and tugged him to the bed, and then onto it.

He wanted to go slow, to take some time to talk to her, to make sure she understood that this didn't mean anything. But that wasn't really an option. As soon as he fell onto the bed beside her, he was kissing her. It was just that fast, like a hammer falling on a nail. Bam. His arms locked around her, his palms skimmed her shoulders and arms, the small of her back where it dipped, her hips, her buttocks. He fed from her mouth as if he were starving, and oddly, that was exactly how it felt; as if he were starving for her, as if he couldn't get enough. He kissed her, licked inside, nibbled on her lower lip and felt her shiver.

And that shiver made him aware of her reactions to him, left him a little less buried in his own. The way her hands were moving over him, over his shoulders and biceps, again and again. She liked the way he felt. Her hips were moving, too, arching in and out against him, as if he were already inside her. And she was opening to him, opening her mouth to his tongue, and opening her thighs until the top one slid over his. His erection pressed against her then. He felt moisture and heat, and he moaned aloud. This was too much. Too good. Too hot. Too intense.

He needed this.

He backed up a little, to give himself a breather, because, damn he wanted this to be as good for her as it was clearly going to be for him. He moved his hand between them, touched her center, gentle and tentative, exploring and curious. At least until she moved and took his questing fingers inside her. She moaned his name and tipped her head back and wriggled against him. She was hot. And so ready. No foreplay necessary.

"I want you so much, Cory," she whispered. "Please don't make me wait."

He slid his fingers in and out, and used his thumb to stimulate her even more. Not because she needed it, but because he wasn't sure how long he could last once he was inside her. And he wasn't sure how much longer he could wait to be there.

He slid his mouth from hers, and lower, seeking and finding a breast, a nipple, warm and stiff, and then he sucked and nipped at it while he worked her with his hand, until she was shaking all over and begging him for more.

Okay, time then. Enough waiting. He was about to push her onto her back, but she beat him to the punch. She rolled him onto his, instead, and straddled him. He was surprised, and turned on more than he thought any man had ever been. And then she slid herself over him, took him deep inside her, and he was on the verge of insanity. She held his shoulders, bouncing up and down over him, making her breasts dance for him. He gripped her hips hard, to add more depth to his thrusts, and she didn't resist. If anything she drove down harder, took him more fiercely.

She was panting, taking him and panting. Her head tipped

back, and her eyes squeezed closed, while her lips parted. "Yes," she whispered. "Yes, come on, *yes!*"

He had to force himself to hold back, to give her time. And then her words changed to whimpers as her orgasm overtook her. He felt her spasming around him, squeezing him, milking him toward a climax that was going to rock him right to his core. Steeling his will, he eased his pace, backed off a little. "Okay," he whispered.

"Okay, what?" She drove down over him, taking him deeper again.

"I'm close, I have to…."

"Don't you dare stop." She pumped herself harder over him, taking him deeper. "Give it to me, Cory."

And that was it. He was no longer capable of holding back, much less withdrawing. Too late. He groaned as he poured into her, held her hard to take him, and shook all over while he went off like a geyser. *Damn,* it felt good.

She collapsed on top of him, and he held her there, waiting for the blinding pleasure to ebb. It took awhile. She lay on him, stroking his shoulders, kissing his neck and his face and his chest. She was saying something. That it was good, or was it good for him, or something, but he couldn't speak just then. He could barely hear. He was overwhelmed.

He didn't think sex had ever been that good before. And when his head started to clear a little, he told himself that was because he had no memory. But he had a pretty strong feeling that was a lie.

And then his head cleared some more and he realized what he'd just done. He opened his eyes, gazed up into hers. "Damn, Selene, you shouldn't have—"

"Yeah, I should."

"We didn't have protection."

Her smile was slow and her eyes all-knowing. "I know my cycles as well as I know the moon's. I'm not getting pregnant tonight. And I promise you, I'm safe for you in every other way."

"I believe you," he said, amazed that he meant it. "But how do you know I am? I don't even know—"

"I do. I know. It's all okay, Cory."

He felt the shock ripple through him. "You telling me you trust your…powers…that much?"

"Mm—hm."

"But Selene, that's just not logical."

She propped her elbows on his chest, rested her chin in her hands and stared down at him. "Is that what you trust? Logic?"

"Absolutely. It's the only thing you *can* trust, the only thing it makes sense to trust."

"Maybe for you. Not for me. And my intuition hasn't steered me wrong yet. It never will. I know that."

Damn, she was frustrating. She didn't make sense. "You sound just like my father," he blurted.

Her eyes narrowed, then probed. "Go on. No, no, don't think Cory. Just talk. Just open your mouth and let the words come."

Cory closed his eyes, as memories swamped him. "He was so sure he and my mother were meant to be together forever. It was over for her years before she died. She wasn't happy with him. I think—I think she might have even fallen in love with someone else."

"Did you know who?"

"No. I never even knew he existed, for sure. But I know she wanted to leave Dad. She wanted it so much, for so long. For years she stayed for Casey and me. When we were grown and on our own, neither of us thought the marriage would last. But he held on so hard. So unbelievably hard."

"What happened?"

He opened his eyes, stared into hers. "I asked her once, why she stayed. I didn't really expect an honest answer, so it shook me when she gave me one. He told her he'd kill himself if she left. And she didn't have any doubt he meant it. So she stayed. She gave up her life, her freedom, first for her sons, and then just to keep a dependent, depressed, alcoholic husband alive.

She never did leave him, not until she died. And he's been trying his best to follow her to the grave ever since."

"I'm sorry, Cory." Her hand was on his cheek. He hadn't even realized that his eyes were burning until he felt her cool touch, so soothing.

"She was a good woman, my mother. She deserved to be happy."

"She's happy now," she told him.

"Oh, come on. You gonna start talking about an afterlife or—"

"Not if you don't want me to."

He was silent a moment, while his brain told him he didn't want her to. He didn't believe in that bullshit. Religion was an opiate for the masses. That was what he believed.

But his lips parted, and his own voice said, "What do you witchy types think happens to people when they die?"

Her eyes had something in them that seemed to be reaching out and bathing him in warmth. She looked at him as if she absolutely adored him. "There are as many theories as there are Witches. Most believe in some kind of reincarnation. Most also think there's a period in between, when we dwell in another realm. Some call it the Summerlands."

He wanted to scoff at her, and instead he asked, "What do *you* believe?"

"I believe all we have to do is look to nature to tell us all we need to know about ourselves. Death is like winter. It's a rest period, not an ending. Just part of an ongoing cycle. Spring always comes. Morning always follows night. When a tree falls, its seeds spring up into saplings that grow into new trees. Its flesh rots to nourish the earth, that grows the grasses and grains that feed the animals and people. I don't think there's any such thing as death. Not the way most people think of it, at least. I think we go on. And I think we return. Life follows death like spring follows winter like dawn follows midnight. It's all the same."

She lay down again, not waiting for, or apparently even expecting any sort of reply. He didn't know what he would say if he had to give one. He only knew she was something else. Something different. Wise way beyond her years and somehow … special.

She snuggled close to him, relishing the feel of his arms around her, his chest beneath her head, his heart beating hard and steady there. It was….

"It was perfect," she whispered.

"Thanks. It was good for me, too."

Good? She hoped it was way more than just good for him, but he probably wouldn't admit it, even if it was. He was still skittish, and that was okay. She didn't need him to confirm what she already knew. She knew it with her heart, with her soul, with her intuition, with every breath she drew. She *knew* he was the one. And it was perfect.

He was already drifting off to sleep. She could feel the way his breaths slowed and deepened, feel his body relaxing beneath hers. She would never sleep tonight. Not if her life depended on it. She was too excited, too crazy in love to even think about sleeping. She could hardly wait until morning, when he would stir awake, and she would make love to him all over again. And then maybe they would shower together and do it again. And dress each other and do it again.

She loved him. She absolutely loved him. And there wasn't a single doubt in her mind that he would love her, too, because it was so perfectly clear to her that this was meant to be.

She lay still, enjoying his warmth, his body, his closeness, until he was sleeping soundly, and then she slid carefully out of the bed, too restless to lie still. There was so much to think about. The way she'd found him, in the midst of death and disaster and danger. The way she might not have found him at all, otherwise. Not that she believed her own happiness was so important that Tessa's life had been sacrificed just so she could find it. That wasn't the way things worked. But it was a gift. Maybe the universe had chosen now to send him to her, because he was the only light in the midst of so much darkness. Maybe she couldn't have withstood the loss and the fear without him.

They had to get through this. The current situation, the current disaster, and that was no understatement. They had to find out who was after him and why. They had to put this matter to rest, end it, find Tessa's killer and put him away. Cory had to find the truth about his past, heal his broken mind and regain the still-missing parts of his memory. She couldn't expect him to rush headlong into a future with her until he found his missing past.

That thought brought another, as she paced across the room and tugged on a T-shirt. His brother likely held the keys that could unlock Cory's mind. And while Casey couldn't be of much help to anyone right now, Selene thought maybe there was one way he could.

The planning calendar they'd found on his poor, wounded body in the woods. Surely it would tell them *something*. An address, a last name, a telephone number…something.

She went to the backpack where they'd stashed the thing, dug it out, and moved to the farthest corner of the room, where she sat on the floor and turned on a small lamp. Then she flipped open the pages, and began reading them.

And then she stopped, and everything she thought she knew evaporated like so much mist in the summer sun.

Cory & Kelly's Anniversary: 10 years. Party @ 2:00.

Her breath caught in her throat, but a sob squeaked out before she clapped her hand over her mouth. Her eyes shot to the bed, to the man in it, who was even now, rolling over, blinking awake and frowning at her.

She couldn't digest what she'd read on that page. It

couldn't be real. It couldn't be. And yet it was there, in black ink on a white page. Words that were like knives in her soul.

Cory came out of the bed, beautifully naked, and walked to where she sat. "Selene? What's wrong?"

She sniffled, brushed an angry hand across her eyes. "Apparently, I am. Or I was."

"About what?"

"About…us. Oh, God, Cory, about everything." She held up the planner in trembling hands, still open to the page with the entry.

He took it from her, frowning as he read what was written there, and then he shot her a look of surprise and worry.

"Does it jar any memories for you?"

He closed his eyes, set the calendar on the small round table, turned and paced away from her, snatching his shorts off the floor and pulling them on as he went. "Actually, a few things did come back to me last night. While I slept, I guess."

She tried hard to keep the tears from streaming down her face. "I don't understand. I was so sure."

"Sure of what, Selene?" he asked, and he turned to face her again.

She felt the way his gaze moved over her face, taking it all in, her heartbreak, her tears. He couldn't seem to look her in the eye. "Of you," she said. "Of us. That we were…meant to be."

He lowered his head. Seemed he couldn't look at her tears, either.

"What did you remember, Cory?"

Sighing, he walked to the edge of the bed where they had so recently made such exquisite magic together, and sank down. "We were following a truck, Casey and I. I remember us taking our wallets and stuffing them under the seats, in case we were caught. Clearly our wallets were taken by the men who attacked us, or the police would know who I am by now."

"True… But you said *caught*. Caught doing what?"

He glanced up at her. "Damned if I know. The truck

stopped at a diner. We stopped, too, went inside. Ordered coffee. Then the guys from the truck left again, and we took the coffees to go, and followed them again."

"It was a car that stopped behind you on that dirt road, Cory. Not a truck."

"Yeah. A red sports car. The truck led us up there, and then—I don't know—things got fuzzy. I couldn't keep up with the truck. I couldn't seem to steer right. I wound up veering off the road, dizzy and sicker than hell."

She rose to her feet, came across the room closer to him. "Was Casey sick ,too?"

"Yeah. He was slurring his speech, nodding off."

"The coffee?" she asked.

"I think so. Someone slipped us something. As soon as we came to a stop, that red car skidded to a stop right behind us. Men got out. They had guns. We got out and ran, and after that…." He shook his head in frustration.

She came to him, put her hands on his shoulders. "Cory, that's a lot. It's coming back to you, bit by bit. And that was a really big chunk of memory, important memory. You'll have it all soon."

He nodded. "I wish I knew if he were all right."

"We can call the hospital, check on him."

"That would be good." He lifted his head, and she stared down at him, lost for a moment in his eyes. She started to tip forward, to move in for a kiss, but stopped as the memory of that entry, and what it might mean, came to life once more, demanding attention.

"What about that entry in your brother's planning calender?" she asked, her words a bare whisper. He didn't answer, so she rushed on. "I can't believe it means what it seems to mean. It can't be right. My heart wouldn't steer me this far off base."

He licked his lips, averted his eyes.

"Cory?" Her heart started to ice over, as if a freezing wind had blown across its surface. "Does that name—Kelly—does it mean anything to you?"

He licked his lips. "I'm not sure. But I think…I think she might be my wife."

She gasped and flinched away from him, feeling for all the world as if he'd just slipped a tiny, razor-sharp blade between her ribs and right into her heart.

"I'm sorry, Selene. But maybe we'd better cool it for a while. Until I get my head straight, at least."

She tried to read his face, but her eyes were too wet with tears to let her see him clearly. But even without seeing his eyes, she knew, she sensed that he wasn't nearly as devastated by this revelation as she was. How many times had her sister Mel warned her? *Never let yourself be more into a guy than he is into you. It only leads to hurt. Let him do the chasing, let him pursue you, make him woo you and win you, and don't give your heart too soon. Don't give it at all, not until you're sure of him.*

Well, she'd ignored every bit of that advice, hadn't she? Made an idiot of herself over this man, this stranger, all based on a gut feeling. An intuition.

But I was so sure!

Maybe it was wishful thinking. Maybe she'd been wrong the entire time.

She forced her hands to return to her sides, told herself it wasn't appropriate to be touching him, not if he were married.

But she'd slept with him.

"We didn't know," she said, maybe to herself. "Neither of us knew." She focused on him, saw guilt in his eyes. "I give you my word, no one outside this room will ever hear about it from me."

"I appreciate that. Especially knowing how seriously you take promises you've made, and secrets you've vowed to keep."

"Are you…are you okay?" she asked.

He lowered his eyes. Of course he felt guilty, he'd cheated

on his wife last night. "I wish I could undo it," she said. "This is totally my fault, Cory, I was so sure….I'm—I'm sorry."

"It's all right."

She shook her head slowly. "No, it's not. It's really not."

He guessed he'd learned something about himself in the wee hours of the morning. He'd learned that he had a conscience. He must have, because it was beating the hell out of him. He'd also learned that he was a total asshole.

The name Kelly didn't mean a thing to him. It didn't spur a single memory, or a single emotion. Nothing. It was just lines of ink scrawled on a calendar. Nothing more. Sure, the notation suggested he might be married. But to be honest, he didn't think so. He hadn't been wearing a ring. There was no telltale mark on his finger, as if he'd been wearing one prior to the attack. There was one on his right hand, a nice, wide one, that matched the size and shape of that class ring.

And yet, he'd led her to believe otherwise. It had seemed like a good idea at the time. She was getting way too serious about him. All her talk about fate and predestination—for the love of God—after all of three days acquaintance. What the hell was he *supposed* to do? It wasn't like he could ditch her—not when her life might be in danger because of him.

He shouldn't have had sex with her. He knew damn well that had been a mistake, had known it even as it happened. After that—hell, she was more infatuated than ever. He had to cool her off, had to do something to slow her down, get her to let go of this certainty that they were somehow meant to be. It was insane anyway. And wasn't it just as cruel to let her go on believing that nonsense as it was to shoot her crazy dreams down?

He sat across from her at a booth in a small diner later that morning. They'd stopped for breakfast on the way to Texas. There was a deep hurt in her eyes. Deeper than he thought it should be.

They ordered breakfast, and then he went to the pay phone in the back to call the hospital and check on Casey. By the time he got back to the table, the food had arrived. He had pancakes and sausage. She had a Belgian waffle. He had coffee, she had herbal tea. They couldn't be more opposite if they tried.

"How's your brother?" she asked as he sat down.

He glanced at her. "You tell me."

She lifted her brows, and he shrugged. "Use your ESP or whatever you call it."

"Yeah. Right. Don't rub it in, okay?"

He frowned and then got it. "I wasn't. I was serious, you've been right on the money so far."

She shook her head.

"You knew when those guys were coming to the cabin. You found Casey in the woods. You—"

She held up a hand. "Don't. Don't try to humor me, Cory, you don't believe in it, you never did, and maybe you were right all along. Frankly, right now, I don't believe in it either."

"Oh, come on Selene, don't say that."

"Why not? It's true. I was wrong Cory, about the most important thing ever. How can I trust in my own feelings, my intuitions, my powers—in anything ever again?"

"Selene—" He reached for her hand, but she pulled it away.

"I've been stupid and more than that, I've been selfish. Indulging in romantic fantasies when one of my best friends is dead and the rest are in danger."

"You've been knocking yourself out to protect them, to find the truth," he argued. "You're doing all you can."

"Just tell me how your brother is doing."

Hell. Maybe he'd done more than just break her heart this morning. And he was damned if he knew what to do about it.

"They wouldn't tell me anything. Denied any gunshot-wound victim had even been brought in."

She nodded slowly. "The police are keeping it quiet. The

killer left him for dead, they probably figure it's best to let him go on believing that."

"Was that a psychic thing or—"

"Educated guess." She nodded at his plate. "Your breakfast is getting cold."

For some reason he didn't have much of an appetite.

She pushed away from the table. "Be right back." Then she walked back to the pay phone, and made a call of her own. She returned two minutes later. "He's stable, but still unconscious. They've got him under guard, but discreetly, and the hospital staff are under orders not to tell anyone anything about him. They were all over your phone call until I told Jimmy it was just us. He said he'd call them off, but I imagine they'll know exactly where we called from by the time we tip the waitress."

"Then we should hurry."

She nodded. "No reason to panic. There's no way for them to know where we're going. I imagine they'll assume I'm heading for Mexico."

"Why would they assume that?"

"I disappeared the night my best friend was murdered. In some peoples' minds, that makes me the most likely suspect, even though Jimmy says the chief is pretty much convinced I'm innocent."

He closed his eyes fast and hard. What the hell had he done to this beautiful young woman's life? Sighing, he wolfed down a few bites, gulped the coffee.

"Don't rush, Cory. What's going to happen is going to happen."

It was almost as if she didn't particularly care what happened. He latched onto the first thing he could think of to snap her out of it. "Whatever is going to happen, can go ahead and happen— but not until after we've warned your friend in Texas."

Her head came up, her eyes holding a bit more life than before. "You're right. Gotta keep our priorities straight here."

She took a big drink of her tea, and got to her feet. Her waffle was barely touched. "Let's go."

Caleb sat beside Marcy as the police—the State Police, who had taken over the investigation—questioned her. He could have wished for a more conservatively dressed client, but she refused to "conform to the authorities' notion of what looks respectable." Her words, verbatim. She wore a black leather mini-skirt with pointy-toed, ankle-high boots and black stockings. Her camouflage-print tank top showed off the Nile Goddess tattooed on her arm. Every piercing on her body sported a jewel, from the dozen or so in each ear, to the one in her nose, to the one in her belly button. She wore so many necklaces and bracelets that she jangled every time she moved, and her jet-black hair matched her eyeliner and nail polish.

"I told you, I have no idea where Selene might be going. And it's ridiculous what you're thinking. She had nothing to do with Tessa's death. She loved Tessa."

"She left town on the night of the murder. She called from Texas, so we assume she's heading for the border. You were with her just a few hours prior to that murder, Marcy," the detective said. "Look, you don't want to be charged as an accessory in a double homicide, do you? Just cooperate."

"I think my client has answered all your questions," Caleb said. He was nervous. This was a State Police detective in charge of the case now. He was no longer dealing with a handful of good ol' local boys, who knew and loved the Brands. This guy wouldn't give Selene the benefit of the doubt, or a crumb of a break. "Marcy came forward of her own free will, and has been more than cooperative. You and I both know she's no accessory. And threatening her isn't going to give her knowledge she doesn't already have. So either arrest her, or we're out of here."

The detective eyed him, lowered his head, shook it. "You shouldn't have this guy representing you, Marcy. You know the chief suspect is his sister-in-law. Any advice he gives you is liable to be more for her sake than your own."

"I think that's slander, Detective. And being a lawyer, I would know."

"It has to be a lie to be slander."

"And it is." He reached for Marcy's hand.

She took it and rose to her feet, turned for the door, but paused and turned back to the detective, jewelry clinking and clanging like church bells. "Caleb is an honest man, and the best attorney for miles around. I trust him. And I trust Selene."

"You just be sure you don't trust them all the way to a jail cell, Marcy. Even if you end up cleared in the end, it wouldn't look good for you in that custody battle you have coming up."

She narrowed her eyes on him, lifted her dagger-tipped hand, forefinger and pinky extended, the others folded down. "You son of a—"

"Easy, Marcy." Caleb covered her hand with his, pushing it down before she could fling whatever she'd been about to fling at the detective. A curse, he suspected. And hell, he didn't need that on the video of this interview.

She shot him a look, then glared at the cop. "Don't you ever threaten me again, Detective. Just…don't."

He stood there with his brows raised and one hand hovering near his gun, as if he'd felt the full impact of the shot she'd just been about to fire.

Caleb didn't know what he thought about all this Witch-craft stuff. But there had always been something very real and very special about Selene. And he was seeing now, that the same applied to her friend, Marcy, but in a different way. And he had to admit to a certain curiosity about it all.

He banked that for the moment, though, and took Marcy back out to the car. They got in. He drove. And he said, "You know, he has a point about Selene being my sister-in-law."

"Would you sell me out to save her?"

"Of course not, but—"

"Wouldn't matter," she said. "If there was a way I could get her out of this, I would."

He sighed, nodded. "I'm worried about her. We all are. She's not safe out there alone, especially not with this guy. She doesn't even know him."

Marcy smiled a little. "Yeah, she does."

He sent her a questioning look.

"Not the way you're thinking. It's just…well, hell, Caleb, you might as well know the truth. I'm pretty sure this stranger of hers is going to be your next brother-in-law. Probably better get used to the idea."

He lifted his brows. "I think you'd better expand on that. Are you telling me she's been seeing this guy—that she knew him before—"

"She never set eyes on him before that night. But she thinks he's her destiny, and I agree with her. You know she's never wrong about shit like this. And you don't have to worry. If Selene thinks he's all right, then he is."

He sighed, more worried about his kid sister-in-law than he had been already. "He was being chased by killers, Marcy. That doesn't exactly suggest he's some kind of stellar citizen."

"Oh, come on. He could be a cop for all you know."

It *had* occurred to him. But if there were a cop missing from anywhere within a few hundred miles, he thought the local police would have heard about it by now. "I don't think Selene's in any real danger of being prosecuted for this. That cop was blowing smoke. They want her back here so they can question her, but they'd have to be idiots to still suspect her in any real way, when all the evidence points to someone else. I just wish there was some way we could make sure she's all right."

Marcy glanced at him. "You want me to tell you what I wouldn't tell them."

"It would help. And it wouldn't go further."

"You wouldn't get into trouble for keeping something like that to yourself?"

"I might. But Selene's more important. She's family, Marcy."

She licked her lips, then slowly, she nodded. "She's going to a campground in Texas to find the fifth member of our circle. She's at a campground there for the weekend."

"You got a name for that campground?"

She held his gaze, and nodded.

Chapter 11

"This is it. Right there," Selene said, pointing to a carved wooden sign at the end of a narrow dirt road.

"Merry Meet Campground. Cute."

"It's a common greeting among Witches. Merry meet and merry part, and merry meet again."

"Uh-huh." She seemed anything but "merry." She seemed...deflated. Her usual boundless spirit seemed to have gone to sleep. "You suppose they get a lot of business?"

"By all accounts, they get all kinds. They run a great campground, and most non-Witches wouldn't recognize the name as anything all that unusual."

"I suppose not." He took the turn onto the dirt road, and followed it for a mile, before finally coming to a log structure marked Office. He parked in a small area, where only one other vehicle rested.

"This won't be easy. Maybe you'd better wait here," she said.

"Why would it be hard? I mean, she's a witch and you're

a witch, so can't you just tell them that and they'll let you talk to her?"

"Uhm, no. Just because I'm a witch it doesn't mean I'm entitled to crash someone else's party. People register in advance and pay to go to these things, and once in session, they're closed and tightly guarded to protect the attendees."

"Well, I'll come along, if you don't mind."

She frowned at him, tilting her head a little to one side. "Still don't trust me?"

It surprised him that not trusting her hadn't even entered his mind. He was thinking about protecting her. Which made sense, right? He was the guy, he'd brought disaster raining down on her life, and there were killers after them. Naturally he was feeling protective.

"You think my being there will hurt your chances of finding her?" Answer a question with a question. Great way to avoid giving an answer.

"Not really. I just think—"

Someone tapped on his window, and he damn near jumped out of the seat as he swung his head around.

A heavyset, smiling woman with a mop of brown curls stood there in a Born Again Pagan T-shirt, and a pair of khaki shorts with numerous pockets. He rolled down his window. "Hello."

"Merry meet," Selene called.

The woman met her eyes, and her smile grew warmer. "I'm afraid we're closed for a private event this weekend."

"I know, the Gathering. One of my coveners is here, and while I know it's against the rules, it's really important that I see her."

The woman's smile died. She lowered her eyes, shook her head. "I can't even confirm whether she's here or not, hon. We guarantee our guests' privacy—"

"I know. I know that, believe me. But…Bonnie, is it?" she asked, glancing at the woman's name badge. "Bonnie, her life is in danger. I'm not exaggerating."

Bonnie's gaze snapped back up to Selene's, wide and horrified. But still torn.

"Look, let me give you her name and a note," Selene said quickly. "You don't have to confirm or deny she's here. Just get the note to her if she is." She was digging into the glove compartment for a scrap of paper even before she finished speaking.

Bonnie nodded. "I can do that much. That's not violating anyone's privacy. Okay, I'll do that."

"Thanks." Selene had located a pen and was scribbling a note, while Cory was beginning to feel as if he was nothing more than a seat cover. The two seemed to have forgotten his presence even as they talked around him.

Selene passed the note to Bonnie, reaching right across his chest to do so. "Tell her I'm staying close by until I hear from her. I put my cell number on the note. Okay?"

"Okay." Bonnie took the paper.

Selene didn't let it go. She held it, gnawing her lower lip. "I didn't tell her about Tessa." She looked at him as if for advice.

And he knew right then that she hadn't forgotten his presence for a minute. "You can't tell her something like that in a note, Selene. If she was as close to Tessa as you were—"

"I know. But she has a right to know."

"She'll call you. You can tell her then. Face to face."

"But what if she doesn't call? What if she doesn't realize how real the threat is, without knowing what's already happened?"

Bonnie covered Selene's hand with her free one. The other still held one edge of the note. "She's your coven mate. Perfect love and perfect trust, right?"

Selene met the other woman's eyes and nodded. "Perfect love and perfect trust. If I say she's in danger, she'll believe me. She'll call."

"She'll call," Cory repeated.

Selene gazed at Cory again and seemed reassured. "She'd better." She let the other woman take the note.

"There's an inn, in town," the helpful Bonnie said. "A nice

one. Should be vacancies, this time of year. Go back to the end of the road and take a right. Three miles down, on the left. the Cactus Rose."

"Thanks."

"Before you go, Selene…" She stabbed Selene in the eyes with a probing look. "Is there any chance this trouble followed you down here? Any chance it's liable to show up at this campground?"

"We weren't followed," Cory said. "I'm sure of it."

He glanced at Selene, saw the troubled look in her eyes and wondered at it.

"It wouldn't hurt to be extra cautious, Bonnie. Just in case."

Bonnie looked worried. More than worried, she looked scared. She glanced at the name on the note, and lifted her brows. "Erica Jackson?" Then she shook her head.

"She might be using her craft name. Starshadow," Selene said. Then she looked at Cory and nodded. "Let's go."

He waved to Bonnie, put the car into gear, drove around a loop, and headed back the way they had come. But the troubled look on Selene's pretty face didn't ease. And it worried him.

"Tell me. What's wrong?"

She sighed, gave her head a shake, almost as if trying to shake something out of it. "Nothing. Probably nothing."

"I can see there's something."

She waved a hand at him. "Turn right here, remember?"

"I remember." He took the turn, and decided to try changing the subject. He didn't like seeing her so worried. "So how about those shorts she was wearing huh? Had enough pockets to hold my entire collection."

"What collection?"

He glanced at her, and then realized he was remembering again. In vivid detail. "Birds of prey," he said. "Miniatures, wood carvings, ceramics, clay, pewter."

"No wonder you recognized my feather. You're into raptors."

"Yeah. Accipiters, buteos and allies, eagles and falcons, even the vultures." He could see his little collection even now. It sat on shelves in his log cabin, shelves he'd made of hand-hewn pine planks, all stained and polished to a rich lustrous shine.

In fact, he could see more. He could see his living room. Cozy and neat. Hunter-green plaid curtains in rich flannel. A fireplace. And something he'd said aloud just now was ringing a loud bell in his brain. Accipiters, buteos, allies...falcons.

Nowhere, however, did he see any sign of a wife.

"Which hawk is your favorite?"

"Redtail," he said. "Same as yours."

She smiled. "Maybe we have a few things in common after all, huh?"

"Maybe we do." The bell was still ringing. And it finally came clear. "Falconer," he said then. "It's Falconer."

"What is?" She studied him as he drove. "You're a falconer?"

"I don't think so. But that's my name. Cory Falconer. Cory Michael Falconer."

She smiled, and he sent a smile back at her. Their eyes met, and that spark flared between them, but then her smile died slowly. And he knew she wanted to ask if he remembered there being a Mrs. Cory Falconer, and he wasn't sure how the hell to answer her if she did. He didn't want to admit there was no hint of that sort of memory in his mind. Would he really recall a bird collection and not a wife? And wouldn't he then have to admit that he never had felt that was true? And wouldn't that just set her off again on her tangent about them being soul mates, destined to be bound forever? He didn't want that.

What he wanted...was to kiss her. To kiss her breath away.

He was saved from the question she was about to ask by the sight of the inn up ahead. "There it is," he said. "Vacancy. Score."

"Yeah. Cool."

They pulled into the parking lot, and Cory went in to register them, proud as hell that he could sign his actual name.

He was easily pleased, wasn't he?

As she signed in beside his name, he glanced at her profile, the way her hair fell down to veil her face, so he could only see the exotic tilt of one blue, blue eye between the fringes of pale blond.

No, he wasn't easily pleased. Not easily at all.

All through the long drive from Oklahoma, she'd felt that something wasn't right. But her instincts were so off target that she didn't trust them.

Goddess, how could she have been so wrong?

She gave herself a mental shake. She had to get over it, get her focus off Cory, and how sure she'd been, and how wrong she'd been. To seal it she asked herself if any woman in her right mind would be this heartbroken, this devastated at losing a man she'd only known for a few days. Losing a man she'd never really had.

Well, okay, she'd *had* him. But she'd never *really* had him. Not the way she had thought she would. Not to call her own. Not to be his own. Not to be loved by him.

And that was what she wanted. She wanted him to love her. It was stupid that she wanted it, even now. Wanting something like that was wrong. It would only cause him pain to love one woman while being married to another. Why would she wish that on him? Was she honestly that selfish?

Maybe. Because she did wish it, deep, deep inside her, she longed to have him turn to her, sweep her into his arms and tell her that he couldn't help himself. That he loved her. She didn't want him to be in pain. She didn't want to cause him trouble. But she craved his love.

And didn't every woman want that? Every woman who loved a man, even if she new they had no chance, no future? Didn't every woman ache, deep down, to have the man she loved tell her that he loved her, too? Wasn't that kind of hard-wired into the female heart?

Ah, hell, she just wasn't sure of anything anymore.

She mulled these things over as they walked from the inn's office to their room, which was a tiny cabin that was a separate building. All the cabins were. The sidewalk twisted among gardens lush with natural, native plants. Plants that didn't need watering in this dry climate in southwestern Texas. And it occurred to her that they were not that far away from El Paso, or Quinn, just beyond it.

"I have relatives not far from here."

"You do?" he asked, and he looked at her as if he were interested. "Who?"

Did he really want to know? she wondered. Did he honestly care about her relatives or her family background? Could he, maybe, care about her? This thing had felt completely one-sided, at the start. But maybe—hell, did it matter? If he had a wife, did it really matter?

Yeah, it did. To her it did. "Too many to name. The Texas branch of the family is huge. I haven't seen most of them in a long time. Too long."

"So maybe when all this is over, we should pay them a visit."

She met his eyes. "When all this is over, Cory, you'll be going back to Big Falls, collecting your brother and heading home to…to wherever you're from. To your collection of raptors. And your wife."

He flicked his eyes away, just briefly. Guilt again. He must remember her, if he were feeling this guilty about being with Selene. She just knew it. He didn't want to hurt her by talking about it, but hell, how likely was a man to remember a bird collection and not a wife?

He probably loved her. He probably missed her, ached for her, now that he remembered her, and he was probably racked with guilt for making love with another woman.

She had to turn her head away quickly, so he wouldn't see the tears that sprang into her eyes. Blinking rapidly, she pointed to the cabin at the end of the walk. "That would be it," she said, noting the number 7 on the door. "I'm really sorry there's only one available. But…nothing will happen, Cory. I promise."

Her tears blinked dry, she glanced up at him when he didn't answer. And she could have sworn she saw real regret in his eyes.

No. That was probably just her own wishful thinking. She stopped at the door, waited while he unlocked the cabin, and then walked through the door while he held it open for her. She eyed the tiny sofa, more like a loveseat, just big enough for two, and the single bedroom, with the big fluffy bed. Just one.

And she heard him mutter something that sounded like, "I must be out of my freakin' mind."

She thought she must be out of hers, as well. Or would be, by morning, if she had to spend the entire night in this cozy place with him and not touch him. Not even kiss him. Goddess, this was clearly set up as a love nest. A romantic getaway. A place designed for intimacy, privacy and comfort.

Maybe she should just sleep in the back of Kara's station wagon and call it good.

At least they'd brought some sleeping bags.

Cory had tried every position in his sack on the floor, but none made sleep any easier. He wasn't uncomfortable, oddly enough. In fact, he had the feeling he'd spent a lot of nights in a lot of sleeping bags. No, it wasn't his bed on the floor keeping him awake. It was her.

He wanted her. No matter how hard he tried to sleep, all he could see when he closed his eyes was her face, the way it had looked the night before, when she'd been on top of him screwing him senseless. It had been good. More than good. It had been phenomenal. And he wanted more. It was killing him how badly he wanted her.

But he was doing the right thing. She didn't just want sex, she wanted hearts and flowers, and that just wasn't his thing. He might not have his memory back, but he knew that much. There was no doubt. It made him want to cut and run for his life when she started talking about destiny and soul mates and fate.

He'd stopped tossing and turning a while ago.

She hadn't. She wanted it, too, but for all the wrong reasons. And all her reassurances about just taking it one day at a time and seeing what developed, didn't ring true. She wanted forever.

He wanted no part of forever.

He estimated he'd been lying there, aching for her and fighting off fantasies about what would happen if he got up and went over to the bed, for about two hours, when she got up.

His heart sped up, because his first thought was that she was coming to him, instead. She was going to shimmy into this sleeping bag with him and—

But no. She wasn't coming toward him. Even in the room's pitch darkness, he could see that. She tiptoed across the room to where her backpack rested, picked it up, and then headed for the door. It took her several seconds to open it, and he knew she was trying to be quiet, trying not to wake him. She was sneaking out.

What the hell was she up to?

It crossed his mind that he didn't suspect her of being up to anything underhanded. His notion that she'd had anything to do with knifing him or with the man who had, had evaporated a while ago. But he was worried about her. He got out of his sleeping bag, pulled on his jeans, and walked quietly to the door, then peered through it. She didn't go toward the car. Instead she walked around behind their cabin. What the hell?

He opened the door, and as silently as he could, he followed her. Five steps later, he wished to God he'd thought to put on his shoes, as he stepped on one pebble after another. Walking as if over hot coals, he kept going behind the cabin. It was easier to see her outside than it had been in the cabin. The moon was lopsided, but big, and bright in a clear, starry sky. It was warm. Even the breeze, what little there was, was warm.

He crept where she led—down a small hill, over a path that

wound through trees. She couldn't possibly know where she was going, could she? She hadn't told him she'd ever been here before.

No, he didn't think she did know. She stopped a couple of times, looked around, then moved on as if not finding what she was looking for. Whatever the hell that was.

Finally, the third time she stopped, she nodded, and veered off the path into a small clearing. It was only a few yards in diameter, sprouting stiff, dry grasses and weeds. But it seemed to be what she wanted. She moved into it, and he found a stump, concealed by the trees around her, and sat down to watch.

Was she meeting someone here? Her friend had never phoned. He'd half expected to find that she was sneaking into that campground to find the elusive Erica—Starshadow, he thought with a shake of his head—herself.

But no, that wasn't it. And she wasn't meeting anyone, either. He realized that as she began tugging items from her backpack. A tiny vial. A paper packet. An incense stick. Four candles. She set them in the four corners of the little clearing, lit them one by one. Then she lit the incense from one of them, let it burn for a moment, and shook it out. She closed her eyes, and leaned close to the spiral of smoke that rose from its end, sniffing it as if she loved its scent. Then she wafted the smoke over herself, using her free hand, moving it from her head to her feet and back again. She moved, then, waving the stick around, as she moved in a circle from candle to candle, spreading the smoke.

Soon, though, her movements became more than just that. They became a dance. She stepped, and spread her arms and turned slowly. She bowed and dipped and spun and whirled. She arched her back, raising her arms to the skies, then moving them snakelike, lower again. She was the most incredible thing he'd ever seen. There was music, there must be, but it was music only she could hear.

Or maybe she *was* the music.

She was something, that was for sure. Outside in her T-shirt and panties, dancing by candlelight. The way she moved, the sense of freedom in it, hell it got to him.

She set the incense down, sticking its stem into the sandy soil, and picked up a candle, dancing it around the circle. Then she replaced the candle, took the vial, and danced with that, spreading droplets of whatever was inside it in her wake. Finally, she picked up the tiny paper packet. It looked like sugar or salt from a restaurant. She tore it open, poured its contents into her palm, and danced the circle once more, scattering it all around her.

When she finished, she moved toward each of the candles, pausing a moment at each one, facing outward, skyward, opening her arms, whispering words he couldn't hear. And when that was done, she moved to the center of the spot she'd chosen, and sat down, her legs crossed, her forearms resting on her knees.

"My kingdom for a drum," she muttered. Then she smiled as if she'd made a joke, as if there were others there to share it with her. "I know. It's just a tool. I don't need it to journey. Hell, I have the best drum anyway, right here." Lifting one hand, she pressed her palm to her chest. "I'm just not sure how well it's working right now. Help me out, here, guys."

Huh? Guys? What guys? He looked around the clearing, but no one came out of the trees. No one showed up.

She took a few deep breaths. Really deep, and after each one she paused a moment, then exhaled fully and kind of loudly. And then she lay back, right there on the ground, and she crossed her arms so both palms were resting on her chest, over her heart. She closed her eyes.

And that was it. She didn't move. She just lay there. And he was damned if he knew what to do. He thought maybe she'd fallen asleep after awhile, and considered going over there and waking her. But he decided not to interrupt, because it wasn't as though it had been accidental. Maybe she just couldn't sleep in the room. Maybe she made a habit of walking out into the middle of nowhere in her underwear and sleeping on the ground without a blanket. She was nutty enough that he could buy that theory.

But hell, it wasn't too wise a move, not while they were targeted by killers. In the end he decided to wait it out a while, see what happened. It wasn't an unpleasant excursion, after all. He hadn't been sleeping anyway. And it was a nice night, and hell, looking at her lying there with her legs exposed clear to her hips wasn't exactly a chore. She had great legs. Short, sexy legs.

Hmm. And no bra under that T-shirt, either. Nice.

He shifted his position, and told himself to stop wanting her so much.

It didn't work. He wanted her anyway.

A half hour passed, more or less. He wasn't sure, because he wasn't wearing a watch. But finally, she opened her eyes and lay there a minute, staring up at the sky. She frowned, took another deep breath, and sat up. She took her time, as if she had to get her bearings before getting to her feet, and then she swirled around the circle again, waving her arms and whispering words and snuffing her candles, all but one. She left the incense burning—it was nearly gone anyway. She dug a notebook from her backpack. It had a pen in a pocket inside the cover, and she took it out, sat down by the remaining candle, leaned over it and began writing.

He managed to let her go on for another ten minutes, before he finally decided to let her know he was there. But before he could get to his feet, she lifted her head, looked in his general direction and said, "You can come over now, if you want to."

He lowered his head, closed his eyes. He should have known, he thought. "How did you know I was here?"

"Just did. And that's odd, isn't it? I mean, isn't that just totally out of whack?"

Getting up, he moved to where she sat on the ground and

sank down beside her. "Why is it out of whack? You've been telling me all along that you're a Witch."

"Because my skills have totally deserted me. At least, that's what I've been feeling since…well, since we found out about…Kelly."

"Is that why you're out here? Trying to…I don't know, get your powers back."

"I was journeying."

"Uh, beg to differ, babe, but you were just lying there."

She glanced at him and smiled at his lame attempt at humor. "A shamanic journey. It's not a physical one."

"I see."

"I doubt it." ·

He shrugged. "So where did you go on this journey?"

"Into the Upperworld. Talked to my guide. Took a look around."

"And what did you find out?"

"I had arrows in a quiver. As I walked the tips cut through the sides of the case that held them, and poked me in the back. It hurt."

He thought, and not for the first time, that maybe Selene Brand was a little bit nuts. "Does that…mean something?"

"I think it means my skills, my weapons are just as sharp as ever. But maybe I don't like what they're trying to tell me. Or maybe I'm not listening because the truth hurts."

Or maybe, he thought, she was dead on target all along and he was letting her believe something he had no reason to think might be true for his own purposes. Hell, she'd been right about everything else. What if she was right about the two of them?

No, no way. He was not going to spend the rest of his life with this adorable little fruitcake just because she thought it was fated.

"So what were you writing?"

She glanced down at the notebook. "Just jotting down everything I saw and what I think it meant. You tend to forget if you don't get it down when it's fresh in your mind."

He glanced at the notebook. It was thick, and open to a spot well past the middle. "That whole thing is full of... journeys?"

"Yep. It's my Journey Journal." She giggled a little. It was good to hear, good to see a grin on her face again. She'd been so troubled and preoccupied today, not only with worry for her friends and the situation, but because she'd thought her so-called powers had failed her. He'd done that to her. And damn, he regretted it. He wanted to keep her mood upbeat, or as upbeat as possible, given the circumstances.

"Listen, you know, maybe this Kelly thing isn't what we're thinking it is, after all." He could have kicked himself for blurting it. Why the hell was he messing with her like this, giving her hope when there wasn't any?

Too late, though. There it was right in her eyes. Hope and surprise and a dozen other things. "I figured you'd remembered her by now."

"I didn't say I had remembered her, did I?"

"Well, no, but I assumed you were just trying to...you know, spare my feelings."

He closed his eyes. "Why do women always assume they know what men are thinking? So what else have you assumed, Selene?"

She shrugged. "That you remembered her, were missing her, feeling guilt-ridden for having cheated on the woman you love, couldn't wait to get back to her—"

"I haven't remembered anything about any wife."

She tipped her head to one side. "But you said you had a feeling it was true."

"I lied."

"You lied?" She blinked, lowered her head, then raised it again and glared at him in disbelief. "You *lied?*"

"It seemed like a good idea at the time."

"How does lying about something like that ever seem like a good idea?"

"Look, you kept going on about us being meant for each other, and I'm just not interested in anything like that. Not now. Maybe not ever, okay? I just thought it might…slow you down."

"Well, it did."

He felt like a jerk. "The truth is, I don't know, Selene. I don't know what the notation meant. I swear that's the truth. I don't know that I don't have a wife, but I don't feel that I do."

"Hell."

"I'm sorry."

She looked at him, seemed about to say something, then stopped and jumped to her feet. "Something's wrong."

"What? What do you mean?"

"I don't know." She turned slowly, facing the direction of the campground. "It's Erica. She's in trouble, Cory. We have to go."

She bent only long enough to snuff the remaining candle and toss it and the journal into her backpack, then she slung it onto her shoulder and ran back toward the cabin.

He ran, too. And he was hoping to God she was wrong this time. Not only because he didn't want there to be another dead Witch on his conscience, but because if she was right about this, and so many other things, then how the hell could she be wrong about him? About them?

He darted into the cabin. She slung the backpack onto the bed and yanked her jeans on. He pulled on a shirt, shoes without socks, and grabbed the keys. And then they were racing for the car, and driving like hell for the campground.

They were almost there when he heard the sound there was no mistaking.

She sent him a look, her eyes wide and round. "Was that—?"

"Gunshots. Rifle, I think."

"Oh, Goddess, no."

"Chant or something, baby. I'm driving as fast as I can."

She closed her eyes, and started chanting.

Chapter 12

As they sped toward the campground, Selene didn't know whether to be angry that Cory had lied to her or relieved that maybe he didn't have a wife after all. The latter would be pretty stupid, she supposed, because it might very well turn out that he really was married, whether he remembered it or not. She couldn't think of too many other reasons his brother would have a note about his and Kelly's anniversary party in his date book.

Being angry about his lie would be pretty counterproductive as well, though. She'd probably scared him into that by being so open about her feelings. He was conservative, a planner, a slow, methodical, practical kind of guy, she thought with a roll of her eyes. And apparently, a little bit gun-shy when it came to commitment. Okay, more than a little bit gun-shy. The man was downright terrified of it. And it was no wonder, given what he'd told her about his parents.

She didn't know what to think anymore.

And there wasn't time to decide, because they were turning now, onto the campground's access road, and she had far more pressing matters to worry about. Her friend, Erica, and all the other campers. "Goddess, protect them all," she whispered.

"Amen to that," Cory muttered.

A large form swooped out of the sky, crossing in front of the car so suddenly and so closely that he hit the brakes.

"Jeez, was that an owl?" Selene asked.

"Yeah. A great horned owl." He looked toward where it had gone, but there was nothing there. "Scared the hell out of me." He put the car into motion again.

Selene put a hand on his forearm. "Pull over, Cory."

He frowned at her.

"Come on. That was a sign. A warning. The owl was telling us to stop here."

"The owl was telling us…? Selene, how do you suppose the owl knows and why on earth does he care enough to bother telling us anything?"

She scowled at him. "It's not so much that he knows and is trying to warn us. It's that there's a vibrational energy of danger here, and he was reacting to that."

"Vibrational energy. Uh-huh."

"Look, this is no time to debate the legitimacy of signs and omens. Just pull the car over and let's go on foot from here."

He shrugged and steered the car off the road. They got out and started walking. "What I wouldn't give for a weapon."

"We've got the best weapons there are," she said. "Our brains, our senses, and nature itself. We're working in harmony. The bad guys aren't. Everything on the planet is going to fall in our favor here. Everything in the whole freaking universe."

"I hate to bring it up, Selene, but that didn't exactly help your other friend and her husband."

"I know that. But she had no idea she was even in danger. She was taken completely by surprise. We know what we're getting into."

"Do we?"

He looked at her for a long moment. She thinned her lips, swallowed hard. "As best we can."

"Selene, maybe you should wait back at the car, or better yet, back at the inn. Let me check this out. Hell, we should have called the police when we heard the shots."

"They've been called."

He lifted his brows.

"Believe me or don't. But we can't have been the only ones to have heard the shots. Someone would have called."

"That makes sense. So why don't you wait for them, fill them in when they get here?"

She kept on walking. "You're trying to protect me. That's sweet."

"Yeah, I'm a sweet guy."

"Cory….look." She put a hand on his arm, and he stopped walking, lifting his head to stare ahead. The campground's office stood just a few yards distant. Its door stood open, and a shape lay on the ground at the bottom of the steps.

"Is that—?"

"Bonnie," she whispered, and she started to run, but Cory gripped her arm and held her back.

"Take it slow, Selene," he said, and he pointed to the red sports car in the parking area. "That car was at Tessa's cabin. And I think it's the one that followed Casey and me before all this came down. It belongs to the killers, and we don't want to walk right into their sights."

She knew he was right, but it killed her to move slowly. He closed a hand around her, and tugged her into the trees, off the path. They cut through the woods, for cover, moving slowly and as quietly as possible, though it seemed to Selene every step she took made as much noise as a bear crashing through the forest would.

They kept under cover for as long as possible, then hesi-

tated at the edge of the woods nearest the little building, listening, barely breathing.

"Stay here," he said, and before she could disagree, he was
gone, darting across the open patch of grass between them and
poor Bonnie. He was kneeling beside the woman a second or
two later. No one had shot him, as Selene had half expected.
And she didn't wait before racing after him.

She crouched beside him. "Is she—?"

"Still breathing," he said. "I told you to wait."

"Yeah, I'm not so big on being told what to do. Ask my
mother about it sometime." She leaned closer to the fallen
woman. There was a bandage wrapped around her belly, and
a lot of blood on her torn-open camp shirt. "Bonnie?" Selene
patted her cheek. "Bonnie, wake up. Tell me what happened."

The woman moaned, but said nothing.

"Don't move."

The voice was male, and it came from just inside the cabin.
Selene's eyes shot to the doorway, and she saw a form sil-
houetted there. She lifted her hands.

"Who are you? What are you doing here?" the man asked.

Cory spoke. "We were staying at the inn, heard gunshots
and came to try to help." He glanced at the woman on the
ground. "This woman needs an ambulance."

"I've already called one." The screen door creaked open,
and the man came out. He wore camping clothes like Bonnie
wore, had tattoos covering the length of both arms, long
brown hair pulled back in a ponytail and a scruffy beard. He
knelt beside them. "Two carloads of men pulled in about
twenty minutes ago. That red car there, and a Jeep Wrangler.
Bonnie came out to tell them we were closed for a private
event. I wasn't even watching. I heard the shots, and came
running to find her lying here bleeding, and the men and the
Jeep gone."

"They all piled into one vehicle and left?"

He looked up, big dark eyes in a young, worried face.

"They didn't leave. They went into the campgrounds. I think part of them took the Jeep and the others went on foot." He swallowed hard. "I was on the phone with nine-one-one when I heard more shots."

"Oh my God," Selene said. "The campers…."

"I couldn't leave Bonnie to warn them—to help them."

"If you had you might be lying somewhere with a bullet in you, too," Cory said. "I'll go check on them."

"*We'll* go check on them," Selene said. "You stay here and tell the police what happened. They should be here any second."

She got to her feet, and Cory did, too. She was a little surprised, and a lot relieved that he didn't argue with her. It would only waste time and she thought he knew it.

"Take the fork to the right, that's where everyone's camping," Bonnie's friend said. "The west fork is just for the vendors and they wouldn't have opened until morning. Beyond that is the larger parking area, where the campers leave their vehicles."

Cory clasped her hand again, and they moved, fast and in a half crouch, off in the direction the man had indicated, veering off the trail and into the woods to follow the path without walking on it in the open.

Together they moved through the trees. Until Cory stopped, frowning.

"What? What is it?"

"I…this is really familiar."

"This campground?"

"No, just something about these woods." He narrowed his eyes, looking around. "Casey and I were in a forest like this one, before we came here. There were golden eagles nesting there, and some redtails a few miles away. We were checking on them."

"Checking on them?"

"There were men in the tree. Taking the fledglings from the nest."

Her brows shot up in surprise. "Why?"

"It's a billion-dollar industry. Young raptors are smuggled into Mexico, sold there, right out in the open sometimes."

Frowning, Selene tilted her head. "You're some kind of wildlife officer, aren't you, Cory?"

He stared at her, and nodded. "National Organization of Wildlife Officers. That's what the initials on the ring stand for."

"And your brother—?"

"Him, too."

She nodded.

"We let the men go, hung back to follow them. Figured we could do more good by getting to the higher-ups in the smuggling ring. They were just flunkies. Low men on the totem pole."

"So that explains the truck you were following. They must have known you were on to them, and set up the rest."

He nodded.

"But you don't know who they are. They stopped you from catching them, though. They could have gone on with their plans unhindered. Why are they so determined to kill you?"

"Maybe there's more. I just haven't remembered it all yet." He clasped her arm, looking ahead. There were clusters of tents and campers lining the road there. Camper doors and tent flaps stood open. Coolers and water bottles, backpacks and shoes were strewn everywhere. And there were no signs of life. No people, no voices, no movement. And thankfully, no bodies.

"I think everyone left in a hurry."

He nodded in agreement. "We know who they were after. If they found Erica, they wouldn't have worried about the others, so long as no one saw their faces. Would you know Erica's gear if you saw it?"

"Yeah. Her tent is a big red dome model, brand-new, and she always has dream catchers hanging from the trees around it."

He nodded, and clasped her hand again. "Let's find it then."

"I just hope they didn't find her first."

They emerged from the trees, and moved carefully and

silently along the narrow, pine-needle carpet of road. Eventually, Selene spotted Erica's tent, and pointed. "That's it. That's her site."

His hand tightened on hers, and they moved closer. Erica's gear was strewn everywhere, her site much more messed up than anyone else's. "They knew this was hers," Selene whispered. "How, Cory? How could they know?"

"I don't know. But listen, if they ransacked it like this, they must have been looking for her, right? Which means she wasn't here when they came for her."

She stared at him, her eyes widening. "She got away?"

"Looks like."

She stared at the woods around them. "But they went after her."

"They don't quit easily. So yes, they probably went after her."

"Then we're going after them." She faced the sky, her jaw clenching. "Which way?"

"I don't know, Selene."

"I wasn't asking you," she said, and she closed her eyes. "Which way?" she asked again.

In the distance, a hawk screeched. Her eyes popped open. "Thanks." And she started off in the direction from which the sound had come.

"You've gotta be kidding me," he said. "Listen, Selene, don't you think we should look for a trail, some kind of sign or—"

"That was our sign."

He lowered his head and shook it.

"Cory, hawk is my totem. And, I believe, yours as well. But even if you don't believe in that—well, hell. When's the last time you heard a redtail cry at night?"

His brows drew together, and he shivered visibly.

Selene took his hand again. "This way."

Cory was awed by her. He supposed he shouldn't be, but he was. She rummaged around the abandoned campsites, gathering up what they might need—bottles of water, a small box of granola bars—and stuffing them into their backpacks. It took her all of fifteen minutes. While she did that, he used a flashlight to examine the tracks in the woods.

"Anything?" she asked, coming up to him with one pack on her shoulders, and another in her hands.

"Looks like people just scattered. Heard the shots and ran like rabbits. They headed in a dozen directions."

She nodded. "They'll lay low until they're sure it's safe, then head for the office, the road, their vehicles."

"Where are all their vehicles anyway?" he asked. She held the backpack and he turned and slid his arms into it, then hiked it up onto his back.

"At most campgrounds, they pull into the campsite area, unload their stuff, then take the cars to a parking area and walk back. Remember, Bonnie's friend said the parking lot was down the opposite fork, all the way at the end."

"I bet that's where they'll head."

"Yeah. But not Erica."

"Why not?"

"Because she would make the same guess we did, that everyone would head that way. If she ever got my note, then she knows she's the one the killers are after. She's not going to lead them to the others. She'll lead them in the opposite direction." She pointed. "Which is exactly where the hawk seemed to be."

He was skeptical. Her logic was flawed. It only held if Erica was selfless enough to put herself at greater risk in order to save countless others. But that defied human nature. She'd run for her car out of a sheer sense of self-preservation.

And as for the hawk—well, hell, he didn't know what to make of that. But despite thinking that she was full of it, he followed where she led.

"I hear sirens," she said at length.

"Yeah, I hear them, too. The cavalry has finally arrived."

"I hope Bonnie's still alive." She trudged fast, through the undergrowth, angling sharply uphill. "And I hope to Goddess that Erica is."

Vidalia Brand had been fielding phone calls all evening, trying to get straight on exactly what was happening. When her son-in-law, Jimmy Corona, had phoned to start jabbering on about a siege taking place at some campground in Texas, she hadn't understood what the hell he was talking about, much less what it had to do with her. Until he'd said the lines she had probably known he was going to, all along.

"Selene's there."

"What?"

"One of the women with her that night out by the falls was at this campground for the weekend," Jimmy said. "Selene and that wounded stranger went down there after her, to warn her. But the killers apparently got there around the same time. The police are on the scene, trying to sort everything out."

Gripping the phone tighter, she said, "Is Selene alive?"

"As far as I know, Vi. I'm on the scene. She's not among the—uh—that is—"

"The dead? By God, Jimmy, what's happened down there?"

"One wounded, three dead. So far. The police have surrounded the campground, and are closing in from all sides. Most of the campers scattered, many made it to their cars and left. Those still in the woods are being located and brought out to safety."

"Who's the girl?" she asked.

"Vi, I—"

"I know about Marcy, because she came forward. I've noticed two other good friends of Selene's seem to have vanished without a trace this week, though I hate to think— just tell me, is it Erica or Helena?

"Erica."

Erica Jackson, the minister's daughter. Lord have mercy. "I'll inform her father."

"She's still missing, Vi. And frankly I think the police may have cast their net too small. I think chances are Erica and the men who are after her were already well off the campground property by the time the cops sealed it off."

"If they are, Selene and that stranger are likely right on their heels."

"I'm doing my best, Vi. I promise, I'll try everything possible to bring Selene home safe."

"I know you will. And I hope you won't mind that I'm sending some more help."

"Help?"

She sighed. "She's my daughter. My youngest. My *baby*, Jim. I'm throwing everything I've got at this one."

She pressed the cutoff button, then dialed a number she hadn't dialed in a long time. And when the deep voice answered she knew it well.

"Hello Garrett. This is your Aunt Vidalia."

"Aunt Vi? Well, I'll be—hey, how are you? How are the girls? It's been way too long since—"

"No time for small talk, son. My youngest is in trouble. I need your help."

The jovial tone of his voice turned deadly serious. "Selene? Where is she?"

"Merry Meet Campground. Town called Locklan in Texas."

"Selene is *there?*"

"You've heard what's happening then?"

"I'm the law here, Aunt Vi. That town's only thirty miles from Quinn. Of course I've heard. What's Selene doing there?"

"Ah, hell, Garrett, it's a long story. Just you get there, all right?"

"Don't worry, Aunt Vi. She's as good as home."

"I'll be down there just as soon as possible, Garrett. But don't wait for me. Do whatever needs doing."

"You got my word on that, Aunt Vi."

She nodded, not doubting it for a minute. There was no reason to doubt. When a Brand was in trouble—any Brand—the rest would get there to help, come hell or high water. It was the unwritten code of their bloodline. And while her end of the clan had grown distant from the Texas branch of the family, she knew they would never let her down. Not when it mattered. Not when one of their own was at risk.

"We need to stop, Selene. We've been tracking them for six hours. They're just too far ahead."

"They'll get farther if we stop to rest."

"I have a feeling they won't."

She frowned, staring hard at him. "What do you mean?"

Cory licked his lips, not wanting to frighten her, but all too aware of her strong feelings about having a right to know all there was to know and make her own decision. "All these guys wanted was to silence the witnesses. Right?"

"Right, as far as we know."

"So then why haven't they just shot your friend and left her? Why are they hanging around here, wasting time following her on this wild-goose chase?"

"They haven't caught up to her yet."

"No, but with those high-powered rifles and scopes, they could have picked her off from a distance. Unless she's found a way to make herself completely invisible."

"I wouldn't rule it out."

He glanced at her, unsure if she were kidding, and then decided he didn't want to know. Instead, he focused on her uneven gait and the grimace in her face every time she stepped on her right leg.

"You're limping."

She shrugged. "Twisted my ankle a little a ways back. It's nothing."

"Sit. Rest. They know we're following them, and that's what they want. They'll wait."

She went utterly still, staring at him as if she thought he was insane. No, it was more as if she *wished* she thought that. But she didn't.

"That's what they're doing, then? Luring us up here after them?"

He shrugged. "I guess we'll know when we get there."

"But if that's the case, Cory, it'll be an ambush! They'll wait for us in the spot most advantageous to them."

"So we'll wait for the time most advantageous to us," he said.

"What time would that be?"

He smiled at her. "The Witching hour?"

Rolling her eyes, she punched him in the shoulder. "Dammit, Cory, this is no time for joking."

"I'm not joking. We need to wait until after dark. We both know our way around the woods. It'll leave more time for more help to arrive. And it'll have them so confused wondering what we're waiting for, that they'll be off balance."

"And what do you suggest we do until then?" she asked.

He glanced her way and then got stuck in her eyes. It was tough to drag his away, but he managed it. Not, however, before his stomach had knotted up tight, and his throat closed off to the point where he couldn't even swallow.

Damn, she hit him hard. Just a freaking glance. That was all it took.

"How about we rest a bit? Maybe have a snack and some water."

She nodded, found a suitable spot and slid the backpack from her back. She lowered it to the ground, and turned, to end up standing very close, so close her breath fanned his face.

"Damn," she muttered.

He thinned his lips. "I'm...sorry."

"Sorry for what?"

"This." He pulled her into his arms and kissed her. He

didn't know if he had a wife, and at that moment in time, he didn't particularly care. He wanted to kiss her just then more than he wanted his heart to beat another time in his chest. And from her reaction, he thought she wanted it just as badly.

And more.

He wrapped his arms around her, held her enfolded in them, in him, and cradled her head to his chest where his heart thundered. Fingers threading in her hair, he whispered, "I want you so much, Selene. I don't know if it's right or wrong. I don't know about the future—or the past for that matter. I only know I want you, right here, right now, I want you more than I want to breathe."

Her hands slid around his nape, and she tipped her head up to press her lips to his yet again. But when she broke the kiss, there were tears brimming in her beautiful eyes and she whispered, "I want you, too, Cory. But I can't. Not…not until I know you're really free."

He thought his heart broke when her words made themselves clear in his brain. It was a blow, and it hurt. And yet, grudgingly, he admired her for having the strength to say them, when he knew she was feeling the same burning hunger he felt.

Nodding, he eased his arms from around her. She sank a little, as if her knees were weak, so he clasped her elbows, hating the few inches of space between his body and hers.

"One thing," she said. "No matter what else happens, I need you to know…that…I love you."

He closed his eyes.

"You don't have to say it back. I know it's too soon."

"Selene, it's just that I—"

"I know." She pressed her fingertips to his mouth, to save him having to answer. "You probably think I'm a complete fool to feel so much so soon. But I've never said it to any man before. I love you. And I probably always will."

Chapter 13

She didn't wait for him to answer, and it was just as well, because he didn't know what to say. Instead, she stood on tiptoe, and pressed her mouth to his. His entire body reacted, every thought driven from his mind as he kissed her back, twisting his arms around her waist to hold her close to him. Every sense in him was filled with her, and everything in him seemed to sing because of it. It felt good to hold her, to kiss her. He couldn't think of anything he wanted to do more.

When he lifted his head, she tugged free of his arms, turned and walked to the big rock, where she sat down again. And he was left standing there, dazed, turned on, confused, with his heart racing and his erection throbbing.

The sun was finally climbing in the sky, and he felt frustrated, uneasy, jittery. He couldn't wait to be moving again, despite that they'd barely rested ten minutes. He was nervous with her declarations of undying love, and his inability to respond in kind. His mind was at war with his conscience, his brain telling him to go ahead and lie to her. Not only would it spare her having to know the truth—for now—it would probably get him laid again, and right now that was a pretty high priority for him.

Maybe he could have gone for it, if she were any other woman. But she wasn't. She was crazy, irreverent, slightly nutty Selene Brand. And he liked her. He couldn't lead her on or lie to her, because she was just trusting enough to believe him. It would never occur to her that he would say he loved her if it wasn't absolutely true. And that meant the hurt would be a hundred times worse later on, when he had to leave her to reclaim whatever remained of his forgotten life.

Hell.

She sat on the rock, basking in the rising sun even while remaining as alert as a doe with fawns to protect. Every one of her senses seemed open as he looked at her. And he took a moment to try to attune his own, try to figure out what she was seeing, hearing, feeling. He looked around, letting his gaze slide easily from one thing to another: the sky, red-orange now as the rising sun chased the purple away, painted clouds, like long fingers reaching for each other. The air was growing warmer on his skin as the sun beamed down, and he felt the chill of the night fading beneath the onslaught. Birds twittered and chirped all around them. It seemed the more he listened, the more of them he heard.

He glanced back at her, saw her close her eyes, tip her face up to the sun, and felt something inside him twist into hard knots. Damn, he was drawn to her. Just looking at her there, he felt things writhing around in his gut. Things he didn't recognize or recall having felt before. What was this?

He felt cruel for not returning her feelings. And clearly, he liked her, genuinely liked her. Maybe more than that. Maybe…. He shook that away and focused on her sitting there. He wanted her. Burned for her. There was a voracious need gnawing at his gut, and he didn't think he could quiet it—maybe not ever.

So what was that telling him? Could he possibly be feeling more than just fondness for her? More than just sexual desire? Was that even possible, for him? He didn't think so.

God, he had to get some distance, give himself some space to think, to figure this out, logically and rationally, something he couldn't do when he was close to her.

"I'm going to take a walk," he said at length.

She snapped to attention, got to her feet. "I'll come with—"

"No, no. Rest here for a few more minutes. I just want to circle out a ways, see if I can pick up any sign of them."

Tipping her head to one side, she searched his face. "We don't need a trail to follow, Cory. Look." She pointed.

He looked. There, soaring against the backdrop of the red-orange sky, was a hawk, circling in loops, dipping and rising again, crying now and then.

"A little morning hunt. Probably thinks she sees a field-mouse or—"

"She's showing us the way."

He made a skeptical face at her. "If it's all the same to you, I'll go check around for a trail anyway."

"Suit yourself." She slid down the rock, lay on her back and opened her arms. "I'm going to listen to Earth while you're gone. She may have some advice."

"Right. You do that."

"I will." She rolled over, lying face down, her cheek pressed to the earth.

Cory dragged his gaze away from her, forcibly suppressing the thoughts the sight of her brought to mind, and turned to take his walk and clear his head.

Selene lay there for awhile, letting the earth sooth her wounded heart. Loving a man who didn't love you back, she decided, wasn't healthy for her. She felt a lot of hurt, and that wasn't a good thing. She spent way too much time being sad, and wishing for something that might never be. When had she become that kind of woman? The kind so desperately needy for affection from a man? The kind of woman she'd always silently pitied.

When she'd lain there long enough, she began to feel the gentle pulse of her heartbeat, where her chest pressed to the ground. After a time, she imagined she could feel the heartbeat of the Earth, too, pounding in perfect rhythm with her own, but louder, stronger, deeper. Solid and powerful, the Earth promised it would always be there for her, to replenish her, to comfort and sooth her, to heal her.

And then, suddenly, the sound went silent.

Something's wrong.

She rolled over fast, eyes flashing open, then squinting in the sun. An instant later that sun was blocked out by a dark silhouette.

"Where is Cory Falconer?"

She frowned, shielding her eyes with one hand to try to see better. "Who?"

"Falconer! We know you were with him in the hunting cabin. Where is he?"

The earth was silent. That told her that she must be silent, as well.

"You mean that guy you stabbed back in the woods of Big Falls? That *was* you, wasn't it?" There was a grunt, but she rushed on. "So that's his name. He couldn't remember, you know. Couldn't even remember what happened to him, who he was, where he was from."

"I'd heard as much. Is it true?"

"You mind if I sit up? The sun is burning my eyes."

A hand came down, gripped the front of her shirt in a fist, and jerked her upright, into a sitting position. She blinked her vision into focus, and got her first good look at her attacker. Blond-haired, tanned, with crow's feet around his blue, blue eyes. He looked like an aging surfer.

"Is it true Falconer has amnesia?"

She nodded. "Yes. I only helped him when he left the hospital because the police suspected me of trying to kill him that night. Thanks a lot for that, by the way."

The man shrugged but didn't interrupt her.

"I thought he could tell them what really happened, but he didn't remember. So then I thought I could help him get his memory back, and he would be able to clear me, but no luck."

"So where is he now?" the aging beach boy asked. She stole a look around him, noted no others in the immediate area.

"How would I know?"

His eyes narrowed. "Don't make me hurt you, Selene Brand."

"Hey, easy now," she said, holding up a hand. "Neither of us wants that. I'm just saying, I'm not the guy's keeper. He was no help to me. I decided to leave town."

"To find your friend and warn her," he said.

She frowned. "What friend would that be? No, you're way off. I left town to avoid being arrested. They not only think I stabbed this…Falconer fellow, now they think I murdered my best friend and her husband to boot. I'm heading for Mexico, pal."

"We have her, Selene."

"Have who?"

"Erica."

"Erica who?"

He backhanded her, and her head snapped with the impact. She felt every knuckle driving into her jaw and cheekbone, and she was pretty sure the skin of her cheek was cut on the inside, from being mashed into her teeth with so much pressure.

She brought her head back around, slowly, her head ringing with pain, and lifted a hand to her face to sooth it. "Damn."

"Again, where is Falconer?"

"The last time I saw him, he was in Big Falls, looking for a place to hole up. I haven't seen him since I left town."

He sighed, then straightened and took a more thorough look around the area where she and Cory had been sitting. He

looked at the ground, but it was too hard here to hold any footprints. He looked at her backpack, and she thanked her stars
Cory had taken his with him. There was nothing else to tell the
tale. Nothing he would see anyway. If he was at all in tune he
would feel Cory's presence lingering here. God knew she did.

She knew the moment he decided to believe her. She saw
the change in his eyes, the way his mind shifted from questioning her about Cory, to doing whatever came next. She
didn't think he was capable of directing too many trains of
thought at the same time. Cory was, for the moment, forgotten. The man came to her, gripped her upper arm, and jerked
her to her feet. "You're coming with me."

"Oh, yeah? And where are we going?"

"Wherever I tell you."

She stomped hard on his instep and when he bent slightly
in reaction she pulled her knee up hard and fast to connect
with his chin. But his foot snaked out and hooked behind hers,
tugging forward, so her legs went out from under her and she
landed hard on her back, cracked her head on a rock, and felt
pain explode in her skull.

He loomed over her.

"I'm not going without a fight," she said, panting, blinking
the stars from her vision. "I hope you're up for it, because I'm
going to make this just as hard for you as I can."

He rubbed his chin. "Maybe not. We have Erica," he said.
"I can take you to her, or make one little call on this—" He
held up a walkie-talkie. "And have her shot. You choose."

"You're going to kill her anyway," she accused.

He shrugged. "And you, too, I imagine. The question is,
do you want to die now, or later? Do you want to see your
friend again before you go?"

She swallowed hard. "I'll see her again, either way." But
she didn't want him to take Cory as well, and he could come
back at any moment. There was no sense in both of them
dying. Maybe he could get help, track them, wait for the right

moment. Maybe she could find a way to gain the advantage, and save herself and Erica.

Or maybe Erica was already dead.

"All right," she said. "I'll come with you."

"Good girl."

Cory didn't find any obvious signs to follow, not that he'd expected to. His true purpose in leaving Selene had been to give himself some space, to figure out what the hell was happening to him. He couldn't be falling for her. Even if he thought he might be, it would be stupid to believe it. In the state he was in, how could he trust his own feelings? He couldn't even trust his own mind right now. It had gone from a looming black hole to a jigsaw puzzle with a handful of pieces still missing. Okay, so his memory was almost fully restored. But those missing pieces were big ones. Recent history was still spotty. He still didn't know who the hell this Kelly was. He might be *married,* for God's sake.

Deep down a little voice told him he knew damn well that wasn't the case, but until he knew that for sure, he had to consider it a possibility. Or maybe he was just using it as an excuse to avoid thinking too hard about what he felt or didn't feel for Selene.

Okay, scratch that. He definitely felt something for Selene. He supposed he had to admit that to himself. But he couldn't admit it to her, because maybe it would still remain even after he'd regained the missing pieces of his memory and got his head back in order. But maybe it wouldn't. It wouldn't be fair to her to give her hope when his own emotions were so damned unreliable and uncertain.

He shouldn't have left her, though. He'd only been gone twenty minutes, and feeling guilty as hell the entire time. It bugged him that he couldn't bring himself to say anything when she told him she loved him. But what could he say? He didn't know what he was feeling, or even whether his feelings were real or just some kind of psychological bond with the only person he'd known since his memory had deserted him.

He sighed, and was no closer to knowing his own mind than he had been when he left, as he walked back into the small clearing. He shrugged off his pack. "Sorry I left like that. You were right, as usual. I didn't find anything."

She didn't reply. Probably angry with him for retreating rather than talking to her. Taking the easy out. She had to know he'd left to avoid a difficult conversation, and not to search for any trail.

He was hoping she'd have let it go by now, and he could put off the tough stuff until later. But maybe not. He turned to face the music, but he didn't see her there, on the ground where she'd been lying only minutes ago.

"Hey. C'mon, Selene, don't be mad." He looked around the area. "Selene?"

Something chattered in a way so angry it almost made his heart stop—and he was spinning around even before his brain registered the familiar voice of a gray squirrel.

The animal was sitting on Selene's backpack. It flicked its tail rapidly, then chattered at him again.

"What the—" He remembered that Selene had told him Squirrel was her friend Tessa's animal guide. Could this mean something, then? It whispered through his brain that maybe Tessa was trying to tell him something, before he brushed the ridiculous notion aside. Since when did he think like that?

He moved toward the pack, and the squirrel took off. He watched it go, then looked around again, kneeling beside the pack. It had been leaning up against a tree trunk when he'd left Selene. Now it was lying on the ground, five feet from the tree, and he was getting a very bad feeling. "Selene?"

His heart hit his ribs like a sledge-hammer. There was a large dusty boot print on her backpack. Not hers, that print, and not Cory's. Rising slowly, he took a more careful look around. There were marks on the ground, as if from a scuffle. And—hell, was that....?

He knelt near the small round cobblestone that protruded from the earth, and touched the red wetness there. Blood.

Hell. "Selene!" He turned in a circle, searching as his heart rate zoomed from alarmed to frantic in the space of a single beat. "Selene, where are you?"

A screech drew him around, and the pounding beat of powerful wings passed so close to his head, he ducked instinctively. The hawk, a redtail, swooped over him, then sped away into the woods below the treeline, with all the speed and maneuvering of a stealth bomber. She rocked up to one side, then to another, zigged and wove to avoid limbs, and then vanished.

He didn't hesitate long. Only a moment. Just enough time for his mind to register that there was something way beyond "normal" going on here. And then he was heading in the direction the hawk had gone, bending to scoop up both backpacks as he passed. He slung one over each shoulder, and they were heavy. He might have to leave them before long. Depended on how far they had taken her, whoever they were.

And he had no doubt whatsoever that Selene had been taken. He blamed himself. He ached with guilt, and damn near burst with worry as he recalled the fate of Selene's friend. "If those bastards hurt her, I'll fuckin' kill them." His own anger astounded him, but he didn't take time to question it.

The hawk screeched from somewhere beyond his line of sight, and he adjusted his course. "I'm coming," he said.

Garrett Brand's big, white oversized Ford pickup truck kicked up a cloud of dust when it slid to a stop in the campground's small parking lot. By the time the other vehicles—pickups, SUVs and a Mustang, filled all the spaces around it, there was so much dust one could barely see.

But he didn't need to see. He got out and absently brushed

the dirt off the star pinned to his chest as he listened to other doors slamming.

Garrett's baby sister Jessie and her better half, his own deputy, Lash, got out of one pickup, and his brothers Wes and Ben climbed out of another. The SUV doors opened, and more Brands poured out. Elliot and Adam, Luke and cousin Marcus. The women—aside from Jessie, who was the best tracker in the entire state of Texas—had remained at the ranch. Most had wanted to come along, but since the entire Oklahoma branch of the family were even now making their way into Texas, the ranch needed to be manned. Those Okie Brands were going to need a home base, and this could drag on a while.

His siblings and cousin gathered around Garrett, though he towered over all of them, except for Ben, who was nearly his size and ten times as graceful, what with the martial arts and all. Wes stood closest to him, shoulder to shoulder, as always. Black eyes and blacker ponytail gleaming in the morning sun, Wes said, "Aunt Vi and the crew here yet?"

"It'll take them a mite longer. It's further off, but Aunt Vi was working on a charter plane to fly them to the nearest airport." Garrett glanced at his watch. "Should be here in the space of another hour, though."

"I should take a look around, see if I can pick up a trail," Jessie said. She hauled all five foot two inches and hundred-ten pounds of herself away from them, heading along the trail.

Garrett almost called after her to be careful, then bit his lip at a swift look from Lash. Jessie hated being watched out for. And Lash had it down to a science anyway. "Wait up, hon," he called. "I'm coming with you in case you need muscle as well as brains."

She rolled her eyes at him, but waited.

Garrett saw cops milling around, several sending curious looks after the two trackers, and likely getting ready to intervene. So he stepped over to them and asked who was in charge. His gang trailed behind him, silent and keeping their distance, but only until they were needed.

He was directed to a white-haired, tired-looking man in a suit a size too big. Garrett, who'd had enough experience with people not to judge them on appearance alone, approached the man, and extended a hand. "Garrett Brand, sheriff up from Quinn. I bent your ear on the phone earlier."

"Brand." The man clasped his hand, his grip surprisingly firm, his nod sharp. "Special Agent Chapel, FBI."

Garrett nodded. The Feds were involved because state lines had been crossed and this had all the earmarks of a hate crime, Selene and her murdered friends being Wiccans and all. People tended to misunderstand that sort of thing around these parts. Hell, he might have been a mite troubled by it, too, if he didn't have a bona fide shaman and a full fledged Buddhist for brothers. They'd pretty much enlightened him about the more 'outer edge' spiritual systems. Wiccans cast spells, and that scared people. But Wes and Ben insisted they both did pretty much the same sort of thing, just in different ways. The differences were all semantics and details, was all.

"Good meetin' ya." Garrett looked around. "What's the latest?"

"Campground owner is in ICU and not talking. Her partner says two carloads of men pulled in, she went out to tell them the place was closed, and they up and shot her. Then they headed back toward where the camping areas are." He pointed as he spoke.

"How's the owner doing? She going to pull through?"

"It's touch and go right now. She's only thirty-two years old for crying out loud."

Garrett shook his head slowly. "So did the partner say how many men there were?"

"Five, he thought. That red car there, that was theirs. No plates or registration. No insurance cards or inspection stickers. VID number's been filed off. Forensics will find any trace evidence. There has to be something. They had a Jeep, too, took that on into the grounds with 'em."

"What went on in there?" Garrett asked, looking along the winding trail that disappeared into the woods.

"They went in shooting, demanding to know where Erica Jackson was. Had a photo of her and everything. The campers scattered."

"Casualties?"

"Three dead, two injured. The rest are all accounted for. Except for Erica Jackson, that is. She was last seen running up the mountain into the forest. One witness says the killers went in the same direction a short time later, on her trail. Everyone else got the hell out of there. We rounded them up and questioned them one by one in the parking lot, then sent 'em into town to find a place to hole up until they can come back for their gear."

"And my cousin?" Garrett asked. When the special agent just frowned at him, he reminded the man, "The blonde who got here before the cops did?"

"Right. Selene Brand. She was with a feller. Cory something. They spoke to the campground owner's partner, then went on into the woods in search of Erica. They're out there now, far as anyone knows."

Garrett nodded slowly. "Okay. So we've got five armed killers chasing one preacher's daughter—"

"Preacher's daughter?" The agent looked aghast. "What the hell was a preacher's daughter doing here? This was some kind of Witchcraft festival."

Garrett held up a hand. "That's hardly relevent here, Special Agent Chapel. I was just nutshelling this thing. We've got five armed killers chasing one unarmed preacher's daughter through the dense forest. We've got a ninety-five pound witchling and an amnesiac fresh out of the hospital chasing the bad guys, and we've got…."

He paused, glanced at the agent with brows raised, waiting for him to fill in the rest. The man nodded. "We've got cops and agents set up in a perimeter covering five square miles and closing slowly. I have a map in here, I'll show you."

"Suppose they moved farther than that before you locked it up?"

"They couldn't have," the old man said. But Garrett had a feeling they just might have managed.

"Maybe, just for the hell of it, I'll take my team out a few miles beyond your perimeter, hmm? That way we're not getting in your way or traipsing over your jurisdiction, and we can cover the areas you can't."

"That's not a bad idea, Brand." The man looked over at the others who stood waiting, just as more vehicles began to roll in.

Garrett grinned as Vidalia piled out of a pickup big enough to require a stepladder for a woman her size. More shocking was the fact that she was carrying a shotgun so tall its butt-to-muzzle distance was about the height of Vi's shoulder. Double-barrel, ten-gauge, side-by-side. And he didn't have a doubt she knew how to use it. That thing would blow a hole in a man the size of a freaking grapefruit. And that was just on the way *in*.

She was a beauty, his Aunt Vi. Curvy and small and fit. Not a line on her face and hair like black satin. Seemed more likely to be the older sister of the bunch than their mamma, but he knew better.

Behind her were her daughters, Maya, Edie, Mel, and Kara. Each of them had a gun and a gun-toting man in tow. The fellow with Kara had been there waiting, and he wore a police uniform.

"All those folks deputies of yours, Sheriff Brand?"

He glanced back at the federal agent, gave him a wink. "Sure are."

"Look an awful lot like a pack of armed vigilante civilians to me."

"I'll keep 'em in line. And like I said, we'll work outside your perimeter." He waved at Vi, cupped a hand and shouted to Wes. "Grab the walkie and call Jessie and Lash back. We've got a better starting point."

"Will do."

Aunt Vi and her family marched into the crowd of Texas Brands, and while the sisters and husbands stopped there, as introductions were obviously being exchanged, Aunt Vi kept right on moving through the pack and up to where Garrett stood talking to the agent. She stopped, cradling the gun in her arms, across her chest.

"I'm Vidalia Brand," she announced, as if the name should mean something to the agent. "And I'm here to find out just where my daughter is, and what you are doing about getting her back here." One fine, dark eyebrow cocked up, and one foot tapped impatiently as she awaited her answer.

Chapter 14

Cory followed the hawk. It would fly out of sight, and he would head in the direction it had gone until he couldn't tell if he were still on course. And without fail, when he got that far, the hawk would scream in the distance, pulling him back on the mark. He knew it was ridiculous to follow a raptor through the forest like this in hopes it would somehow, magically lead him to Selene. He knew it, and his brain was arguing with him the entire time, and yet he couldn't quite stop himself. There was nothing else to follow; there were no other signs to go by.

At least, not for awhile.

And then there were.

The first was a bracelet, glittering and flashing in the speckled sunlight that filtered down through the canopy. It hung from a tiny limb, right about at eye level. He stopped and took it carefully, and the images flashed in his mind. Selene dancing in the moonlight, around that circle outside the inn, her arms extended over her head, moving sinuously, the bracelet catching and reflecting moonbeams. The memory hit him so hard he damn near doubled over in pain. God, if anything happened to her....

He couldn't think that way. Couldn't bear to think that way, it would cripple him. The thought of some bastard putting his hands on her, hurting her. Hell, he already had, hurt her. That had been her blood back there on the stone. And God only knew what else he'd done.

No, he couldn't let those thoughts paralyze him. But he couldn't quite wipe them from his mind either. And another thought distracted him from the task at hand, too. The realization that he had actually been right to follow the hawk. It had honest to goodness led him in the right direction, for as long as he had needed it to, right up to the spot where Selene had managed to begin leaving signs for him to follow.

He walked on, and in another hundred yards or so, he found another sign. This one, her necklace. Her pentacle, suspended from its chain. Again, she'd left it at eye level for him to find. She was leading him to her.

He took it and draped it around his own neck, wondering why she would leave it behind, when she'd told him what a powerful symbol it was, how protective its powers, and how much stronger she felt when she wore it.

She might need that kind of strength. And yet, she'd risked doing without it, just to give him another sign. Hell.

He kept following. Every scrap of jewelry she'd been wearing showed up, appearing in branches and dangling from twigs every hundred yards or so. And she'd been wearing a lot of jewelry. Even the earrings, three pairs and one single, for a grand total of seven pieces, dangled one by one. A hoop hanging like a Christmas ornament from a pine tree. A wire piercing a thick ash leaf. A post, thrust into the trunk of a white birch like a thumbtack in a cork board.

When the jewelry was gone, he started spotting scraps of

fabric, and even, once, a hank of her silvery-blond hair, thick enough to make it visible, and wound around a tiny limb. He winced when he saw that, thinking how much it must have hurt her to yank that much hair out. And damn, he didn't want her doing that any more. Her hair was too beautiful to waste that way.

He picked up the pace, telling himself to move faster, get to her before she ran out of things to leave behind her.

And just then a familiar crackling sound brought him to a grinding halt.

The walkie-talkie rasped again, and this time he shoved the pack off his shoulder and turned it around, and dug into it. He'd forgotten they had the things. Much less left them on. He was surprised the battery had held out.

He got the walkie-talkie, a small, bright yellow one, already tuned to channel 13, and turned up the volume.

"Do you hear me, Falconer?"

That voice. It stroked strings in his mind that played discordant sounds. It was familiar, and yet he couldn't place it. Damn this memory thing!

"Come in, Falconer. We have your little Witch with us, now, so you really have no choice. If you're out there, respond. If you're not, there's really no reason for us to keep her alive any longer."

His thumb twitched on the button. He raised the walkie to his lips, opened them to reply, and heard another static belch, followed by Selene's voice. "This is stupid, you trying to make me talk to someone who isn't there, just to prove you really have me. I told you, I left that stranger back in Big Falls and haven't seen him since."

There was a sound that made him clench his jaw so hard his teeth hurt. The sound of a hand on flesh. A slap. A whimper, involuntary and probably as stifled as Selene could manage. The bastard had hit her.

"Fine. I'll talk to him. Give me the damn thing." There was a spurt, and then another. "Hey, person in the woods who doesn't

exist. Or, hell, for that matter, how about sending this out to the
entire band of people in the woods who don't exist? God knows
the entire Brand clan must be fanning into the forest by now. This
is Selene. I'm alive and well, and in the hands of the bad guys.
There are five of them, all armed with—Ow!"

The static burped again as the walkie was no doubt yanked
away from Selene.

There had been a message there for him. He was sure of
it. She'd told him about her family, about how there was a
whole branch of Brands in Texas, and how when one was in
trouble the entire clan tended to come to their aid. No doubt
this so-called siege was big news. And there had been plenty
of time for her family to get here by now.

What was she telling him? To wait for them? To go back
down, hook up with her kinfolk, and then come on after her
again?

Right. No way in hell.

He lifted the walkie to his mouth again, hoping there was
help on the way, but not willing to bet Selene's life on it.

"This is Falconer," he said after keying the mike. "What
do you want me to do?"

The shack in the woods smelled musty from years of disuse.
When the man opened the rickety door and shoved her inside,
Selene thought it was probably something that had been used
by hunters a half century or so ago. God knew it was too far
from any road to make it handy. They'd hiked through the
forest for more than eight hours, most of it uphill. She had no
idea how this bastard knew his way around the Texas woods so
well. He didn't sound like a Texan. Or an Okie, for that matter.

She stumbled through the door at her captor's brutal shove,
caught her footing and managed not to fall to her knees, then
brushed herself off and took a look around.

The first thing she saw was....

"Erica!" Selene raced across the room to where Erica sat

on the floor in the corner, her hands bound behind her back, her feet tied together at the ankles. She had tear stains on her face, and red, puffy eyes.

Selene fell to her knees, and hugged her friend. "It's okay, baby. It's okay. I'm here." She reached for the rope at Erica's ankles.

"Oh, no you don't. No one said you could untie her."

She whirled on the man who had brought her here, certain now he was the leader. There were two other men in the cramped cabin, and she'd glimpsed two outside, standing watch. "Her skin is raw. Look how red it is. At least loosen them."

"No, but I'll make sure yours are even tighter."

"You don't want to mess with us, mister."

"Hank." He nodded, and one of the other two thugs came to her, jerked her around, and, pulling her hands behind her, began binding her wrists.

"Hurt her, Hank. I owe the bitch."

Selene felt anger rise up from somewhere deep, and in a voice that didn't sound anything like her own, she began muttering what she remembered of an ancient Sumerian curse.

"A-na-am, er-se-tam, na-ra-am, bi-i-it e-er-ru-bu, la-te-er-ru-bi-i-ma!"

The guy tying her wrists jerked his knot tight and backed away. She turned slowly, glaring at him, her eyes narrow. Taking a single step toward him, she repeated the curse, and thought hard of its meaning in English even as she chanted it, phonetically, in a language no one had heard spoken in at least two thousand years. "By heaven, by lakes, by the river, the house I enter, you shall not enter!"

She put her anger behind her words, felt power rising up through her as her kundalini uncoiled, and writhed up her spine, empowering and igniting every chakra center along the way.

"A-na-am, er-se-tam, na-ra-am—"

The man who'd been tying her backed all the way to the

door. Her anger alone should flatten him, she thought. It was burning out of her pores now, and she did nothing to tame it.

"*—bi-i-it e-er-ru-bu, la-te-er-ru-bi-i-ma!*" she growled.

He got the door open and stumbled through it.

She turned her attention to the leader now, primed with power, brimming with it, feeling incredible and invincible. *"A-na-am, er-se-tam—"*

He clocked her in the jaw. She couldn't block the blow because her hands were tied behind her, and it took her with so much force, her head snapped up and her body slammed down, hard, onto the floor.

"Shut up, Witch." He jerked his head at the one thug remaining in the room. "Slap some goddamn duct tape over her mouth, and then tie her ankles. Her hero ought to be here pretty soon, and then we can dispense with the bunch of them."

She willed Cory not to come, willed it with everything in her. She could have wept when she'd heard his voice coming over the static-laced airwaves via the walkie-talkie. She'd been trying to tell him to keep quiet, to wait for her cousins and siblings to arrive. But he'd fallen for their garbage and replied to their threats, asking what they wanted him to do.

The leader had given him directions to this cabin, told him to be here within three hours, giving him ample time, she was sure. And he'd do it, too.

The dumb ass. She loved him.

Thug number two was smacking duct tape over her mouth. The ropes on her wrists were already chafing. He gripped one of her bound arms, just above the elbow, and dragged her to the corner to set her beside Erica. Then he knelt and tied her ankles, using the tape instead of rope this time.

"She'll be quiet," Erica said. She sounded hoarse, as if she'd been doing a lot of yelling, or maybe she just hadn't been given anything to drink. "You can take the gag off. Please?"

"You shut up, honey, or you'll be gagged right along with her," the leader said.

Then he turned to glance out the window. "Great. Hank's out there filling the other guys' heads with tales of this voodoo bullshit. Get out there and set 'em straight, Larry."

The big guy nodded, and strode out the door.

Only the leader remained. He pulled out a rickety chair, and sat down at a rickety table, shaking a yellowed and fray-edged newspaper into a suitable shape, and looking for all the world like the dad from a 1950s sitcom. All he lacked was a pipe and a cup of hot coffee.

When his attention was caught, Selene met Erica's eyes, told her without a word that she was up to something, then turned, millimeter by millimeter, until her back was angled slightly toward Erica's. Erica frowned, then she got it, and it was her turn to turn, ever so quietly, ever so gradually, until her back was angled toward Selene's. Selene stretched out her fingers, and felt just what she'd hoped to feel. The rope around Erica's wrists. They leaned closer, pressing their shoulders together to conceal the work their hands were doing as they stretched their fingers to painful lengths and picked at the knots that held each other captive.

Erica was smart. She leaned her head forward and closed her eyes, pretending to be asleep. Good move. Selene just rested against her, trying to move as little as possible, and stilling her fingers each time the creep glanced their way. When she stilled, Erica did, too, not even needing to open her eyes.

As she worked patiently and tediously at the knots, Selene kept finding Cory, wandering through her mind. She just couldn't seem to stop thinking of him. Sometimes she relived the times they'd been together, the way he'd touched her, the way he'd made her feel, the things he'd whispered while making love to her. Those thoughts made her want to arch her hips and sigh, an urge she barely caught in time to prevent it. Goddess, but she had it bad for that man.

She managed to stop reliving their passion, but it only led to her imagining what the next time might be like—if there was a next time. But this was her imagination, she was in charge. So yes, in her mind, there would be a next time. He would regain his memory and realize there were no obstacles in their way. Kelly was probably an ex-wife, not a current one, and maybe they'd broken up after Cory's brother had made his little note in the date book. That worked. So there would be a next time, and this time, when he drove into her, when he kissed her neck and held her legs up high, and made her entire body sing—this time, he would add the most erotic part she could imagine. He would hold her to him, and stop kissing her just long enough to whisper, "I love you, Selene."

And damn, that would be perfect. Just freaking perfect.

Erica's finger tapped hers, and Selene blinked out of her fantasy and realized her hands had gone still. She'd been too busy daydreaming to keep picking at the knots. And this was too important, so she got back to it.

It was frustrating, working with just the tips of her fingers. Her wrists and hands ached from the straining she was giving them before the first hour had passed. But eventually, the knots began to give, to loosen, and Selene felt hope.

When the knots came free, the two women's hands clasped for just a moment. Then they relaxed, leaving the ropes, loose enough now to shake off at a moment's notice, wrapped around their wrists for appearance's sake.

Garrett had led the gang, armed with maps, guns, and walkie-talkies, into the woods from a point a couple of miles up the road, around a bend which should cut off some of the walking time. They'd been discussing who should enter the woods where, and which way to head, when his radio picked up the transmission addressed to someone named Cory.

He held up a hand, yanking his radio from his belt, and turning up the volume. When the man said something about having "your little Witch," he knew this was important.

"Cory must be the name of the guy she was accused of

stabbing in the woods. That's what started all this. He vanished from the hospital," Vidalia explained.

Jimmy Corona nodded. "She's been traveling with him, she told me as much on the phone, but I couldn't get any more out of her."

"Wait, listen!" Vidalia shouted, as another voice came over the radio. "That's Selene!"

They all leaned closer, listening to Selene insist there was no one with her, and then try to tell this Cory fellow to wait it out, that her family would be there to help him soon. Garrett hoped to the Almighty he would take that advice.

But the man didn't. He was on the line a few moments later, asking the bastard for instructions.

And the man replied by giving detailed directions to an old hunting shanty where they wanted him to come, alone, naturally. They always told you to come alone. Garrett rolled his eyes, and noted that Lash was already scribbling the directions the man gave on a notepad.

The radio went silent, then crackled again. "You have three hours."

And that was it. Three hours. Hell.

Lash leaned over the map with his scrawled notes, and when Jessie shoved her way in between him and Garrett, Garrett let her. Between the two of them, they managed to pinpoint the cabin's probable location on the map, marked it with an X, then shoved the map back toward Garrett.

He looked it over. "There's a road that'll take us pretty close," he said, tracing the snaky line that represented the road across the page. "It's the only way we're gonna make it in time. Cory's got quite a head start on us."

"Good plan," Vidalia said. "I'm looking forward to having a talk with this fella."

"Vi, it's gonna be rough going." Garrett thought that even as strong and fit as she looked, he wasn't sure a woman her age could make the trek.

She lifted her brows and fixed him with a look. "Well, now, Garrett, if you think you can't handle it, you can certainly wait in the truck. But it don't look all that tough to me."

"Or to any other mamma, when her baby's waiting at the end of the trail," Jessie told him.

"Any other mamma isn't Vidalia Brand," Melusine put in. "Frankly, she can hold her own better than anyone else here."

He nodded. "Okay. I won't mention it again."

"You hadn't better," Vi said. "Let's get this show on the road." She started for the nearest vehicle.

Crouching in the woods outside the small hunting shack, Cory took stock of the situation. There was a man guarding the front door, another guarding the back, and he had no idea how many inside. If he walked right up to them, he would probably be signing his own death warrant. And Selene's, too.

Selene.

God, being this close to her, knowing she was just beyond that lopsided door, was almost too much to take. Everything in him churned. He was shaking, literally shaking all over as thoughts chased themselves through his mind. Had they hurt her? Were they hurting her even now? Was she even alive?

The idea that she might not be filled him with thick, suffocating darkness. His chest felt empty; there was a black void where his heart should be.

Swallowing hard, he backed a safe distance away, and keyed the mike on the walkie-talkie. "I'm close," he said. "But how do I know the women are still alive?"

The radio crackled, a female voice came over it, but not Selene's. "This is Erica. We're all right."

A second later it crackled again. "It's me," Selene said. And the relief that washed through him nearly deafened him to what came next. "Don't risk your life for us, Cory—ow!"

He gripped the walkie so hard he cracked its plastic casing. "Don't hurt her again." His voice was unrecognizable, even to his own ears. He'd never sounded like that before. Memory or no, he knew that for a fact.

"Get your ass in here, Falconer, and I won't have to."

The voice was familiar. It tickled the edges of his memory, teasing something to life there. Something he could almost grab hold of. Almost.

"Those women didn't see anything that night," he said. "They don't know who the hell you are. There's no reason to kill them."

"They've seen me now."

"And whose fault is that?" he demanded. "Look, I'm the one you want. Send them out, and I'll come in without a fuss."

There was no reply. But a second later the cabin's door slammed open so hard it banged into the outside wall, broke off at the upper hinge, and hung there, crookedly, by the bottom hinge alone. Selene was shoved outside, but not alone. A man had one arm hooked around her shoulders, holding her back flush to the front of his body, like a shield. His other arm held a gun, its barrel pressed to her temple.

"By the powers of the Dark Goddess, you will suffer for this!" she shouted.

"Shut up!"

"I curse you by the sun! I curse you by the moon! I curse you by—"

He drew back and clocked her in the head with the butt of the handgun. She went limp in his cruel grasp, her head falling forward, even as Cory lunged upright.

A hand on his shoulder shoved him right back down, and a voice he didn't know spoke from close to his head. "Easy, fella. You've got back-up now, just take a breath."

He turned, and found himself face to face with a big man who wore a star on his chest. "Garrett Brand," the man said. "I'm her cousin. And so are most of them." He nodded toward the woods behind him as he spoke. "Exceptin' for her sisters and in-laws and her mamma—well, hell we can save the introductions for later, I s'pose."

Cory scanned the brush, and saw at least a dozen others lurking in the trees. Several men, and handful of women. One of the women strode up to him, and he thought she had to be Selene's oldest sister. The resemblance was there, in the shape of her face and the exotic tilt of her eyes, though where Selene was light, this woman was dark.

"You him?" she asked.

"I'm Cory Falconer," he said.

"The fella that brought all this down on my daughter."

"Your daughter?" He was stunned, and more than slightly intimidated. "Believe me, Mrs. Brand, I tried to protect her. I never meant—"

She gripped his chin in a firm hand, staring at him with narrow, piercing eyes. "Well, I'll be." Then she thinned her lips, sighed as if in some sort of capitulation. "I suppose you may as well call me Vidalia, then." She released his chin, took his hand. "Don't look so scared, son, we've been in worse spots than this one. I daresay those fellas don't have a clue what kind of mess they've got themselves into."

He swung his gaze back to where the man stood, holding a limp and nearly lifeless-looking Selene in his arms, shouting at him to come out, to show himself.

"I have to go before he hurts her anymore," he said.

"Takes more than a blow to the head to hurt that one," Vidalia Brand said.

"He knocked her unconscious."

"No, son. He just pissed her off, you'll pardon the language."

Someone moved just to the left, and Cory swung his head that way. It was a copper-skinned, black-haired man, leaning against a tree, with a rifle braced on one of the branches, pointed right at the man who held Selene.

"Don't," Cory whispered. "You could hit her."

"Not in this lifetime," the man said. "Go ahead on out, I've got you covered."

Another voice chimed in, a female voice. "I've got the one

in the front," she said. Elliot's gone around back to cover that one. The rest of you back us up, and Lash, you keep a bead on that door in case any others come out."

"There's another hostage in there," Cory warned.

"Yeah, we know," Garrett said. "Go on, we're ready."

Cory swallowed hard, drew a breath, reminded himself that this was Selene's family. If they were anything like her, he could trust them. She certainly did. He nodded, then stepped out of the trees and into the open, raising his hands high. "I'm here," he called. "I'm coming in."

Chapter 15

Selene had to fight every instinct in her not to go stiff with fear when Cory stepped out into the open. She could see him, barely, through the slits of her eyelids. He stood there, hands up, with at least two guns trained on him.

"That's more like it," the man holding her said. "Get on inside. We've got some talking to do before I blow your head off."

Cory moved closer, until the bad-ass holding her said, "that's far enough. Hank, check him for weapons."

The man who'd been guarding the front of the shack hurried toward Cory, quickly searched him, then turned to the apparent leader and nodded once.

"Bring him inside."

Hank gripped Cory's arm, even as Cory lowered them to his sides, and hustled him to the door. The man holding Selene stood aside until Cory was in, then he came in, half carrying, half dragging her. Hank remained outside, probably to resume his job of playing lookout.

Once inside, the bastard released Selene with a little shove. She fought the urge to catch herself, and just let her body stay limp, preparing for the impact with the floor. It didn't come. Cory's arms snapped around her first, kept her from falling. Then he scooped her up and moved toward the back of the room, where Erica was still bound and waiting. He lowered her to the floor, carefully, and as he did, she swore his lips brushed her temple. His hands brushed over hers, behind her, and she moved hers apart while his were there, so he would know she was neither truly bound, nor truly unconscious.

He went still for just a moment. Then she felt a relieved sigh whisper from his lips and he moved them close to her ear. "Careful."

She nodded, just barely, her cheek rasping over his. "You, too."

Then he leaned her against the wall and straightened away from her, turning to face his would-be killer. She'd had to work hard to maintain the illusion of being knocked out to this point. But the hardest part of all came when she heard Cory suck in a sharp breath, and say, "Kelly?"

Did he just say Kelly? The Kelly from the datebook? The Kelly with the anniversary?

"Thought you had amnesia, pal. Guess not, huh?"

"I did. Do. But it's coming back to me now. It was you. You were the one Casey and I spotted in the forest, robbing nests of fledgling hawks and eagles."

"Bingo."

"Jesus, Kelly, why?"

He did! He said Kelly! Selene's hand closed on Erica's and squeezed hard—because she had to hold on to something to keep from jumping to her feet and asking questions.

"Oh, come on, Cory. Why do you think?"

"Money." The word emerged on a sigh that held pure disillusionment. "I never would have thought—"

"No, and you never should have found out. You or your freaking brother. Tell you the truth, I hated killing him a lot more than I'm gonna hate killing you. Barely more than a kid."

"That didn't stop you from doing it, though, did it?"

"There's too much at stake, Cory."

"Then why am I still alive?"

"Because I need to know—who else have you told?"

"Okay, he's inside," Garrett said, keeping his voice low. "We can't waste any time. Wes—"

"Already on it." Before Garrett finished speaking his brother was in motion. He leaned his rifle against a tree, drew a blade from his side, and crept soundlessly out of the cover of the trees. Ben saw him going, nodded once to Garrett, and slipped out just as silently. Seeing Wes move like a big cat was one thing. Wes was lean and wiry. But watching a man as big as Ben move with so much stealth and grace never ceased to amaze Garrett. He couldn't have done it himself, and didn't care to learn.

Ben crept toward the front of the shack, while Wes slid around to the rear, out of sight. As Garrett watched, Ben slid up behind the man guarding the shack in front, and the guy never even felt him coming. Didn't hear him, didn't see him, didn't sense him. One minute he was standing there alone, looking in one direction and then another. The next, he made the mistake of putting his back toward Ben, and Ben struck. Glided up to him, snapped his big arms around the guy, and choked him out cold.

He was dragging the unconscious fellow back into the cover of the trees, when Wes came along with his man slung over his shoulders. Dead or unconscious, Garrett wasn't sure which. Wes didn't have a lot of patience for men who would hurt a woman. And these two were guilty of that, and then some.

"See to it they don't cause any trouble, ladies," he said,

nodding toward Selene's mother and sisters, and his own kid sister Jessie. "The rest of us are going inside to get them out."

Jessie made a face. But before she could present him with the inevitable argument, Vidalia Brand spoke up. "Makes sense. Too many of us will just get in each other's way. But are you sure Selene and her friends won't be hurt, you all go charging into that cubby hole at once?"

"There are still too many of us," Garrett said, looking at the men, all of them eager to move, around him. His own brothers, Wes, Adam, Elliot and Luke. His cousin Marcus. And Selene's brothers-in-law, Jimmy, Wade, Cal, and Alex. Counting himself that was nine men. There wasn't room in that shack for nine men. His Aunt Vi was right.

"We don't know how many are in there," Alex said. Garrett racked his memory to place the man. The big city PI, Melusine's husband and a man who knew his job. He had a reputation that reached well beyond Garrett's neck of the woods. "We should try to lure them out."

"And maybe sidle up close enough to get a peek inside," Jimmy Corona, the former Chicago cop put in.

"Probably could get a look through one of those filthy windows," Wes said. "I can go up nice and quiet, take a peek."

Garrett nodded. "Keep your ass covered, Wes. Don't expose yourself to any pot-shots, and get right back here."

"They won't know I'm within a hundred miles," Wes promised, and he was off again, slipping up to the building.

Selene was supposed to be unconscious still. It had only been five minutes, after all. She figured she could squeeze fifteen out of the act. But then she got the distinct feeling of eyes on her, to the point where it made her risk opening her eyes and looking toward the direction from which that energy seemed to come.

For just an instant she thought she glimpsed someone beyond the dirty window, peering in. But it was so brief she almost thought she had imagined it. Would have thought so, if not for that feeling.

She *never* mistrusted her feelings. Okay, she had for a brief span of time, but never before. And never again.

It was someone all right. And not one of the thugs, but a spiritual person. His aura was huge. A second later, there was a noise from outside. Sounded like a rock hitting the side of the building.

Kelly jumped to his feet, then nodded to one of the two other thugs in the room. "See what's up."

One of the men nodded, drawing his weapon and moving to the door. He frowned as he stared outside. "I don't see Larry." He hurried to the other side of the shack, looking out the back. "Hank, either."

"Shit." Kelly turned an angry glare on Selene. "You did this, didn't you? You and that mumbo-jumbo you were babbling at us earlier!" He moved toward Selene as he spoke, lifted a foot to kick her in the ribs, but Cory launched himself from his chair before he could land it, and knocked the guy to the floor.

They struggled; a gun went off. And Cory rolled onto his back, with blood pumping from beneath his hand where it was pressed to his belly.

Selene was on her feet, falling to her knees beside him, her unbound hands no longer a secret as she pressed them to him. "No, dammit, no!"

And then before she could even feel the pain of being grabbed by her hair, the place exploded. The back door smashed in; the front door smashed in; bodies poured through both, and one hurled itself through the side window, hitting the floor, somersaulting and landing crouched with a gun drawn. Kelly and his two men were disarmed and beaten senseless within a minute, and then everything was still again.

Jimmy and Garrett were snapping handcuffs on the bastards, and she was on her knees again, beside Cory.

He was conscious, and clearly in pain, but his eyes only searched her face and he asked, "You okay?"

"Am I okay? Cory, why did you attack a guy with a gun just to keep him from kicking me?"

He closed his eyes. "I'll tell you later."

"Tell me now." He didn't reply and she leaned closer. "Cory? Cory!" But there was no response.

Casey Falconer burst into the hospital's nearly empty waiting room, looking frantic and frightened. Selene rose from the vinyl chair, a foam cup of stale coffee clutched between her palms. "You look a lot more like your brother when you're not unconscious," she said.

He frowned at her. "You know my brother?"

"Yeah."

"Is he—"

"In surgery. The bullet missed his vital organs, but he lost a lot of blood, despite my best efforts. They're not saying much more than that."

Casey closed his eyes, lowered his head, and his breath rushed out of him. He looked tired. Of course he was tired, given what he'd been through. Selene moved closer, took his upper arm in a gentle hand. "I think you should sit down, before you fall down, okay?"

Nodding, he let her lead him to a chair, then sank into it.

"Coffee?" she asked.

"No thanks." He lifted his head, met her eyes. "I'm Casey Falconer, by the way."

"I know," she said. "How did you get here, Casey?"

"I came around in the hospital, and there was a cop there waiting to talk to me. Chief Wheatly?"

"Yeah, he's an old friend."

"I told him who I was, what had happened, asked about my brother. He filled me in, but told me no one knew exactly where Cory was at that point. I spent one more night in the hospital, then when he told me about what was happening, I signed myself out, insisted on riding down here with the chief."

She smiled. "I'm glad you came. Cory's been worried about you."

"So how did you know who I was?" he asked.

"I was with your brother when we found you in the woods where those bastards had left you for dead." She held up a hand. "Selene Brand."

"Guess I owe you one, Selene Brand." He took her hand, squeezed it briefly.

"Well, I have a suggestion that'll make us even," she said.

He frowned at her. "Shoot."

"Cory...he's been having trouble with his memory. Some kind of reaction, we think, to whatever those animals drugged you guys with. We um...we glanced through a little date book we found in your pocket, you know, looking for some kind of clue as to what was going on. Why someone was trying so hard to kill the two of you. And there was this notation."

As she spoke, she tugged the tiny planner from her own pocket, flipped it open to the page in question, pointed to the note as she turned the book to him, handed it to him. "Can you tell me what this means?"

Casey took the book, looked at his note, furrowed his brows and looked at her again. "Cory and Kelly anniversary. Ten years. Party at two."

"Yeah, that's the one."

He tilted his head to one side. "You and my brother have something going on, Selene?"

"Not if he's married, we don't." She averted her face as she felt it getting warm. "The leader of that gang of bird smugglers— Cory called him Kelly. I was hoping...maybe somehow—"

"Kelly McGuire is a wildlife officer. Well, he was one, before he decided to use his position to line his own pockets at the expense of the wildlife he was paid to protect. He and Cory were hired on the same day. They would have been celebrating ten years on the job next month." He closed the notebook, shoved it into his breast pocket.

"Then—Cory doesn't have a wife?" She was holding her breath, she realized, as she awaited his answer.

"Cory can't commit to a long-distance carrier, Selene, much less a woman. His car's a lease so he can get a different one every two years. He rents his house in case he ever wants to move. No. He doesn't have a wife."

She smiled slowly.

"So you and my brother *do* have something going on," Casey said.

She shrugged. "He's my soul mate."

The expression that came over Casey's face when she said that made her smile. His eyes went kind of wary and wide, and his jaw went slack.

"Yeah, that was pretty much his reaction, too," she said. "But it's true. Of course that doesn't mean I can say what the outcome will be."

His eyes narrowed and he seemed to be studying her. "I have the same issues, you know."

"I thought you might. Because of your parents, right?"

He lifted his brows. "Apparently, his memory wasn't entirely wiped out."

"It's been coming back in bits and pieces. But you know, just because your parents weren't happy together, doesn't mean no one can be. If anything, you both learned from their example—at least learned what not to do." She shrugged. "I have a feeling you're both going to make great husbands, if you ever get over your issues. Hell, you'll be so attuned to the women you choose to love, you'll make sure they're happy. I know it."

He was staring at her hard. "They told me you were some kind of a Witch."

She nodded. "And sometimes a little psychic, too."

"You really think that can happen?"

"You really want to know?"

Casey was staring at her a little oddly when the doctor

came through a set of double doors toward them. They both got to their feet, and it surprised her when Casey's hand curled around her shoulder.

"Ms. Brand," the doctor said, nodding to her. "And you are?"

"Casey Falconer, Cory's brother. How's he doing, doc?"

"He came through the surgery. We've repaired the damage and given him transfusions."

"But—?" Casey prompted.

The doctor sighed. "If his body can withstand the shock it's been through, he should make a full recovery. If not…well, the next few hours will tell."

"Can we see him?" Selene asked.

"We're moving him into ICU. You can both sit with him there. I'll send a nurse for you as soon as he's settled."

"Thank you, doctor." They both muttered the words together. Casey slid his arm fully around her shoulders and squeezed. "Hang in there. He's more stubborn than you know."

"Oh, believe me, I know."

He looked down at her. "Why are you here all alone, Selene? Don't you have any family or—"

She started to laugh, had to cup a hand over her mouth to stop herself. "Sorry," she managed. "It's just that—well, up to about ten minutes before you got here, there were so many Brands in this waiting room the hospital was threatening to have them bodily removed."

"Oh."

She smiled. "Four sisters and brothers-in-law, plus my mom. And then there are the half siblings—got three of those, plus an entire ranch full of cousins, and all their spouses, and kids, and—well, you get the picture."

"So where are they?"

"Her mother is still here," Vidalia said from across the room. She came closer, her eyes on Selene. "How's he doing, daughter?"

"Surgery went well. The next few hours are going to tell

the tale. I thought you went back to the Texas Brand with the rest of them."

Vidalia nodded. "I sent them on without me. We...didn't have much of a chance to talk with them all milling around. And we need to."

Casey cleared his throat. "I'll uh—step down the hall to that bank of vending machines. Can I bring you back anything Mrs. Brand?"

Vidalia broke off staring at Selene long enough to send him a smile. "You must be Casey Falconer," she said. "Forgive my manners. Vidalia Brand."

"Nothing to forgive, ma'am. How's hot cocoa sound?"

"It would hit the spot. And call me Vidalia."

He nodded, turned and left them alone. Selene stiffened her shoulders once he was out of sight, dreading what was coming next. Her mother had never had the chance to finish dressing her down. She decided to beat her to the punch.

"I'm sorry about running off like that, Mom."

"If you hadn't, you'd have been in your room that night when that killer came looking. I shudder to think what would have happened then." Vidalia shook her head and hugged herself. "No, I think your intuition was right on the money, child. Then again, it usually is."

Selene looked at her mother slowly, unsure what to say. She wasn't screaming at her.

"The uh—the Reverend Jackson and I have been doing some studying together, since you've been away."

Oh, no. "Studying?"

"Yes. We started with that book you left lying on the kitchen table for me. Which I read with a healthy dose of skepticism, believe you me. It painted this Witchcraft thing in the most flattering light, it was clearly biased. So we did a little more digging."

Letting her head fall forward until her chin nearly touched her chest, Selene whispered, "And no you doubt found all

kinds of crazy sources that told you Witches engage in wild
orgies, torture black cats and sacrifice babies to Satan."

"Well, yes, there were a few of those. But I'm not a stupid
woman, Selene. I could see those sources were nothing but
propaganda. Besides, Witches don't even believe in the devil,
much less worship him."

Selene brought her head up slowly, opened her eyes, met
her mother's.

"And besides, between the Threefold Law and the Wiccan
Rede, I can't see how there's room for torture or sacrifice at all."

"Just who have you been talking to, Mom?"

"Oh, lots of people. Though I wasn't buying a lot of what
they told me—not until I had a chat with your cousins, Wes
and Ben. I admit, now, I don't like the words you're choosing
to use. Witchcraft. Makes it sound like something dark and
evil, when the truth is it's nothing more than nature worship
and folk magick."

"That's exactly what it is."

"Well, I just don't know why you don't call it that, then."
She sighed. "Anyway, I'm sorry I overreacted. But it's as
much your fault as my own. You should have told me long
ago, Selene. Talked through this with me. Your assumptions
about how I would react were as misguided as mine about
what this Witch thing was all about."

"You're right, Mom."

Vidalia nodded firmly. "Well, then, it's settled."

"Miss Brand?"

Selene turned to see a smiling, gorgeous young nurse
waiting for her. "Yes?"

"You can go in to see Mr. Falconer now. I'll take you back."

"Oh, but his brother—"

"You go on," Vidalia said. "I'll send him on when he gets
back. Just tell me where."

"Through those doors," the nurse said. "Fourth door on the
right. Room 307. Then she led Selene through and into the

hospital room. Just inside the door, though, she froze—literally. Her skin got goosebumps, she shivered with the chills that raced up her spine and her hands felt like ice.

He lay there, his skin pale except for the slightly blue tint beneath his eyes. The sheets were pulled up to just past his hips, and his chest was bare, except for the leads taped in place there, which, she guessed, were what caused the heart monitor to beep and make wavy lines across its screen. A white bandage encircled his waist. There was an IV line in his arm, another lead clipped to the tip of his forefinger, and tubes feeding oxygen into his nostrils.

He looked fragile, as if he were hovering somewhere between life and death, as if the slightest breeze could send him one way or the other.

She almost didn't dare to move nearer. And then she couldn't stop herself. She tiptoed up to the bed, and leaning close, clasped his hand in hers and lifted it to her lips. It felt cool to the touch. Startlingly cool, and she couldn't help the tears that welled in her eyes as she sank into the chair beside his bed. "Cory, I'm here," she whispered. "You're going to be okay."

He didn't reply, so she bent even closer, brushing her cheek over his, closing her eyes because the rasp of his whiskers felt so damned good. "Cory."

The door opened, closed again. She straightened and blinked at the tears in her eyes.

"You really do have a thing for him, don't you?"

"I love him." She brushed at her eyes, and turned slightly in her chair. Casey handed her a cup of cocoa.

"You love him?"

"You sound surprised."

"Most women don't get that involved. Not with him. I mean, he's usually pretty up-front with them about his— well, his intentions."

"He was with me, too." She shrugged. "I didn't listen." She

took a deep breath, sighed. "Well, hell, I might as well get to work." She took a big drink of the just-warm-enough cocoa, then set the cup on the nightstand.

"To work…doing what?"

She was standing by then, leaning over and laying her palms on the top of Cory's head. "Healing him. What else?"

"Oooh-kay."

She worked on Cory while chatting with Casey for the better part of an hour before he opened his eyes and blinked her into focus. His smile, when it came, was so warm, his eyes so full of emotion, that she almost lost her breath.

"Hey, beautiful," he whispered.

"Hey, yourself. You feeling better?"

"I'm hurting like hell, but I'm really glad to see you in one piece. You okay?"

"Better than okay, now that I'm pretty sure you're going to be."

"How's Erica?"

"Grieving for Tessa, but physically fine. I have a surprise for you." God, the way his eyes held hers, the way they seemed to be searching….

"What surprise?"

"Your kid brother is here. We've been getting to know each other while you've been napping."

He lifted his brows and looked past her, and she knew when he saw Casey, because his smile grew wider. Casey came up beside her, leaned down to clasp his brother's hand in a tight-fisted grip.

"About time you woke up, pal. I was getting ready to douse you in cold water, but uh, your girlfriend here thought some of her hocus-pocus would be a little more effective."

Cory managed a smile. "Have a little patience, Case. You must have been out a lot longer than I was." He shifted his gaze to Selene. "Wasn't he? How long was I—?"

"Only a few hours."

He closed his eyes in what looked like relief. "Good. That's good."

"Why?" Casey asked. "You have a pressing appointment or something?"

"Yeah, I do. Case, pal, I know we've got some catching up to do, but uh—"

Casey looked from his brother to Selene and back again. "Actually, I wouldn't mind getting to know the gorgeous female I met in the waiting room a little better. You mind if I take off for a few minutes? Maybe...I don't know, a half hour?"

"Thanks, little brother."

"Yeah, yeah. See you later, okay?"

Cory nodded, and Casey surprised the heck out of Selene by leaning over and kissing her cheek before he left. While he was close, he whispered, "From the look in my brother's eyes, hon, I'm beginning to think you really *are* some kind of Witch."

So she *was* seeing something in Cory's eyes. Something more than what had been there before. It wasn't all in her head, because his brother saw it, too. Suddenly her stomach was churning, and she didn't know what to do with her hands, other than clutch them together in her lap to try to still their shaking.

Cory sat up, winced a little as he did, and she jumped out of her chair, hands going to his shoulders to help him. And then she stayed there, caught in the spell of his eyes. His hands closed around her waist, and he kissed her. His mouth pressed to hers, gently, at first, but when her lips parted and her arms slid around his neck, it grew more urgent. His mouth opened and closed over hers in a slow, sexy rhythm, as he pulled her so hard against him she nearly fell into the bed.

When he finally broke the kiss, Selene was breathless and aching for more.

He still held her, still stared into her eyes. "I don't have any wife," he said.

"I know."

"I remember everything now. All the pieces have fallen into place. I live in Perry, a small town out toward Tulsa. Have a big, empty cabin. A rental. And the most precious thing in it is my collection."

"The raptors."

"Yeah," he said, and the look in his eyes grew even more intense. "I'm a wildlife officer, have been for ten years."

"I know."

"You've met Casey. He's the only family I have, besides my father."

"Cory, why are you telling me all this?"

He slowed down, took a pause and a breath and seemed to think for a moment before speaking again. "Well, I've met most of your family. I've gotten to know you pretty well over the past few days. I thought now that I remembered, you should know more about me."

"I want to," she said, easing up a bit, and turning to sit on the edge of his bed. She used the button on the side to raise the upper part, so he could lean back without lying down. "I want to know everything."

"I want to tell you everything."

She'd been looking at the button on the bed, but the tone of his voice brought her gaze back to his, fast. "Why?"

"Because I'm in love with you, Selene."

Tears welled in her eyes so fast, so deeply, she couldn't blink enough to keep them from spilling over. How often had she dreamed of him saying those words to her?

He pulled her close again, and this time she lay across his chest, her head on his shoulder, his arms holding her. Nothing could feel as wonderful as being in his arms, she thought.

"I didn't think I wanted a relationship, a commitment. But I do, Selene. I want it with you. It's just like you said, all the fears and doubts vanish when you meet your soul mate."

He gripped her shoulders, lifting her a little, so he could look her in the eyes. "I think you're the one, Selene. I think you were right all along. We're meant to be." He searched her eyes for a long moment, then squeezed her shoulders gently. "Aren't you going to say anything?"

She'd been trying, but her throat was so tight, and now her face was wet with tears to boot. She waved a hand at her cheeks, to dry them, drew a breath and tried to swallow to free her voice. It was squeaky and soft, but at least she got words out. "What's to say? I've been telling you this stuff for days now."

"So…you still feel that way? I mean, I didn't screw it up, taking so long to figure out what I was feeling?"

She smiled through her tears, sniffled and wiped a cheek with a knuckle. "I said I'd love you forever, Cory. It hasn't been close to forever yet."

He smiled, finally. That sexy, slow smile she loved so much, and his bedroom eyes closed as he kissed her again.

"Damn," she whispered, when their lips pulled apart. "There's gonna be one hell of a party at the Texas Brand when they let you out of here."

"You think so?"

"Yeah. Cause, uh, the last single Brand has finally met her match."

"Not quite," he said. "There's still Vidalia."

"You have been paying attention, haven't you?"

"I love your family, Selene. They were amazing out there. Treated me like I was one of them."

"You are," she told him. "From now on, Cory, you are."

Author's Note

This novel contains instances of a modern-day Witch practicing her skills in a number of ways, including the healing
power of Reiki (an eastern tradition), the use of Pow-Wow
(Pennsylvania-Dutch folk magic), and Shamanism, among
other methods. While some see conflict in this, it is precisely
the way modern Witches work. Shamanism, while seen by
many as a purely Native American practice, has actually been
used by cultures all over the world, from Laplanders to the
natives of Peru. Northern Germanic Shamans were said to
travel the skies with the help of sacred reindeer and return
with gifts for their people. Witches have been said to travel
the skies with the help of a magic broomstick. Both tales refer
to the same practice, that of "journeying" into alternate worlds
in search of wisdom and guidance: Shamanism. Today's
working Witches believe that, from the point of view of a
spirit, there's no difference between one religious system and
another. They are all created by man as a means of under-

standing the divine, and any means of bringing us closer to the divine is both valid and sacred. So they use what works, the way great cooks do with recipes: borrowing from traditions old and new, creating new methods from the old and from scratch, keeping those that work best for them and for the job at hand. And it works—Magic happens!

* * * * *

*Experience entertaining women's fiction for every woman
who has wondered
"what's next?" in their lives.
Turn the page for a sneak preview of a new book from
Harlequin NEXT,
WHY IS MURDER ON THE MENU, ANYWAY?
by Stevi Mittman*

On sale December 26, wherever books are sold.

Design Tip of the Day

Ambience is everything. Imagine eating a foie gras at a luncheonette counter or a side of coleslaw at Le Cirque. It's not a matter of food but one of atmosphere. Remember that when planning your dining room design.
—Tips from *Teddi.com*

"Now that's the kind of man you should be looking for," my mother, the self-appointed keeper of my shelf-life stamp, says. She points with her fork at a man in the corner of the Steak-Out Restaurant, a dive I've just been hired to redecorate. Making this restaurant look four-star will be hard, but not half as hard as getting through lunch without strangling the woman across the table from me. "*He* would make a good husband."

"Oh, you can tell that from across the room?" I ask, wondering how it is she can forget that when we had trouble getting rid of my last husband, she shot him. "Besides being ten minutes away from death if he actually eats all that steak, he's twenty years too old for me and—shallow woman that I am—twenty pounds too heavy. Besides, I am *so* not looking for another husband here. I'm looking to design a new image for this place, looking for some sense of ambience, some feeling, something I can build a proposal on for them."

My mother studies the man in the corner, tilting her head, the better to gauge his age, I suppose. I think she's grimacing, but with all the Botox and Restylane injected into that face, it's hard to tell. She takes another bite of her steak salad, chews slowly so that I don't miss the fact that the steak is a poor cut and tougher than it should be. "You're concentrating on the wrong kind of proposal," she says finally. "Just look at this place, Teddi. It's a dive. There are hardly any other diners. What does *that* tell you about the food?"

"That they cater to a dinner crowd and it's lunchtime," I tell her.

I don't know what I was thinking bringing her here with me. I suppose I thought it would be better than eating alone. There really are days when my common sense goes on vacation. Clearly, this is one of them. I mean, really, did I not resolve less than three weeks ago that I would not let my mother get to me anymore?

What good are New Year's resolutions, anyway?

Mario approaches the man's table and my mother studies him while they converse. Eventually Mario leaves the table with a huff, after which the diner glances up and meets my mother's gaze. I think she's smiling at him. That or she's got indigestion. They size each other up.

I concentrate on making sketches in my notebook and try to ignore the fact that my mother is flirting. At nearly seventy, she's developed an unhealthy interest in members of the opposite sex to whom she isn't married.

According to my father, who has broken the TMI rule and given me Too Much Information, she has no interest in sex with him. Better, I suppose, to be clued in on what they aren't doing in the bedroom than have to hear what they might be doing.

"He's not so old," my mother says, noticing that I have barely touched the Chinese chicken salad she warned me not to get. "He's got about as many years on you as you have on your little cop friend."

She does this to make me crazy. I know it, but it works all the same. "Drew Scoones is not my little 'friend.' He's a detective with whom I—"

"Screwed around," my mother says. I must look shocked, because my mother laughs at me and asks if I think she doesn't know the "lingo."

What I thought she didn't know was that Drew and I actually tangled in the sheets. And, since it's possible she's just fishing, I sidestep the issue and tell her that Drew is just a couple of years younger than me and that I don't need reminding. I dig into my salad with renewed vigor, determined to show my mother that Chinese chicken salad in a steak place was not the stupid choice it's proving to be.

After a few more minutes of my picking at the wilted leaves on my plate, the man my mother has me nearly engaged to pays his bill and heads past us toward the back of the restaurant. I watch my mother take in his shoes, his suit and the diamond pinkie ring that seems to be cutting off the circulation in his little finger.

"Such nice hands," she says after the man is out of sight. "Manicured." She and I both stare at my hands. I have two popped acrylics that are being held on at weird angles by bandages. My cuticles are ragged and there's marker decorating my right hand from measuring carelessly when I did a drawing for a customer.

Twenty minutes later she's disappointed that he managed to leave the restaurant without our noticing. He will join the list of the ones I let get away. I will hear about him twenty years from now when—according to my mother—my children will be grown and I will still be single, living pathetically alone with several dogs and cats.

After my ex, that sounds good to me.

The waitress tells us that our meal has been taken care of by the management and, after thanking Mario, the owner, complimenting him on the wonderful meal and assuring him that once I have redecorated his place people will be flocking here in droves (I actually use those words and ignore my mother when she rolls her eyes), my mother and I head for the restroom.

My father—unfortunately not with us today—has the patience of a saint. He got it over the years of living with my mother. She, perhaps as a result, figures he has the patience for both of them, and feels justified having none. For her, no rules apply, and a little thing like a picture of a man on the door to a public restroom is certainly no barrier to using the john. In all fairness, it does seem silly to stand and wait for the ladies' room if no one is using the men's room.

Still, it's the idea that rules don't apply to her, signs don't apply to her, conventions don't apply to her. She knocks on the door to the men's room. When no one answers she gestures to me to go in ahead. I tell her that I can certainly wait for the ladies' room to be free and she shrugs and goes in herself.

Not a minute later there is a bloodcurdling scream from behind the men's room door.

"Mom!" I yell. "Are you all right?"

Mario comes running over, the waitress on his heels. Two customers head our way while my mother continues to scream.

I try the door, but it is locked. I yell for her to open it and she fumbles with the knob. When she finally manages to

unlock and open it, she is white behind her two streaks of
blush, but she is on her feet and appears shaken but not stirred.

"What happened?" I ask her. So do Mario and the
waitress and the few customers who have migrated to the
back of the place.

She points toward the bathroom and I go in, thinking it serves
her right for using the men's room. But I see nothing amiss.

She gestures toward the stall, and, like any self-respecting
and suspicious woman, I poke the door open with one finger,
expecting the worst.

What I find is worse than the worst.

The husband my mother picked out for me is sitting on the
toilet. His pants are puddled around his ankles, his hands are
hanging at his sides. Pinned to his chest is some sort of Health
Department certificate.

Oh, and there is a large, round, bloodless bullet hole
between his eyes.

Four Nassau County police officers are securing the area,
waiting for the detectives and crime scene personnel to show
up. They are trying, though not very hard, to comfort my
mother, who in another era would be considered to be suffer-
ing from the vapors. Less tactful in the twenty-first century,
I'd say she was losing it. That is, if I didn't know her better,
know she was milking it for everything it was worth.

My mother loves attention. As it begins to flag, she swoons
and claims to feel faint. Despite four No Smoking signs, my
mother insists it's all right for her to light up because, after
all, she's in shock. Not to mention that signs, as we know,
don't apply to her.

When asked not to smoke, she collapses mournfully in a
chair and lets her head loll to the side, all without mussing her
hair.

Eventually, the detectives show up to find the four patrolmen all circled around her, debating whether to administer

CPR, smelling salts or simply call the paramedics. I, however, know just what will snap her to attention.

"Detective Scoones," I say loudly. My mother parts the sea of cops.

"We have to stop meeting like this," he says lightly to me, but I can feel him checking me over with his eyes, making sure I'm all right while pretending not to care.

"What have you got in those pants?" my mother asks him, coming to her feet and staring at his crotch accusingly. "*Baydar?* Everywhere we Bayers are, you turn up. You don't expect me to buy that this is a coincidence, I hope."

Drew tells my mother that it's nice to see her, too, and asks if it's his fault that her daughter seems to attract disasters.

Charming to be made to feel like the bearer of a plague.

He asks how I am.

"Just peachy," I tell him. "I seem to be making a habit of finding dead bodies, my mother is driving me crazy and the catering hall I booked two freakin' years ago for Dana's bat mitzvah has just been shut down by the Board of Health!"

"Glad to see your luck's finally changing," he says, giving me a quick squeeze around the shoulders before turning his attention to the patrolmen, asking what they've got, whether they've taken any statements, moved anything, all the sort of stuff you see on TV, without any of the drama. That is, if you don't count my mother's threats to faint every few minutes when she senses no one's paying attention to her.

Mario tells his waitstaff to bring everyone espresso, which I decline because I'm wired enough. Drew pulls him aside and a minute later I'm handed a cup of coffee that smells divinely of Kahlúa.

The man knows me well. Too well.

His partner, whom I've met once or twice, says he'll interview the kitchen staff. Drew asks Mario if he minds if he takes statements from the patrons first and gets to him and the waitstaff afterward.

"No, no," Mario tells him. "Do the patrons first." Drew raises his eyebrow at me like he wants to know if I get the double entendre. I try to look bored.

"What is it with you and murder victims?" he asks me when we sit down at a table in the corner.

I search them out so that I can see you again, I almost say, but I'm afraid it will sound desperate instead of sarcastic.

My mother, lighting up and daring him with a look to tell her not to, reminds him that *she* was the one to find the body.

Drew asks what happened *this time.* My mother tells him how the man in the john was "taken" with me, couldn't take his eyes off me and blatantly flirted with both of us. To his credit, Drew doesn't laugh, but his smirk is undeniable to the trained eye. And I've had my eye trained on him for nearly a year now.

"While he was noticing you," he asks me, "did *you* notice anything about him? Was he waiting for anyone? Watching for anything?"

I tell him that he didn't appear to be waiting or watching. That he made no phone calls, was fairly intent on eating and did, indeed, flirt with my mother. This last bit Drew takes with a grain of salt, which was the way it was intended.

"And he had a short conversation with Mario," I tell him. "I think he might have been unhappy with the food, though he didn't send it back."

Drew asks what makes me think he was dissatisfied, and I tell him that the discussion seemed acrimonious and that Mario looked distressed when he left the table. Drew makes a note and says he'll look into it and asks about anyone else in the restaurant. Did I see anyone who didn't seem to belong, anyone who was watching the victim, anyone looking suspicious?

"Besides my mother?" I ask him, and Mom huffs and blows her cigarette smoke in my direction.

I tell him that there were several deliveries, the kitchen staff going in and out the back door to grab a smoke. He stops me and asks what I was doing checking out the back door of the restaurant.

Proudly—because, while he was off forgetting me, dropping by only once in a while to say hi to Jesse, my son, or drop something by for one of my daughters that he thought they might like, I was getting on with my life—I tell him that I'm decorating the place.

He looks genuinely impressed. "Commercial customers? That's great," he says. Okay, that's what he *ought* to say. What he actually says is "Whatever pays the bills."

"Howard Rosen, the famous restaurant critic, got her the job," my mother says. "You met him—the good-looking, distinguished gentleman with the *real* job, something to be proud of. I guess you've never read his reviews in *Newsday*."

Drew, without missing a beat, tells her that Howard's reviews are on the top of his list, as soon as he learns how to read.

"I only meant—" my mother starts, but both of us assure her that we know just what she meant.

"So," Drew says. "Deliveries?"

I tell him that Mario would know better than I, but that I saw vegetables come in, maybe fish and linens.

"This is the second restaurant job Howard's got her," my mother tells Drew.

"At least she's getting *something* out of the relationship," he says.

"If he were here," my mother says, ignoring the insinuation, "he'd be comforting her instead of interrogating her. He'd be making sure we're both all right after such an ordeal."

"I'm sure he would," Drew agrees, then looks me in the eyes as if he's measuring my tolerance for shock. Quietly he adds, "But then maybe he doesn't know just what strong stuff your daughter's made of."

It's the closest thing to a tender moment I can expect from Drew Scoones. My mother breaks the spell. "She gets that from me," she says.

Both Drew and I take a minute, probably to pray that's all I inherited from her.

"I'm just trying to save you some time and effort," my mother tells him. "My money's on Howard."

Drew withers her with a look and mutters something that sounds suspiciously like "fool's gold." Then he excuses himself to go back to work.

I catch his sleeve and ask if it's all right for us to leave. He says sure, he knows where we live. I say goodbye to Mario. I assure him that I will have some sketches for him in a few days, all the while hoping that this murder doesn't cancel his redecorating plans. I need the money desperately, the alternative being borrowing from my parents and being strangled by the strings.

My mother is strangely quiet all the way to her house. She doesn't tell me what a loser Drew Scoones is—despite his good looks—and how I was obviously drooling over him. She doesn't ask me where Howard is taking me tonight or warn me not to tell my father about what happened because he will worry about us both and no doubt insist we see our respective psychiatrists.

She fidgets nervously, opening and closing her purse over and over again.

"You okay?" I ask her. After all, she's just found a dead man on the toilet, and tough as she is that's got to be upsetting.

When she doesn't answer me I pull over to the side of the road.

"Mom?" She refuses to meet my eyes. "You want me to take you to see Dr. Cohen?"

She looks out the window as if she's just realized we're on Broadway in Woodmere. "Aren't we near Marvin's Jewelers?" she asks, pulling something out of her purse.

"What have you got, Mother?" I ask, prying open her fingers to find the murdered man's ring.

"It was on the sink," she says in answer to my dropped jaw.

"I was going to get his name and address and have you return it to him so that he could ask you out. I thought it was a sign that the two of you were meant to be together."

"He's dead, Mom. You understand that, right?" I ask. You never can tell when my mother is fine and when she's in la-la land.

"Well, I didn't know that," she shouts at me. "Not at the time."

I ask why she didn't give it to Drew, realize that she wouldn't give Drew the time in a clock shop and add, "…or one of the other policemen?"

"For heaven's sake," she tells me. "The man is dead, Teddi, and I took his ring. How would that look?"

Before I can tell her it looks just the way it is, she pulls out a cigarette and threatens to light it.

"I mean, really," she says, shaking her head like it's my brains that are loose. "What does he need with it now?"

Silhouette

nocturne™

**WAS HE HER SAVIOR
OR HER NIGHTMARE?**

HAUNTED
LISA CHILDS

Years ago, Ariel and her sisters were separated for
their own protection. Now the man who vowed
revenge on her family has resumed the hunt, and
Ariel must warn her sisters before it's too late.
The closer she comes to finding them, the more
secretive her fiancé becomes. Can she trust the man
she plans to spend eternity with? Or has he been
waiting for the perfect moment to destroy her?

On sale December 2006.

In February, expect MORE
from

as it increases to six titles per month.

What's to come...

Rancher and Protector

Part of the
Western Weddings
miniseries

BY JUDY CHRISTENBERRY

The Boss's
Pregnancy Proposal

BY RAYE MORGAN

Don't miss February's
incredible line up of authors!

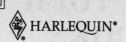

REQUEST YOUR
FREE BOOKS!

2 FREE NOVELS
PLUS 2 FREE GIFTS!

Silhouette® Romantic

SUSPENSE

Sparked by Danger, Fueled by Passion!

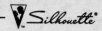

SPECIAL EDITION™

Silhouette Special Edition brings you a
heartwarming new story from the *New York Times*
bestselling author of *McKettrick's Choice*

LINDA LAEL
MILLER

Sierra's Homecoming

Sierra's Homecoming
follows the parallel lives
of two McKettrick women,
living their lives in the
same house but
generations apart,
each with a special son
and an unlikely new
romance.

December 2006

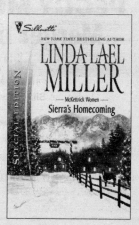

Don't miss
DAKOTA FORTUNES,
a six-book continuing series following
the Fortune family of South Dakota—
oil is in their blood and privilege
is their birthright.

This series kicks off with
USA TODAY bestselling author
PEGGY MORELAND'S
Merger of Fortunes
(SD #1771)
this January.

Other books in the series:
BACK IN FORTUNE'S BED by Bronwyn James (Feb)
FORTUNE'S VENGEFUL GROOM by Charlene Sands (March)
MISTRESS OF FORTUNE by Kathie DeNosky (April)
EXPECTING A FORTUNE by Jan Colley (May)
FORTUNE'S FORBIDDEN WOMAN by Heidi Betts (June)

Silhouette®

SPECIAL EDITION™

Logan's Legacy Revisited

THE LOGAN FAMILY IS BACK WITH SIX NEW STORIES.

Beginning in January 2007 with

THE COUPLE MOST LIKELY TO

by

LILIAN DARCY

Tragedy drove them apart. Reunited eighteen years later, their attraction was once again undeniable. But had time away changed Jake Logan enough to let him face his fears and commit to the woman he once loved?

Silhouette®

COMING NEXT MONTH

INTIMATE MOMENTS